Shifting Allegiances

A novel by
AMAKA LILY

Copyright © by Amaka Lily

All rights reserved. No part of this publication may be reproduced, stored in a retrieval system, or transmitted in any form or by any means, electronic, mechanical, photocopying, recording or otherwise, without the prior written permission of the author.

Original and modified cover art by Nina Mathews Photography and CoverDesignStudio.com

ISBN-13: 978-1500133795
ISBN-10: 1500133795

Note

This book is a work of fiction. Names, characters, places, and incidents are either the products of the author's imagination or are used fictitiously. Any resemblance to actual events or locales or person's living or dead is entirely coincidental.

Dedication

To every immigrant who has experienced culture shock.

Acknowledgements

I won't be a good Nigerian if I did not thank God first. I thank God for giving me life. I thank my family and friends for their support. I also thank America and Nigeria for providing fodder for this book.

Table of Contents

Prologue- An introduction

Chapter 1- First impressions of America.

Chapter 2- An Idle Mind.

Chapter 3- An American Job.

Chapter 4- Tonsillitis.

Chapter 5- An American College.

Chapter 6- African Americans.

Chapter 7- Lawrenceville.

Chapter 8- Strange developments.

Chapter 9- An unexpected turn.

Chapter 10- A new Deka.

Chapter 11- The Scales fall off.

Chapter 12- Nigeria again.

Chapter 13- Diary.

Chapter 14- Return to America.

Chapter 15- Understanding

Epilogue

Prologue

An introduction

SHIFTING ALLEGIANCES

On March 6, 2005, I arrived in the United States of America. Touching American soil was the culmination of a journey that had taken years to achieve, a journey fraught with pain, tears intermingled with hope. I almost wept when the doors of my plane opened up and I witnessed the bright lights of Indianapolis airport.

I could not believe I had finally made it to the Great U.S. of A, the land of milk and honey, the greatest country in the world! I could not believe I had finally made it here!!!

I was happy, deliriously happy.

As I made my way through customs and eventually towards baggage claim, I hummed happy tunes underneath my breath and flashed a big smile at everyone who looked at me. They had no idea how much this meant to me, how grateful I was to be in this country...

Three weeks prior, I had been living a life of frustration. My life had stalled in Nigeria and there was nothing I could do to jumpstart it. I was mired deeply in the molasses of poverty, halted achievement and lack of opportunities. Scattered around me where the ghosts of all the dreams I had dared to dream. Dreams that included entrance into university-*or barring that-* financial stability for my mother- *or barring that-* deliverance from the terrible living conditions we were experiencing.

You see, we were living in one room. Not a studio apartment, mind you… but a 10 by 15 foot space located in the servant's quarters. This was the only type of "home", my mother could afford and it came free, courtesy of a family friend, the latest in a string of "generous" benefactors. Far from ideal, it was still a welcome respite after the frequent movement that had accompanied the previous 7 years.

In this place, we were all together, my mother, 6 sisters and I. No longer split between temperamental relatives and facing the constant threat of eviction or worse, abuse, this was home … our home.

Amaka Lily

But it was cramped, really, cramped, and it was in this cramped place that we ate, read and entertained ourselves. At night, I slept on the floor with five sisters while my mom shared the bed with the baby. Next door was our "bathroom" which consisted of a pit toilet-yes, pit toilet in 21st century Nigeria and a shower stall, separated by a thin wall. At the other end was the communal kitchen where we housed our coal pot and cooked our meals. Both had no doors and anyone could waltz in at anytime.

I still remember that bathroom. I was always on edge whenever I took a shower, fearing that one of the male yard workers would choose that moment to relieve himself and "mistakenly" enter the stall. No I wasn't afraid of getting raped. I was worried that one of them would chance a glimpse of my naked flesh which would have been very embarrassing. I would have been deeply mortified if any of them had seen me in the nude.

Deeply, deeply mortified.

And so I'd trained my ears to pick up the slightest sounds, to be forewarned of approaching footsteps. Unfortunately, every sound I heard sounded like a human approaching. I would hear what I thought were footsteps, scramble madly for my towel, heart beating erratically, rushing to cover myself up. I would then stand there waiting, ears cocked on high alert, half my body covered in wet soap and the other half covered in towel dried soap. I would be panting heavily, ready to yell at the person, only to realize later that no one was coming.

I would then start the whole process of bathing all over again, still straining my ears and doing the same crazy dash when I heard sounds. Truth, be told, I was never surprised by a male yard worker in all the mornings I took my shower. Nevertheless, I could not relax. I anticipated that the day I didn't react to a sound, would be the day that that sound turned out to be human and that would be the end of me.

SHIFTING ALLEGIANCES

I was never so relieved as when my torturous bath came to an end. Never so relieved...

I was in pain.

My skin throbbed with the sores and bite marks left over by the mosquitoes that nightly inhabited our room. Mosquitoes that regardless of how many insect repellants or bed coverings I used always seemed to find their way to my skin. Every morning, surveying the latest damage, I would shed bitter tears of frustration. As a young woman, I desired clear skin but was powerless to protect my body from their relentless defacement. Coupled with the soreness that accompanied sleeping on a hard, stone floor, I was a raw, achy, bundle.

I was hiding a secret

I could not have friends over. In a country where appearances mean EVERYTHING, I could not risk having my friends see the reality of my housing situation. *How was it possible, that I, Njideka Onuoraegbunam, lived in a boys-quarter? How could I explain to my friends that me and my whole family lived in the sort of housing that they kept their house-helps?*

How could I?

How could I?

It was embarrassing, shameful and I was not equipped to handle the certain ridicule that would accompany their discovery. The news would spread like wild fire ...

"*Have you heard where Njideka lives?*"

"*No! Where?*"

"*She lives in a boys-quarter... She and her whole family... In ONE ROOM!!!*"

"*Really?*"

"*Yes oh! They even sleep on the floor*"

"*Ha Ha Ha Ha Ha*"

"*Ha Ha Ha Ha Ha*"

...and so their laughter would ring in my mind

Amaka Lily

It wasn't a case of paranoia.

I had witnessed the vicious skewering of friends by so called friends, skewering disguised as "discussing" another's plight but for the unmistakable gloating detectable even to a deaf person.

It had been my experience, and this has held true, long after I left the shores of Nigeria that people, regardless of their background and mental constitution, derive great pleasure from discussing another's misfortune. It's like people deep down want to feel better than you and your misfortune gives them validation that they are.

Much later, I would discover that there was actually a name for this... *Schadenfreude*....

So I did not want my friends to see my home, but how do you tell a friend not to visit you? How do you prevent friends from coming in without seeming rude?

Luckily, this problem was solved by the presence of our benefactor's dogs. They provided the perfect reason to tell friends, "*If you come to see me, please knock on the gate and wait there. Don't come in... We have dogs ....*" The last statement was an immensely powerful motivator to heed my instructions.

If there's one thing Nigerians dread the most, it is to be bitten by someone else's dog. In a country where poverty reigns supreme and pet care is non-existent, you had no idea - nor did you wish to find out- what diseases an unknown dog was harboring. Furthermore, there was absolutely no financial or legal recourse if you got bitten by someone else's dog. You alone would be responsible for your medical expenses. You and you alone. And, if you were further blessed to be bitten by a rabid dog, suffer madness in addition to your wounds.

Our benefactor's dogs, *Kunle, Waziri* and *Bingo*, had keen ears. Like me, they could pick up the slightest sounds. Unlike me, they could distinguish human sounds from all other sounds

SHIFTING ALLEGIANCES

and would only bark when they heard a human knock. That would usually alert us that there was a visitor waiting at the gate and I would send my sisters to check who it was, and if it was for me, tell them that I was on my way.

From the gate, visitors could not see the boys-quarters. All they could see was the main, beautiful house, where our benefactor lived. When I came out, it appeared that I was coming from the kitchen and what was so strange about a Nigerian girl, and the first born for that matter, working in the kitchen?

Nothing.

In this way, I perpetuated the impression that we lived in a suitable house, and saved myself from my friends scorn. My friends never pressed to enter my home and I never volunteered the reality of my situation. After the initial greetings we would proceed to a nearby *mama-put*[1] which served as my entertainment center.

It was not uncommon to host a friend at a *mama-put*. Even friends with decent houses regularly hosted in such places as it gave us privacy from our family members and allowed us to be loud. I would buy my guests food and we would chat about everything under the sun.

When it was time for their departure, I would walk them to the bus-stop, give them transport money, and wait until they were safely boarded. As I walked home, I would thank my lucky stars that my secret was safe for one more day, but it was an uneasy victory. I always wondered how long I could keep this up. *What would happen the day my secret was discovered?*

I was STUCK

My educational attainment had stalled since I completed my secondary school education four years before. Why? You may ask. Two things: money and connections. Without those, you

---
[1] Local restaurant

could not secure admittance into a Nigerian university. It didn't matter that I was the top scorer in my graduation class. It didn't matter that I had taken all the requisite university exams and passed with flying colors. It didn't matter. For post-secondary education in Nigeria, **merit** counts for nothing. Zilch. Nada.

It was an unfair system.

I watched friends who had been at the bottom of my secondary school classes, get into college before me. I watched people whom were my juniors in secondary school, get into college before me. I didn't want to be at home. I wanted to be with them, be in university, but I was stuck, STUCK, STUCK, STUCK. Without those two requirements, I could not continue my education.

And my friend, being starved of an education is a soul crushing experience. In Nigeria, it is made particularly acute because Education is our God.

Let me repeat.

Education is a Nigerian's GOD.

A person without an education in Nigeria is a person that will never garner respect... the lowest of the low. Our "Stars" are degree holders and the more degrees you have, the more respect will be accorded to you. Instead of athletes, actors or singers, we revere doctors, lawyers and engineers.

The pursuit of education is carefully cultivated in our spirits from a very young age. We are raised to desire it, pursue it, compete for it and if you happened to be one of those children who was ambivalent towards it, flogged until it sank into your thick skull that EDUCATION and EDUCATION only, was the only thing worth living for.

But whereas entrance into primary and secondary schools was a more straight forward process, entrance into a university was anything but. College entrance was a biased and corrupt process and it showed no signs of abating.

SHIFTING ALLEGIANCES

Each year, I would take the JAMB and Polytechnic[2] exams and each year I would exceed the cutoff mark by a huge margin. But yet, when I visited my selected schools, my name was inexplicably absent from the NEW STUDENT boards. It took me a while to understand the system, partly because I was the first person in our nuclear unit to attempt entrance into a Nigerian college and also because I naively believed corruption had not tainted the education process. I was soon set straight by a college student who took pity on me after watching me stand for almost an hour, looking repeatedly at the board for my name, as if hoping that by some miracle it would appear.

He walked up to me and said, *"My sister, I've been watching you for a while. I don't think your name is there. The only way you can get into our college or any for that matter is to either grease someone's palm or have your uncle's father's cousin be the Dean's best friend. And by the way, you are pretty, how can I get in touch with you...."*

I wasn't a lone case.

Thousands of people were in my shoes. Our next door neighbor, Bisola was still awaiting entry, 9 years after she had graduated from secondary school. 9 years!!!

Bisola was a whiz in everything art-related. She could draw, mold and construct anything, I mean anything. Watching her work was like being given a special seat to the divine.

She was that good.

Her dream was to become an architect. Like me, she lacked the wherewithal to secure entry. Unlike me, she had a hopeful disposition that was impervious to doubt. Her faith was so unshakeable that she continued to rebuff the advances of the male suitors that wanted to marry her. She was NOT getting married until *after* she had become an architect. Not before, after.

---

[2] University entrance exams for Nigeria

This resolution had worked out well until she entered her mid-twenties. Her mother had begun to worry that her only daughter may never get married and to a Nigerian mother, there is nothing scarier...

"*Bisola, every body's path is not the same. Perhaps it is not God's will that you become an architect*" followed by entreaties "*...Why don't you consider Dapo? ... He is a good man and he has money*" but no amount of entreaties could sway Bisola. Rather, it made their home a battle ground. I could hear their voices on some nights...

"*Mommy, leave me alone...*" Bisola would say "*... please just leave me alone. I don't want to talk about marriage*"

"*Why don't you want to talk about it? What is wrong with you?*"

"*Nothing is wrong with me. I am just not ready*"

"*What do you mean you are not ready? Isn't 30 years old around the corner? I say isn't 30 years old around the corner? What is wrong with you? Do you want to be an old maid?*"

"*Mommy I will not be an old maid. Don't worry?*"

"*Don't worry? I say 30 is around the corner!!! 30 YEARS OLD! What is wrong with you?*"

"*Nothing mommy, but I am not ready to get married!*"

"*What happens if this does not work out then? What will you do? Will you keep rejecting all the men that are coming for you?*"

"*Mommy, I don't want to talk about that. Also you are beginning to stress me!*"

"*What do you mean stress? Me! Your MOTHER!!! I am stressing YOU? Is that what you call it? Concern for your welfare is now stress?*"

"*Yes mommy, you are stressing me. I have told you before that I will not get married until after I finish university. Not before, After. AFTER mommy. Now please let's drop it. Please*"

SHIFTING ALLEGIANCES

"I will not drop it. I will NOT drop it. You must tell me what is wrong with you! You must tell me why you want to condemn me and you to this life, when your mates and their mothers are doing differently.. You must tell me today. You must tell me TODAY!!!!" and on and on they would go at it.

I didn't blame her mother

You see, every Nigerian girl wants to get married. Every single Nigerian girl! From a very young age, we are conditioned to view marriage as an ultimate goal, on par with education and child bearing, and some would even rank it higher than education. Deliberately choosing to never get married is not part of our consciousness, not part of our vocabulary. Spinsterhood is viewed as a curse and nothing strikes as much fear in the heart of a Nigerian girl, as the possibility of never getting married.

As little girls, we are prepared for our eventual responsibilities of motherhood by being taught to cook, clean and take care of a home. A man can legally divorce his wife if she lacked home-making skills and many Nigerian girls would rather die than be put out for those reasons.

Even I myself, if I were Bisola's age and still not accepted into University, would have gotten married. No doubt about that. But Bisola was unlike typical Nigerian girls. For some reason, she lacked that sense of urgency that was encoded in our genes and was prepared to wait until she had achieved her education, however long that took.

Recently, and to her mother's dismay, she had shaved her hair *gorimapa*[3] and joined a cele-church. She now spent most evenings attending the church's services in order to "*bind the demons that were holding her back from her blessings*"...

But even having the connections and money did not always guarantee placement in your desired major. Many of those

---
[3] Bald

classmates who entered college before me got placed in useless courses, courses that were not only considered financially imprudent but also garnered no respect. Courses such as Fine Arts and Philosophy. And Nigeria is all about respect and status. Every parent wants their child to be a doctor, lawyer, or business person because anything less than that is looked down upon.

Yet, not only did people eagerly scoop these "useless" courses, but there was also a waiting list of people wanting to get into such courses because it was infinitely better to be in the university system than to be at home. At least in the system, you could make the important connections that could put you in your desired major, or failing that, at least graduate with a university degree. You might not get a job with that degree, but you were still better than a person who had never attended college

I WAS FRUSTRATED WITH NIGERIA

This so called *"Lion of Africa"* was more like the *"Suffocator of Dreams"* to me. Even though I had grown up in the country and knew what obtained, I was frustrated with the ceaseless suffering that seemed to accompany everything.

Everything was difficult. This was a country teeming with crude oil and yet we frequently experienced oil scarcity. Oil prices literally increased within hours and if you depended on public transportation, which the majority of the populace did, it was not uncommon to pay one rate on your way to work and double the same rate on your return.

The reason?

"Petrol don go up![4]*"* the conductors would say.

"How e go up so fast?" I would ask *"No be 20 Naira I pay for morning so?"*[5]

---
[4] Gas prices have gone up
[5] How did it go up so fast? Wasn't it just 20 Naira I paid this morning?

SHIFTING ALLEGIANCES

"Na so we see am. Abeg pay me my money. If you no want, come down!"[6]

And of course I would pay. It was either that or walk since those were the only options. Every other transporter hiked their rates. The government couldn't control it. There was absolutely nothing you could do about it.

With the hike in transportation costs, everything else automatically increased. Second to transportation, food was the next most painful increase. At least with transportation, where some hardy souls could take the option of walking, there were no alternatives to food. You have to eat. It was exquisitely painful to watch your money literally dissipate in front of your eyes, painful to see money you thought was sufficient to feed your family, no longer be enough.

Electricity was highly unreliable. It was not uncommon to go weeks without any electricity. In a country as hot as ours, you can imagine how uncomfortable that was. During the day it was tolerable in the sense that you at least had natural light to see with and could move to a cooler, shaded spot. At night, you didn't have that option. You had to be inside your home, and the candles you lit attracted mosquitoes and other critters that made a feast of your body. Coupled with the sweat running down your back, nighttime was truly an uncomfortable existence.

As soon as we experienced a blackout, you could count on hearing wails:

"AAAAAAAAaaaaaaarrrrrgh NEPA"
"That useless NEPA don take light again"[7]

And curses:

"God go punish those NEPA people, tomorrow own today"[8]

---

[6] That's just how it is. Please pay me my money. Otherwise, leave the bus.
[7] That useless NEPA has withdrawn light again

Amaka Lily

The country's sole electricity provider, NEPA, which stood for National Electric Power Authority, was notoriously unreliable, and consequently, a frequently derided entity. It was so bad that if you had a business and wanted it to survive you needed to buy a generator as an alternate source of power. So rare was constant electricity that when it came back on, shouts of "*Praise God*" or "*Nepa don come oh*", rang out.

Corruption also reigned supreme. From our leaders all the way down to street hawkers, corruption was the name of the game. At the university level, it was not uncommon to hear of male teachers holding back their students grades which was essential to proceed to an upper class in exchange for money-if you were a male- or sexual favors -if you were a female-. Grades that you had earned legally and through the sweat of your brow were not automatically given to you. You had to pay for it.

On the job front, a person who had fewer qualifications than you, but knew someone from the company or happened to be from the correct tribe, could land a job before you. Even for government jobs, you had to bribe your way to get in.

Our leaders used their positions to fatten their pockets rather than help to improve our economy. They did it so frequently and so blatantly that we were no longer shocked by it.

In any case, there was nothing we could do about it.
Complain! you say,
and I respond
To whom?

There was absolutely no one to report to. This was a country where law enforcement was a joke. Our policemen openly harassed innocent drivers for bribes and refusing to pay meant either an unnecessary delay -where you still had to pay them- or a trip to the police station where you still had to pay to be

---

[8] God will punish those NEPA agents greatly

SHIFTING ALLEGIANCES

released. These same policemen would be the first to take to their heels when reports of armed robbers, of which there were many surfaced. Some were even in cahoots with the robbers. I had a cousin, Obidi, who once narrowly survived a carjacking, only to arrive at the police station to be reunited with his attacker who also happened to be the sergeant at the station. *What do you think happened?*

In a country where survival was difficult, it was no wonder that thievery became rampant and let me tell you, these were no petty thieves. They came armed with machetes and machine guns and were so brazen, that they occasionally sent letters to their intended victims in *advance* of their attacks, to alert the latter that they were coming.

Such letter recipients never took those letters lightly because as surely as night follows day, those armed robbers would appear.

And my friend, you never want to experience a Nigerian armed robbery.

Those thieves were heartless, HEARTLESS!!! They regularly raped, maimed or killed whoever was present during their operations. They did this because they knew what awaited them if they were ever to be apprehended. Such thieves would first be beaten by a mob and if none of our "police" happened to be around to stop the mob, would then proceed to burn the thieves alive. It was called *Jungle Justice* and was the mode the oppressed populace utilized to deter potential thieves.

One morning, my sleep was shattered by the sounds of a mob congregating in front of our home. Within seconds, I heard the most soul piercing, horrible scream, I have ever had the misfortune to experience.

It was the sound of a thief, being burned alive!!!

Now why the mob chose the front of our home to administer their jungle justice, I would never know. All I know is that I never want to re-experience that sound ever again.

Amaka Lily

Never, Ever, Ever!

It was an otherworldly, gut wrenching, soul piercing sound that reached deeply into my soul. I found myself pitying the thief for his terrible, terrible luck.

That sound really affected me and I refused to leave our home the entire day. Not only did I not want to see his charred remains but I also didn't know how I could talk to members of my community who had participated in this justifiable yet ghastly act. These were things that I had read about and knew happened in Nigeria, but having it happen so close to my home, and by people I saw daily, was just too much to bear.

But with time, I got over it and later, Bisola filled me in on the details of the unfortunate thief's story. He was one of four thieves that had come to rob one of our chiefs. Chief Lekan was one of the quieter chiefs in our quarters. He was very reserved, never ostentatious but rumored to be extremely wealthy. Some people claimed he was deeply into juju[9]. Anyway, the thieves had burst into Chief Lekan's room early that morning, but instead of seeing a sleeping chief, were in fact accosted by a strange wild animal standing alone in the middle of the chief's bed.

I never got consensus on what exactly the "wild animal" was. Bisola said it was a lion, but Mama Dupe who was also present at the mobbing, swore it was a wolf. None of them had actually seen it of course, but had gleaned their answers from the descriptions the unfortunate thief gave during his interrogation. I had a lot of questions myself.

Why had we never seen this animal before? Why did Chief Lekan keep it in his room? Why was the animal present in Chief Lekan's stead?

I did not doubt that there had been an animal present. I just did not think it was an earthly animal. Actually, I suspected

---

[9] Voodoo

SHIFTING ALLEGIANCES

something a lot more sinister, something more in line with *juju*. This being Nigeria, a nation where *juju* was heavily practiced and where stories of supernatural happenings abounded, it was not hard to reach this conclusion. There were a lot of things that happened which science could not explain, a lot of things which as surely as darkness follows daylight occurred on a regular basis, a lot of things which I could not personally explain, but which every Nigerian knows is real.

I know my western readers will be quick to dismiss this juju as "nonsense" but remember, juju preceded all modern religions in Africa and was only labeled "quackery" by the missionaries who could not explain it. Also, think about this, if juju is fake, why has it persevered for generations? *Why do people worldwide continue to practice it?*

What I do know is that the "animal" scared the daylights out of the thieves and in their mad dash to get away, the unfortunate thief fell and his friends left him. It was at that point that Chief Lekan appeared, began shouting "*Ole, Ole*[10]", while simultaneously hitting the thief with a pestle.

The rest as they say is history.

You could not even trust the products you were paying for. Nigerian counterfeiters had so mastered the art of counterfeiting that they were undoubtedly, the world-leaders in that "art". I do not think another country comes close, yes, even China because the intricacy of the products made by our counterfeiters was really, a sight to behold.

They had the ability to duplicate what seemed to you like the real thing, only to discover much later that it was a fake. You could buy something that looked and felt like a shoe, only to arrive home and discover that it was made of cardboard. There were lots of other products which you could obtain from our markets which looked, felt, tasted and smelt like the real

---

[10] "Thief, Thief:

thing, up to the labeling only to arrive home, and discover it was a fake.

And to my Western brothers and sisters, you cannot return or exchange a product after it has been purchased in Nigeria. Every sale is final. Every single sale. Even if there were a return policy, I don't care how soon you returned to the market to complain that you were sold a fake, you would never ever find the seller who sold you that product.

Never ever.

Don't get me wrong, not all Nigerian traders were dishonest. In fact, there were millions of honest, hardworking, truthful traders, but with the rampant corruption, attendant poverty and struggle for survival, you couldn't be sure whom to trust.

There were bad eggs.

You had to protect yourself.

So, you learned quickly to be suspicious and to smell, open or feel whatever it was you were buying to ensure you were buying the real thing. Despite those precautions, I can't tell you how many times I ended up with a counterfeit product, whether it was body cream or anti-perspirant. The worst was when I bought what I thought was a hair relaxer, only to get something that not only wounded my scalp but left me with bald patches.

So this was Nigeria to me in the year 2005.

Corrupt, inadequate infrastructure, zero opportunities for advancement and suffering personified.

Nigeria, My beloved country.

This was just the way life was and without any viable alternatives, most people just bore it. Nigerians are very adaptable and can survive harsh conditions. If there was a blackout, we lit candles, made hand-made fans and went about our evening. If petrol prices went up, we ponied up the extra money and kept going. If like me, you ended up with a fake hair relaxer, you washed it out while heaping curses on the person who had formulated such a concoction and the seller

SHIFTING ALLEGIANCES

who had sold it, "*E no go better for am!*[11]", and then went about your day.

Nigeria was unjust, we all knew that.

It was just how it was.

Many though tried to leave. Those who had experienced living abroad, and kept those ties open, promptly went back. Foreign embassies teemed with endless lines of Nigerians, trying to get the almighty VISA. It didn't matter whether it was to the U.S, London or another African country, people just wanted out, legally or illegally.

Since the late 80's, we had experienced a steady drain of our workforce to other foreign locations. To stem this tide, the government in conjunction with foreign embassies, began placing Herculean restrictions on getting a VISA. Still, that did not deter people from trying. Many Nigerians utilized all sorts of means to try to get out of the country. Some attached themselves to ship containers. Others went via neighboring African nations. Still others obtained counterfeit visas and if they were lucky arrived undetected. The not so lucky ones were promptly sent back or first thrown into jail and beaten for good measure

But that didn't stop the tide.

Nigerian folklore teemed with stories of people who within a year or two of living abroad[12], returned with riches and cars. It appeared that it was definitely better to live in the West. There was 24/7 electricity, great infrastructure, available colleges and easy living. So people continued to try.

Unfortunately, the illegal means the desperate ones utilized contributed to give our country a bad, international image. If there were 10 travelers in an airport, the Nigerian in their midst was automatically considered the most likely illegal traveler.

---

[11] It will not be good for you!
[12] Term we used to refer to all Western countries.

Amaka Lily

The drug trafficking which some bad eggs partook of also didn't help our cause.

Because of this, Nigerians became the recipients of the harshest level of scrutiny leveled on any traveler. Say you arrived at Heathrow airport with a Nigerian passport, you would be subjected to one of the most invasive probes ever designed by man. Every orifice in your anatomy would be carefully probed and examined for drugs.

Every. Single. Orifice.

Your papers would also be thoroughly scanned for any hint of illegality and you would be posed so many questions which you had better have the correct answers for.

It was demeaning, embarrassing, but there was nothing you could do. Absolutely nothing.

It had not always been like that.

My mom regaled me with tales of how great Nigeria had been in her childhood. A Nigeria that was stress-free and clean. A Nigeria that was merit based. A Nigeria where everything worked. A Nigeria she had yearned for as a college student in the states. A Nigeria that she had hastily returned to with my dad in tow, as soon as her studies in America were completed.

A Nigeria that she now viewed with great disappointment.

A Nigeria that for a brief period of my life, I had also experienced.

You see until my father's death, I had lived a very comfortable, middle class existence.

My parents' had run a small consulting practice in the little town of Port-Harcourt. Even though it was a small practice, it had been a thriving practice and we never lacked for clients.

Since the discovery of crude oil in Nigeria, there had been a steady stream of multinationals, eager to invest in our national cake. Port-Harcourt was one of those cities bursting with oil and there was high demand, both from the government as well

SHIFTING ALLEGIANCES

as from multinational companies, for engineers knowledgeable in both Nigerian and Western practices.

This was where my parents fit the bill. As Nigerians' trained in America, they were specially positioned to help these two groups. ...

My parents' had met in the United States, at the University of Tennessee. They had both been accepted into U-Tenn's engineering program and had quickly bonded, once they'd discovered that they were the only Nigerians in that program.

My father, who was a year ahead, told me that when he met my mother, he was very excited because finally, there was a fellow Nigerian whom he could discuss things with. My mother later shared with me the same sentiments. Now that I've lived in the U.S myself, I know exactly what they meant. When you are in a foreign location, you appreciate so much more, people from your home country and it's because, they provide an instant understanding, an understanding which no foreigner, despite how many years they've known you, will ever be able to provide.

Together, they had talked about returning home, of lending their skills to our burgeoning nation. In those days, the 70s through the early 80s, most of the Nigerians who traveled abroad, promptly returned home at the completion of their studies.

They did not remain in their foreign location.

At the time, Nigeria was bursting with opportunities. We were a young, independent nation and we had oil..... lots and lots of oil. Almost every company you found in the West, had a Nigerian counterpart, so there was no reason for any Nigerian to remain in a Western location

My father proposed to my mother as soon as he graduated from the university. I was born exactly nine months later. Two months after my mother's graduation and five months after my birth, my parents' held a garage sale, purchased 2 one -way tickets and headed back to Nigeria

My father had accepted a position with the Port-Harcourt state government and so my parents' settled in that oil rich town. My mother didn't work that first year as she stayed at home taking care of me.

After some months of working with the government, my father began to realize that his dreams of becoming instrumental in our nation's growth were at risk of becoming pipe dreams. Tribal politics, the scourge of many African nations dominated every aspect of the state agency with plum roles going only to Port-Harcourt indigenes. Non natives had to settle for less visible roles and my father an Igbo man, chafed under the unfairness. He couldn't advance if he was not part of those visible roles and there was no way he was ever going to get those roles. Furthermore, he found that he did not like bureaucracy. Having to justify and obtain signatures for the most minimal of expenses severely curtailed his effectiveness.

He could not imagine doing this for the rest of his life.

There had to be a better way.

He began to entertain thoughts of leaving the government and of opening up his own practice. He believed that without the restrictions of the government, he would be a lot more successful in making his mark. Also, with my mother in tow, he would have a double advantage over other consultants.

He shared this idea with my mom. She was on board. They made a plan that my father would continue working until he'd saved up adequately for the business. One year to the day of his hire, my father quit and launched our business in our parlour[13].

His instincts were right.

Multinational companies loved this two-person team who combined western expertise with intimate Nigerian knowledge.

---

[13] Living room

SHIFTING ALLEGIANCES

In addition, my fathers' short stint with the government had exposed him to the right government contacts without which nobody can do business in Nigeria.

The business blossomed.

By year 2, my parents' were able to move to one of the busiest districts in Port-Harcourt. They hired our first staff, a secretary called Uchenna. Every day, my parents would work from morning till night, making calls, drafting proposals, etc.

I was always with them. I can still remember myself waddling around that office, exploring things. They would bring me stacks of old paper and crayons and have me color them. Sometimes Uchenna would carry me and sing me lullabies.

The business continued to explode.

By year 3, they'd expanded to the entire floor and hired even more staff. My parents also moved to a bigger home. When my mother became pregnant with my second sister, she handed the reins over to my dad and spent the remaining 9 years as a full-time house-wife, giving birth and providing the rare input to the running of the company

Life was bliss.

We had a big house, a driver. Life was good.

Ifunaya was born 4 years after my birth. My other sisters Amara, Nonye, Obioma, Adaobi and Chiamaka followed soon after

Seven of us in total and all of us girls.

My father didn't mind. Even though Nigeria is a country where boys are preferred to girls and a boy's naming ceremony is celebrated with more pomp and pageantry than a girl's, my father never made us feel that we were inferior. He was proud of us and always boasted that we were better than boys. He even taught us how to play football and some of my best memories were when he would let us all play against him.

Amaka Lily

Seven girls-including some in diapers- against one man and he would let us score.

Everytime!

God, I miss my father so much. I wish he were alive to see me today.

But that wasn't God's plan. One night my father slept and didn't wake up. He wasn't sick before hand, nothing. He just slept and didn't wake up.

I had never seen my mother cry prior to my father's death and I have not seen her cry since the burial. She was and still is a strong woman but my father's death was just too much for her to bear.

My mother cracked.

She cried and cried and cried.

She stayed in her room most of the time. As the oldest, I made sure my sisters were washed, fed and taken care of. I was 13 years old.

In the daytime, friends and relatives would stop by to comfort and grieve with my mother.

At nighttime, I would sit with my mother and listen to her. She would reminisce and tell me stories of how she had met my father, how nice he was to her, how much he loved us...

I cried too when my father died, but not in front of my mother and never in front of my sisters. I had to show them I was strong, which I really wasn't but as the oldest, needed to be.

Luckily, in Nigeria, we are not required to bury our dead immediately. Burials are an expensive affair and depending on the status of the departed, may require certain customs and rites to be performed per tradition. Also, at a minimum, food and drink must be provided. All of these cost money so postponing a burial to a future date is not unusual and was in fact, the norm. The dead is embalmed while money and arrangements are made for a proper and final internment.

In time, my mother recovered enough to begin planning my father's burial which in Igbo custom was an expensive affair. If my mother didn't bury my father as befitting his stature, our family would be disgraced.

That was not an option.

But when my mother tried calling her employees, she could not reach them. She then went to the office, only to find it deserted. There was not one single employee around. Not one. Even Uchenna, our longest serving employee could not be found. The place had been thrashed and looted of all our equipment. The office phone was ripped from the wall. The door was not even locked.

It was the worst timing ever. My mother just decided to shut it down.

For the burial she dug into our savings. I still remember that burial as if it were yesterday. We all had to wear a special cloth and shave our heads clean. I had to stand beside my mother while she received the mourners.

It was a horrible day.

After the burial, my mother concentrated on finding work. Getting a job proved to be a considerable challenge because my mother who had mostly been a housewife, found herself ill prepared for the new world we were suddenly thrust into. Not only had the technologies changed but most employers now preferred to hire younger, single workers.

Still she persevered and she found a job as an entry level engineer but the salary was pittance and scarcely enough to cover our house rent not to mention our school fees.

It is amazing how quickly a person can fall from grace. How in the blink of an eye one can go from comfortable existence to desperate poverty.

Amaka Lily

Because that's precisely what happened to us
Soon, our rent payments became late. Our school fees became deferred. We started selling our furniture one by one and three square meals became a rarity.
It was frightening.

Eventually, we were threatened with eviction. Something needed to be done. A family meeting with my father's people was called. It was decided that my mother move to Lagos where opportunities were plentiful. She would be able to make more money and advance a lot faster there than if she remained in Port-Harcourt

To give her a fighting chance, she had to leave us behind. Trying to find your bearings career-wise, while towing seven children, would have been very difficult for my mother so it was suggested that we stay with my paternal grandparents until my mom was financially ready to take care of us. In the meantime, she would send us money for our school fees, while my relatives would take care of the housing and other living expenses, for free.

My mother agreed and so we moved to our grandparent's house in Enugu

Coming on the heels of my father's death, being parted from my mother was very difficult to bear. My world as I knew it was suddenly fractured and it was from that moment that I began to view my future with trepidation.

6 months into staying with my grandparents, my grandfather suffered a stroke. He survived but with diminished abilities. It was then decided that we move to another relative's house, Uncle Amaechi, my father's older brother

My friend, if you ever want to know what someone is really like, live with them.

Uncle Amaechi, who used to be so nice when my father was alive, turned out to be a hot-tempered man. He had zero tolerance. Even though he had children, he had not acquired the patience and compassion that comes with raising kids. He could not stand noise and any little sound made him yell. He was also very mean and would strike out unexpectedly. You learnt quickly to stand far away from him. Far, far, away, even when he was speaking to you. Our reflexes became sharper, necessary to dodge any unexpected blows. We stayed with him for two years. After that, we were moved to another uncle's place, Uncle Timothy.

Uncle Timothy was more even tempered. I actually liked him …at first. He never yelled or struck anyone, just always smiled and joked around. But he had one problem. He loved women and was an incorrigible *ashawo*[14]. He would flirt with other women, in front of his wife and female visitors were always stopping by looking for him. What was more surprising was that his wife, my aunt Amaka, never did anything about this. This was not typical. Even though it is perfectly legal, to have more than one wife in Nigeria, it was not common to openly disrespect your wife by flirting with other women. My aunt Amaka never shouted at him to stop and never stopped him from going out at odd times in the night. She also never fought the female visitors who came asking for him. Many women would have beat any woman they thought threatened their marital life.

My aunt Amaka seemed strangely weak.

We later found out that one of his female friends actually had a husband, because he came one day to "talk" to my uncle, with a cutlass in tow. Seeing a stranger striding purposefully to our home, bearing a big cutlass and shouting "*Where is Timothy? Where is Timothy?*" made everyone scatter. The kids, Aunt Amaka, the gardener, everyone took to their heels. Uncle Timothy, that lovable man, turned out to be a coward. He locked himself inside his room and refused to come out.

---

[14] Used here to mean a man who was very fond of women

Amaka Lily

Refused to come out and handle his business like a man.

That was unacceptable. My Uncle, because of his actions had brought this embarrassment upon himself and his family, but when the time came to pay the price, barricaded himself inside a room. Not only that, but he left his own family to deal with it on their own. *What type of a man was that? What if the cutlass holder had killed us all?*

That betrayed husband made our family homeless for nearly two days? No one wanted to enter the house? We stayed outside, taking peeks to see if the man was leaving. He didn't seem to be in a hurry. He made himself comfortable in front of my Uncle's bedroom door and just sat there, not moving. That first night, we slept with the neighbours.

On the second day, my Aunt Amaka had located the man's wife who then arrived and implored her husband to come home. After a lot of entreaties, and perhaps hunger, he left. Anyway, after that fiasco, we never felt completely safe in that compound. *Who knew if the man would come back in the dead of the night to kill all of us?*

When my mother next came to visit, we told her what had happened and she was LIVID. She screamed at my Uncle and it was agreed we couldn't stay at their home anymore. Our next home was to be in Lagos, with another relative, Aunty Chinwekwu.

We were very excited when we learnt we would be moving to Lagos. Not only would we now reside in the same town as my mother, but Lagos was also the Paris of Nigeria. It was very modern, very beautiful and also the seat of all action. Aunty Chinwekwu had a big home and was willing to house us for a while. Unfortunately, once we began living with her, she made us her mini-servants. She made us fetch water for not only her, but her children, our own cousins some of whom I was even older than. She made us do all the housework and if we complained, threatened to put us out.

SHIFTING ALLEGIANCES

God, I hated that woman. She knew that we had no place to go and threatening us with eviction was a wicked way to remind us of that.

One day, deliverance. My mother arrived with the happy news that we were now going to live with her. She had realized that no matter how much she worked, she would never make enough to get us our own place. Even though her Lagos job paid more, it was constantly offset by the fuel scarcity, attendant price hikes and higher cost of living it took to live in Lagos. She no longer wanted to be separated from her children and wanted us to all live under one roof

She had been living in a colleague's boy's quarter and even though it was the tiniest place we had ever seen, we were happy to be with our mother and leave that slave master, Aunty Chinwekwu FOREVER.

And so we all moved.

That was in 2004, 6 years after my father's passing.

Amaka Lily

Because I was the only one in my family to be born in the U.S., I was also the only American citizen. When my father was alive, he had talked a lot about the U.S. and had promised that he would send me there for my university education. I had believed him, and even after he died, had clung fiercely to those dreams. It was the only way I could keep connected to my father. Every night, just before I drifted off to sleep, I would imagine what being in an American college was like. I would think about all the friends I'd make, all the White, Black, Chinese and Indian friends. I would think about the type of education I'd get, one that was obviously superior to what was offered in Nigeria, one where University strikes never occurred.

Those thoughts kept me going. They gave me hope as I suffered the disappointments of not having a home, moving around and living with relatives who were less than ideal.

But as the years passed and financial solvency continued to elude my family, I was forced to shelve those dreams. I had to become practical and concentrated instead on obtaining a Nigerian college education. A one way ticket to the U.S. cost a 120,000 Naira, 6 times what it cost to "secure" your admittance into a university. My mother made 15,000 Naira a month. Cost-wise, a Nigerian college education was the more feasible option.

So I focused on Nigeria, and for 4 years, in 2 different states, had dutifully taken those college entrance exams. I badgered all my friends for the contacts who helped them get into university. I made contact with those people, introducing myself and asking them to help me, hence how I came to know the cost of securing college admittance.

No dice.

Without money, it was like speaking gibberish.

I prayed and prayed and prayed to God to give my mother a better job so that I could enter a university and so that we could

SHIFTING ALLEGIANCES

live in our very own, benefactor free place. I even tried to earn money by teaching lessons to the neighborhood kids, but the money, I made was so little, barely able to make a huge dent on what a Nigerian college admittance demanded.

I still thought about America, but it became more and more like an escape. When life got difficult, I would imagine what it would be like to be in America, to live in a place where there was no suffering, no corruption, paradise on earth and where life was so much easier.

I held on, but each time I didn't see my name on those boards, my hope dimmed a little. Each time something came up to claim my meager savings, my faith further disappeared

Finally, I lost all hope. I stopped thinking about America. It was no use. I'd never get there. I was also never going to rise above my Nigerian circumstances. I was screwed. I felt at the mercy of whatever the capricious gods decided to inflict on me. My future stretched before me, dark and bleak and I no longer wanted to try anymore. I was going to die an uneducated, mosquito ridden, miserable woman.

That was my lot in this hell of a country

These were the types of thoughts that dominated my mind until that fateful day, February 18th 2005, when my mother returned from work with the shocking news that I would be travelling to the U.S., in 3 weeks!!! Apparently, during her lunch break, she was reunited with a classmate whom she hadn't seen since her secondary school days. During their chat, she found out he was now the owner of a travel agency. My mother had mentioned that she had a daughter whom she wanted taken to the U.S. but was unable to afford the cost of a plane ticket. The man had inquired about my status and when my mother mentioned I was an American citizen, had surprised her by saying he could advance me a ticket which my mother didn't have to pay all at once, but rather in monthly installments.

Amaka Lily

I could not believe it. This just did not happen. A Nigerian person was willing to give another Nigerian, a virtual stranger no less, a 120,000 Naira plane ticket to the U.S. and take the stranger's word that she would pay it back in monthly bits. This just did not happen. This just did not happen in Nigeria. *Wasn't this the same country where we did not do credit? Wasn't this the same country where untrustworthy people abounded?*

No I could not believe it. Would not believe it. I had been disappointed so many times in my short life. I could not take the risk of believing anything good could happen to me.

But happen it did, because the next day, my mother surprised me with an airline ticket with my name on it, scheduled for departure to the U.S. on March 6, 2005.

"*No way*", I told my mother, in between sobs

"*Yes oh*" she replied "*Now, you can stop doubting and start preparing*" she finished

The following weeks were a blur. I felt like I was in a dream, going through the motions of preparing for America. I got my hair braided, got a sturdy pair of jeans and some shirts to tide me during the spring. I also made some trips to our relatives to inform them of my impending departure and to get their blessings

The night before I left, my mother called me aside and said to me

"*Njideka, you have been blessed to be given this opportunity to come to America*"

"*Do not forget your family here; DO NOT EVER FORGET YOUR FAMILY*"

"*Never mommy*" I promised "*Never will I forget my family*"

"*Do not forget where you come from*"

"*Never mommy*" I promised again "*I would never forget*"

SHIFTING ALLEGIANCES

"Always keep God in mind, work hard, and I promise he would never disappoint you"
"I will mommy"
"God bless you my child"

March 6 finally came around and I was escorted to Murtala Mohammed airport by all my family members. Two sisters took one hand and my luggage was borne by the other ones. We stayed together, praying and hugging ourselves. To say that I was giddy, would be an understatement. I could not wait to turn my back on this bastard of a country.

When it came time for us to part, that section where travelers are separated from their families, a shot of pain went through my heart and for a second, I wanted to weep.

This was not a dream.

I was indeed leaving Nigeria-which I wanted- but I was also leaving my family- which I did not want. *When would I see them again?* But the thought disappeared just as fast as it came.

I had to leave this country.

I had suffered for far too long here.

"Go well my child and may God bless you"
"Bye Bye Njideka, don't forget us oh" my sisters sang.

I gave one last hug to my family, took my baggage from them and turned away.

But Nigeria wasn't done with me yet.

After I had checked in, I was ushered into a separate room where travelers needed to present their paperwork before going through another gate. When it came to my turn, I presented my ticket and passport.

"Excuse me but I can't let you proceed with this"

"WHAAATTTTTT" my mind went into overdrive. *What was going on? Why couldn't I go on? Was my ticket a fake? Did the travel owner renege on the agreement? Was my passport not valid?"*

"Wh... Why Ma?" I managed to stumble out loud

Amaka Lily

"Your passport indicates you are an American citizen. Can I see your birth certificate? We cannot let you go on without seeing your American birth certificate"

I was not expecting it. My birth certificate was packed with other sensitive material which I had checked in with my luggage. There was no way I could access my bag. I didn't even know where it was in the airport.

I explained all this to the lady agent. She was insistent that I could not continue to the U.S. without the birth certificate and told me to step aside. I started begging. After all I had been through, to be stopped at this point for something I did not know about!!! Oh my God. *What was going to happen to me? Was I going to be sent home? Was I never going to leave Nigeria.*

She then said she would talk to her manager. The wait was torturous. I was deeply worried. After speaking to her manager, she said to me

"We can let you go if you give us a 1,000 Naira fee"

My ears almost fell out of my head. 1,000 Naira!!! I didn't have that type of money on me. All I had was about 100 Naira in spare change. I was broke as hell. *Could she accept that?*

Grudgingly, extremely grudgingly and as if she was doing me a great favor, she accepted my money and I felt very grateful when I was waved through. I hoped that was it. That was the last dime I had. When I finally boarded the plane, I let out a much needed sigh of relief. *God that was close*, but my relief quickly turned into anger, when my seat mate, a businessman, after I told him the narrow escape I just had, informed me that I had just been duped. He said the lady agent had no basis to ask to see my birth certificate and that my passport was more than sufficient. What she had just done was carefully orchestrate a non-event to get herself paid.

SHIFTING ALLEGIANCES

I could not believe it. I could not believe that bribery and corruption extended to our airport. And to think it came from a woman, another woman?

I was pissed.

But there was nothing I could do? *Who would I report to?* It was obviously a scam that all the employees were engaged in. reporting was futile. The only thing I could do was just to continue on my merry way.

God, I was so glad to be leaving that country. The corruption and thievery was just too much. I would never return to it again. NEVER, EVER, EVER.

I thought about America. *Finally I will be in a country where people were honest. Finally I will be in a country where I didn't have to watch my back on a daily basis. Finally I WILL BE ABLE TO PURSUE A COLLEGE EDUCATION!* A happiness I hadn't felt in a long time slowly began to trickle into my bones. It filled me up. I was so happy. My mind began to bring back the dreams I used to have, dreams I'd long buried. I began to think of all the great things I would do in America.

When I stepped off that plane in Indianapolis, I mouthed a prayer of thanks to God. I thanked and thanked God for making me see America in my lifetime. It was indeed a dream come true. I promised God that I would not disappoint him. I promised him that I would ensure that this opportunity was not trivialized.

When I look back to that day, March 6, 2005, I marvel at all my hopes and dreams. I had no idea what was waiting for me in the states, I had no idea at all…

Amaka Lily

If only I could go back to the days of yore
And bask in the innocence of ignorance.

Chapter 1

First impressions of America

SHIFTING ALLEGIANCES

My early days were filled with exploration. America beckoned like a lover wanting to be ravished and I was willing, very willing to comply. Everything about America fascinated me. Everything!

I wanted to touch, see and smell everything.

I was staying with an aunt and uncle, second cousins to my mother. Their whole family had relocated to the U.S. 12 years before my arrival, and they were the only relatives available to house me until I was able to stand on my feet. They also had 7 children, 5 girls and 2 boys, the oldest of whom, Nneka was around my age.

Nneka became my appointed guardian. On a break from college, she was the only one willing and patient enough to show me around. My first teacher, she was the one who introduced me to the mechanics of American society. It was with her I witnessed my first credit-card purchase, with her I rode my first escalator. She never tired of explaining and re-explaining to me how things worked, what things meant that I will forever be indebted to her.

I accompanied her everywhere, on errands, sight-seeing, everything. Any opportunity that arose to breathe American air and witness the sights was eagerly scooped up by me.

In front of our home was a collection of stores, which included the Laundromat and Grocery stores which the family patronized. Since Nneka and I were the oldest, we were usually the ones sent on those errands. To get there, we would use a short cut which really was a trail that doubled up as a bike path. On our walks, we would frequently encounter exercise enthusiasts and dog walkers, both groups trying to get their daily exercise in.

I remember being more than a little taken aback at how friendly American dogs were and how they didn't seem scared of people. As soon as they saw you, they began wagging their tail, the universal sign of friendliness. Sometimes, they would even run up to you and jump on you. It was like they were begging you to touch them. I was not used to that at all.

In Nigeria, humans and canines gave each other a wide berth. You didn't want to be bitten and they didn't want to be yelled at, stoned or end up in somebody's pot. So the few street dogs one encountered, were very fearful and took to their heels at the slightest movement. If a dog approached you boldly, you needed to be scared, because either it was crazy or felt you were encroaching its turf. Regardless of what the reason was, you could be sure of one thing.

The outcome would not be good for you.

So understandably, I was a bit wary seeing dogs approach me wily nily, but after a week of experiencing American canine hospitality and asking questions and doing research, I finally understood why.

American dogs were like children, human children and the American public took great pains to maintain that status quo. They had rights and there were organizations set up to enforce those rights. Mistreating a dog was against the law and a person could be sent to jail for doing just that. There were also things that American dog owners were legally mandated to do, such as bathing their dogs, providing them with reasonable accommodations, taking them on daily walks and having them regularly checked by the veterinarian for diseases.

They even had their own food. This was so different from the way dogs were treated in Nigeria. Nigerian dogs typically slept outside the home, ate left-over's, "exercised" by running away and never saw a hospital in their life.

Dog organizations?

You were not serious.

But the differences didn't stop there. American dogs had dog schools where they were trained on proper etiquette. They also had doggy-day care facilities and even "Doggie Psychologists", who helped sort out their "emotional issues".

SHIFTING ALLEGIANCES

Some owners even took photos of their dogs and hung them around their homes, just as if they were family members, and when those dogs died, gave them a proper burial, complete with casket and mourning.

I had never heard anything like it before.

It was mind-opening, mind enlarging. I had never known that dogs could be treated this way. It was a testament to how great America was that dogs could live lives like this, lives that were better than human beings in a third world country.

It was why American dogs were so bold.

It was why they were so friendly.

Amaka Lily

It seemed as though every other day, we made a visit to the grocery store. The Okafor family was already big by American standards and my addition didn't help matters. There was always something that needed to be picked up, something that had been earlier overlooked or something that had suddenly become a necessity.

The grocery store, *Fresh Groceries*, to my baby American eyes was out of this world. It was fantastically beautiful, fantastically clean. It reminded me of *Kingstime* department store, that expensive Lagos store mainly frequented by foreigners except that this was a thousand times bigger, a thousand times better.

It had everything *Kingstime* had and much, much, more.

When we first moved to Lagos, my mother had begun an annual tradition of visiting *Kingstime* every Xmas eve to procure our Xmas breakfast. It was a treat she started from the time we lived with Aunty Chinwekwu and continued when we moved to our own "home". However, since the store was so expensive, she could only afford to go there once a year.

There were three things which I always looked forward to from such visits, three things which always made me smile and those three things were Ham, Bacon and Sausage.

Oh how I loved the "trio". Perhaps it was because we only had them once a year. Perhaps it was because they were so darn expensive. Whatever the reason was, I loved, loved, loved those items. I could never get enough of it. Never get enough of it. They felt like heaven in my mouth and were absolutely delicious.

When my American trip became likely, I promised myself that once I made it to the states, I would eat ham, bacon & sausage every day of my life!!!

So you can imagine my happiness when I first visited *Fresh Groceries* and saw my beloved items. You can also imagine the joy I felt when I found that they had different varieties of those same items in the store. They had big sausages, fat sausages and skinny sausages. They had beef sausages, chicken sausages and pork sausages. They had thin ham, thick ham and medium ham. They had smoked bacon, regular bacon … you name it.

And they were cheap, very very cheap.

You should have seen me that first day, my inner Shakespeare came out and I began to wax poetic, "*Oh you tastiest of morsels… my soul delights in thee*". Nneka looked at me like I was crazy, but humored me by buying four different kinds of each item.

Another cheap food item in America was chicken. I found it to be cheaper, much cheaper than beef, which was a reverse of how it was in Nigeria. You could buy 10 pieces of huge chicken thighs for just $3.

3 freaking dollars!!!

There were also lots of different kinds of desserts in the store. In fact they had a whole section just devoted to desserts. I had never seen anything like it before. Big cakes, small cakes, plain cakes, fruit cakes, vanilla cakes, chocolate cakes, cheesecake, cookies, muffins, doughnuts, apple pies etc, all freshly baked, all for cheap prices.

I was impressed.

I noticed also that American food manufacturers had taken great pains to cut down on the amount of cooking time necessary to prepare a meal. From chicken which had already been plucked and cleaned, to vegetables that had already been rinsed and cut, Americans had made the cooking process, effortless. No more boiling water, inserting a chicken into it and plucking off its feathers before you could cook it. No more *aroso*[15] that was riddled with stones which you had to take out

---

[15] Local name for rice

carefully lest they break your teeth. No more rinsing and cutting up vegetables.

All the work had already been done for you.

I was impressed. America was even better than I'd been told.

However, I must say that even though I was mostly pleased with American foods, there were some things I had to adjust to, for starters, the beef. It did not taste the way Nigerian beef tasted which was freshly obtained from a cow slaughtered the same day. The beef I ate in America tasted odd. They were like chalk, unflavourful, packed with preservatives. The difference in taste was so clear, that it registered in my mind. Still, I ate them -it is hard for an African to refuse meat- and I continue to eat them, but I still remember how jarring the difference was, the first couple of times I ate them.

There were also some new foods I had to get used to. Like *Farina*, a carbohydrate type of dish like *eba*[16] that was used to eat soup in the Okafor home. It was white and had a very weird taste but after eating it a number of times, I adjusted to it.

Others, like white colored eggs, I simply rejected. The first time I saw Nneka inspecting white eggs to purchase, I almost screamed. I had never seen white eggs before in my life and was certain, a 100% certain that there was something wrong with them. I thought about all the stories I had heard about American livestock being given hormones. I thought about all the articles I'd read about genetic engineering. I truly believed the eggs were a result of a mutation and was unwilling, completely unwilling to subject my body, to its poisoning.

Nneka lost valuable time trying to convince me otherwise. She said that white eggs were harmless and that their color was due to the color of the mother-hen. I did not believe her. I had seen white chickens in Nigeria and they had lain brown eggs.

---

[16] Cooked cassava

SHIFTING ALLEGIANCES

Not white eggs, BROWN eggs. Nneka could believe whatever she wanted to believe but Njideka Onuoraegbunam was not putting white eggs into her body.

Luckily for me, Nneka was flexible and went to another store that sold brown eggs. Even though I found out much later that white eggs are harmless, I still continue to eat only brown eggs till this day. For some reason, my mind still feels they are the only "real eggs".

I also rejected the microwave. The first time I saw that television-looking appliance "warming" food, I knew it was not meant for me. *How does suffusing food with some sort of rays, be it infrared, radioactive or electromagnetic be healthy for a person?*

How can it be?

I believed it was not healthy so till this day, I still heat up my food the Nigerian way, over a stove.

Overall though, I enjoyed American foods. I ate so much of my beloved ham, bacon and sausage that I became tired of them. Imagine that? *Who would have ever thought that was possible?* But get tired I did, that today I don't even eat them.

Still, it was nice to have had that experience.

Amaka Lily

Once a week, armed with the family's dirty clothes, Nneka and I visited the Laundromat. The Laundromat was where Americans "washed" their clothes, except of course, you didn't actually do the washing, a machine did the work for you and another machine, dried the clothes.

When I first learnt that for a few coins plus some detergent, a washing machine washed your clothes for you, I almost died of happiness.

I could not believe it.

My days of hand washing were over. No more standing hunched over a basin, washing clothes with the attendant back ache. No more having my skin peeled or my nails broken by harsh solvents. No more relying on the sun to dry your clothes and being forced to be without clothes if rain chanced to fall. No more ironing either, since Americans had developed a product which you could add to your clothes and which would relax any wrinkles.

Nneka called it a "softener", I called it a "God send".

No more suffering

Life was truly good.

SHIFTING ALLEGIANCES

On weekends, we visited American malls. American malls were what Americans called shopping centers and they were usually enclosed in huge, air-conditioned buildings in the middle of a city. Since we lived in the suburbs, we had to utilize public transportation, specifically, buses to get there.

Now, let me tell you about American buses. These were not the same rickety *danfos* or *molues*[17] that traverse Lagos roads, risking lives while threatening to break down at the same time. No sir. These buses were well designed, fully functional and equipped with the latest in technology.

They were fantastic.

Let's start with the size. These buses were huge. When you got on the bus, there was enough space for one to make his or her way comfortably to his or her seat. I especially marveled at the size of the seats. Having experienced being crammed into buses originally designed for half the occupants with half my rear suspended in mid-air, and the other half resting on hard, metallic seats, this was an enjoyable respite. There was ample space to sit comfortably, stretch your legs and even sleep if you wanted to. The buses were even made to pick up handicapped people as they could be lowered to accept wheel chairs.

I remember thinking to myself: *'This is how it should be. This is how humans should live''*

The buses were also, depending on the season, either air-conditioned or toasty warm. Loud music was discouraged. Also, instead of a conductor yelling the various stops as it approached, a beautiful, well modulated electronic voice announced the stops before hand and thanked you, let me repeat, THANKED you as you disembarked for using their service.

Can you believe it?

---

[17] Danfos and Molues are the local names given to the public buses in Lagos.

Amaka Lily

They were thanking me for using their service. Not swearing at me or telling me roughly to *"Come down "*.

What a blessed experience.

I was also surprised to find that in America, if you wanted to go to an unfamiliar destination but didn't know the way, there was a number you could call, where a person would tell you exactly how to get there, including what buses to use and what times they arrived.

It was AMAZING.

For the first time in my life, I looked forward to riding the bus. It was not only a pleasant experience, but it also gave me an opportunity to gaze at the American populace as the bus went along its way. I couldn't get enough of seeing the modern cars-there were no old cars on the road- or the beautiful people- everyone in America seemed beautiful- or the traffic lights- I was amazed at how they worked.

Traffic appeared to flow smoothly. No potholes, no garbage smells, nothing that was a sore to senses.

It was surreal.

The first mall I ever visited was *Valley on the lakes* mall. Uncle had given me $60 as "Dash money" so that I could buy some clothes since the ones I'd brought with me were insufficient.

I can still remember the first time, I stepped into that mall. I swear, from the moment I entered, till I left, my mouth was agape. I had never seen a building so beautiful and so well laid out. This was the widest and tallest six story building I had EVER been in. Later I would find even bigger and better malls. This mall was filled with all types of stores, choke full with clothes, flashing lights and dance music. It also had many restaurants and entertainment centers. It was simply amazing. I kept swiveling my head to turn around. I could barely keep up with all I was seeing.

SHIFTING ALLEGIANCES

Nneka's plan had been to take me to a variety of stores to give me a sense of their styles and prices so that I could make an informed decision on where to best spend my dollars. The first store we entered, -I would never forget- was called *Raders*. It was filled with typical teenage-hood clothes such as jeans and hoodies. I looked at the first pair of jeans and noted the price.

$24.99.

"*What!*" I screamed "*3,750 Naira for a pair of jeans! No way*"

"*Just try it on...*" Nneka pressed, "*... and see whether it fits. Also, don't forget you are in America now. You can't be converting dollars to Naira*"

But try as I might, I couldn't. I just could not. Every price label I saw was automatically converted to Naira in my head. I could not justify spending 3,750 Naira for a pair of jeans. No way. It was either 750 Naira tops, which worked out to be about $5.

This jeans was ridiculously expensive.

"*Well, you won't find any jeans for under $5 here...*" Nneka continued "*...not unless you go to a thrift shop to buy clothes... but their clothes are used... you don't want that... this is actually a good price for brand new jeans*"

But my mind wouldn't accept it, wouldn't accept it at all. 3,750 Naira could buy you 7 pairs of solid jeans in Yaba Market. 7 pairs of jeans!!! I wasn't going to waste the little money I had on something that was obviously overpriced. This was an expensive store.

"*Let's go to another shop...*" I told Nneka "*...this shop is too expensive*"

"*Alright*"

The second shop we went to was called *Arctic forever*. Now this was more like what I had in mind. Arctic forever was what Americans called a discount store, a store where designer labeled clothes were sold at a discount, as much as 75% less than the true price. This was because, either they were out of season, or the manufacturer made too much of them and wanted to sell off the excess or the manufacturer had mislabeled them such as calling a shirt a medium when it was actually a small.

In any event, it was a great deal.

Brand new clothes for cheap prices?

I was in.

I saw a pair of crocodile colored jeans listed for $10, and it was so pretty, I was willing to pay the full price. Nneka showed me a fitting room where I could try them on, another great service I had never previously experienced.

We did not have fitting rooms in Nigerian markets.

I took three of them with me since they were labeled by sizes and I didn't know what my size was in America. Nigerian clothes, specifically *okrika* [18] which regular people bought, were not organized by sizes. You bought what you thought would fit and hoped that it actually fit.

I tried them all until I found one that fit. But when I tried to close the buttons, I noticed they were missing.

"*What happened?*" Nneka asked as soon as I walked out of the dressing room

"*This one is spoilt…*" I responded "*…no buttons*"

"*You know*"… Nneka continued as I went to look for another pair "*if you had taken this jeans home and found out it was defective, you will be allowed to return it*"

"*WHAAAAATTTT!*" I screamed. I was screaming a lot in those early days. "*You mean they would allow me to return bad clothes? You mean they won't claim that I spoilt it?*"

---

[18] Local name for second hand clothes.

SHIFTING ALLEGIANCES

"Of course they won't. Every store is legally mandated to accept returns. Even if you had worn the clothes for a while and then decided you didn't want it, they would take it back"

"TAKE IT BACK??? After wearing it for a while? Oh that can't be true!"

"It's true! All you need to do is bring your receipt. Sometimes they would even let you return it without your receipt"

"REALLY??? Without my receipt?"

"Yup? And it's not just limited to clothes. You can return anything, shoes, books, bags, electronics, food..., anything at all

"Even if I have already torn open the package? They would still allow me to return it???"

"Yes, of course. This is America, just bring it back and they would take it back"

I almost started weeping right there. I was overwhelmed with emotion. I could not believe that in this country, they would give you, the consumer the benefit of the doubt and allow you to return an item that didn't meet your needs. I really couldn't believe it. It blew my mind away.

This would NEVER, EVER, EVER, EVER happen in Nigeria. Never, ever. First of all, if you go to Yaba market and end up with a defective product, you won't find the seller again. Second of all, if by an act of the gods you managed to find that seller, he or she would tell you that they couldn't take it back since YOU had spoilt it.

America obviously trusted its people and this was something I had never experienced up until that time. It was an unfamiliar but beautiful emotion.

I went back to my searching and found another pair that fit and also had buttons.

Next, I went looking for tops. I found 4 shirts that cost $2.50 each and took them with me.

Amaka Lily

My wardrobe was now complete.
When I went to pay, I was told that it would cost $22.50
"*What?*" I exclaimed for the hundredth time. "*...b... bb.. but I thought the price was $20 for everything*"
The cashier, a woman who was probably tired for the day, looked at me incredulously and said "*The $2.50 is for the taxes ma'am*"
"*What taxes?*" I questioned stammering "*I...I don't understand*"
Nneka chimed in at that moment "*Njideka, every sale in the U.S is accompanied by a sales tax*". She explained "*It is the law. The ticket price is not the price you end up paying and that goes for EVERY SINGLE THING YOU BUY*".
Honestly, I wasn't too happy about the tax portion of my bill. I had never paid sales tax EVER in my life. This was not something we paid in Nigeria. The price you paid was what was quoted. Nothing extra. I worried that this little amount spread over the purchases I would make in the future would cause a dent to my salary...
"*Njideka, didn't you notice that every time we went to the grocery store, I paid taxes?*" Nneka asked as soon as we left the store. Actually, I'd never noticed. Aloud, I said "*No, I didn't*"
"*Well, I've been paying taxes all this while. This is how America is. Everyone pays taxes and it is forwarded to the government. That is why the country works so well*".
I was still thinking about this, until Nneka took me to a store that made me grin from ear to ear.
A dollar store.
A dollar store was a store where everything was sold for $1 and they were brand new, packaged goods with nothing, absolutely nothing wrong with them.
It was just their business model to sell items for $1.
I was in HEAVEN!!!.

SHIFTING ALLEGIANCES

I could not believe my eyes. It seemed like everything you could think of, even clothing accessories, were sold in this store. Food, chocolate, make-up, shampoo, lotion, vitamins, accessories, books, hats, toys, plates, you name it, all for a DOLLAR!!!

I was very happy. My allowance could easily go far in this place, taxes notwithstanding. I was very pleased. My love for the U.S was further deepened as I filled my basket with different types of chocolate.

America was just a wonderful country!

We made many more trips to this and other stores. Of all the outings I did in those early days, visiting *Valley on the lakes* mall was my favorite. No outing was similar to the other and I had a lot of firsts in that mall.

It was in that mall that I rode my first escalator, where I ate my first *McDonald's*. It was also at that mall where I saw my first movie at a theatre and it would always hold a special place in my heart.

One of the things I noticed during those trips was that American stores regularly gave their customers discounts for buying things and that the discounts were legitimate. They did not give you the runaround if you came to redeem an advertised offer. They did not bundle inferior or substandard goods with more expensive items. If they were selling 2 items for the price of one, the second item would not be defective. Both would be equally good. There was no ulterior motive when they gave discounts unlike what I was used to. It was simply to spur sales.

Unfathomable.

It was also on those trips that I noticed that American men were very respectful. They held the doors open for you and allowed you to go into the bus before them. They even gave you their seats if the bus was full, so that you didn't have to stand. I had never seen such gentlemanly behavior before. It wasn't how Nigerian men treated their women.

I was beyond impressed.

At the home front, I was also happy. I shared a room with Nneka and Chibuzo and we had our own personal bathroom. I felt like a queen whenever I took a shower. Hot and cold water came standard at every tap and electricity was on 24-7. Needless to say, I no longer struggled with mosquitoes. It was like they didn't even exist. My skin cleared up and my complexion greatly improved.

Nneka continued to tell me many good things about America. She said that America gave poor people 'food stamps' so that they could be able to buy food and free housing as well. She also said that they had free job training for people who were interested so that everyone in the country could be skilled.

Like I needed any more encouragement to love America?

In those early days, when I turned in at night, I would thank God profusely for the opportunity he granted me to come to this marvelous country.

It was indeed the greatest country in the world.

There was respect for every form of life and dignity for human existence. America also strove to make things easier for its citizens.

It was a great country. It was a wonderful country.

It was my country.

SHIFTING ALLEGIANCES

An idle mind is the devil's workshop

Chapter 2

An Idle Mind

Amaka Lily

By week 4, the thrill was gone. I had explored and over-explored everything that was explore-able in the U.S. I had eaten and over-eaten everything I had fancied. I was now ready for other things, specifically employment. I wanted to work. This was why I had come to America. I had not come here to dilly dally around and waste my time. I had a loan to repay and more importantly, needed to save up for the upcoming school semester.

Now that I was in a country where college admission was merit-based, I was DETERMINED to enroll in school as soon as I could. I had lost 4 years, pining for an education that was beyond my grasp and now that it was finally within my reach, was not going to allow anything, ANYTHING stand in my way.

I felt ready to tackle American employment. I had become conversant with American practices and felt very confident in my ability to handle daily transactions. I could decipher bus schedules, board the bus and navigate the town like a pro. I could slide a credit card and select Credit or Debit. I could order food over the phone and tell them to make it *"To go"*. I no longer walked with a *Johnny Just Come*[19], gait or stared at everything with a look of complete and utter befuddlement.

I was a Native now.

I asked Uncle for some pointers on how to start looking for a job but the response I got, was not what I was expecting...

"To work in America, you first need a social security number"

"Social what???" I didn't think I'd heard correctly *"What is that Uncle?"*

"A social security number is a legal number assigned to you by the U.S. government...." he paused. *"Without that number, no employer can hire you"*

---

[19] "Johnny just come" is a term used by Nigerians to refer to newcomers.

SHIFTING ALLEGIANCES

I was baffled. This was a foreign concept.
Since when did one need a number to work? Whatever happened to just pure desire to work?

"*So even if you want to work...* ", I pressed. "*... They won't hire you?*"

"*Absolutely!*" he emphasized *"If an employer hired you, they could be thrown in jail .... YOU could be thrown in jail. It is THE LAW. You NEED that number to work in the U.S.*"

He continued "*I would ask Nneka to take you to the social security office tomorrow. That is where you can apply for a number. It should take about 2 weeks for you to get your own number since you, yourself are a citizen. Take your birth certificate with you... It shouldn't take long*"

And so the next day, Nneka and I went to the social security office. It was packed. The last time I had seen so many people gathered in one place was at the American embassy in Lagos, but this was different. It was organized and quiet. An attendant asked you what you were there for, and after hearing your response, handed you a particular application form to fill out and assigned you a number. When your number was called, you were to make your way quietly to another section of the office and discuss your issue with a different attendant. I filled out the application form, while also marveling at how efficient American offices were.

"*Number 264*"

I jumped up. I went up to the counter and presented my application and birth certificate to the lady attendant.

"*So you were born in the U.S. and have never been assigned a social security number?*" The woman taking my application peered at me incredulously.

"*No, never Ma!*" I proclaimed. "*I...I.. just came to the U.S.... I've lived in Nigeria all my life. My parents returned to Nigeria as soon as they gave birth to me...*"

"*Hmmh*", she narrowed her eyes, looking at me suspiciously. "*...it is going to take us 45 days to verify that you were actually born in the states. Until that time, we will not be able to assign you a social security number*".

"*What*!!!!" I gasped ". This was way beyond the 2 weeks uncle Ebuka had told me it would take. Then something even more terrifying dawned on me. If this lady was correct, it would be summer before I found a job which meant that I would be unable to save sufficiently before Fall began. This meant that I would not be able to afford college. This meant that I would not be able to go to school. My dreams of college suddenly seemed to be slipping out of my hands...

"*Bu... Bu... But, why should it take so long...?*" I was almost in tears, I didn't want to postpone college for even a minute. I HAD TO GO TO COLLEGE. "*... I mean, I gave you my birth certificate... you have it right there. Why should it take so long to prove that I am a citizen?*"

I didn't understand. I wanted to understand.

"*Well, I'm sorry ...*" she said, "*... it is our policy. We need that time to verify that you were actually born in the states. I'm sorry but it's strange for us to see an American citizen at the age of 20, not have a social security number*". *We would have to verify your birth, and that is the amount of time it would take... Again I'm sorry*"

It was strange because even though she kept saying she was "sorry", she didn't sound sorry. She delivered those words in such a matter of fact, perfunctory tone that was neither apologetic nor comforting. I didn't know it then, but I was getting my first taste of American diplomacy.

I was devastated, but there was nothing I could do. Policy was policy and I was at its mercy.

45 days stretched before me and all I could was wait.

And what a long, interesting wait that was.

SHIFTING ALLEGIANCES

Without a social security number, I couldn't work and without money, I couldn't go out. Uncle Ebuka's generous gift had long since dissipated.

So what does a broke girl do when she has no money? Easy, she stays home.

In May, Nneka began her summer job and my younger cousins enrolled in summer classes. Since Uncle Ebuka and Aunty Priscilla also left in the morning for their various occupations, I became the sole occupant of the apartment starting at 9 am each morning.

It wasn't that bad. Actually it was great. My relatives had cable TV and I used that time to really acquaint myself with American shows.

When I lived in Nigeria, I had loved watching American commercials. You could catch snippets of them from the videos one got from the local market -DVDs were non-existent at the time-. Like a lot of things, the videos were counterfeits but they were the only ones available for sale. Someone who had access to cable, illegally recorded TV movies and mass produced them. Occasionally he or she would forget to stop the recorder when it switched to commercials and that's how it came to be that some of our movies included commercials.

I didn't mind, I considered them a bonus. They were the wittiest, smartest, most visually stimulating and exciting productions ever.

And so in those early days, while I waited for my social security number to arrive, I would sit and watch TV for 5 hours straight taking breaks only to eat or be relieved. I watched everything, all the shows, news and of course all the commercials.

It was around this time that I became acquainted with the likes of *Jerry Springer* & *Maury*. *Jerry Springer* was a show that focused mainly on the bad, depraved sides of American society. It regularly profiled people cheating on their spouses, family members sleeping with family members and things of that nature. It also showcased alternative lifestyles including gays, lesbians, transsexuals and cross-dressers. The participants on the show either came to confess a hidden secret or confront another person for one reason or the other. Predictably, fights broke out and security personnel usually had to intervene.

To say that I was shocked the first time I watched this show, would be the understatement of the century. I kept screaming *"Oh my God!"*, *"Oh my GOD"* because I could not believe what I was seeing, could not believe what was before my eyes. I never knew that people could come out to the world and expose things of themselves, shameful, disgraceful things and have it recorded for posterity.

It was unbelievable.

They were very crass. A lady when asked what red flags clued her in to her cheating husband, would say something like *"Oh, I smelt his dick"*.

WHY WOULD A WOMAN EVEN THINK TO DO SOMETHING LIKE THAT!!!

They also had strange standards. Many of them got extremely livid if a lover had used their tongue in the process of kissing another person. They felt that using one's tongue with another person was much worse than kissing without the tongue. First of all, I didn't know that there were different types of kisses. Second of all, just the fact that your partner kissed another person was grounds for a breakup. Believing that some types of kisses were worse than others just did not make any type of sense to me.

It was shocking, very shocking to me. Many times, I would shout at the TV, scream, *"God will punish you!"* or *"YOU BASTARD!!!"* to the participants who had committed particularly despicable acts. I could not help myself. It just

SHIFTING ALLEGIANCES

came out. Other times, I would just sit stunned, too shocked to say a word.

Now that I write this, I am so glad our neighbors weren't around at the time those shows aired, because they would have thought I was a certified lunatic for screaming the way I did.

But at the time, it was new to me. I had grown up in a society where people took great pains to maintain their external image, a society where your reputation meant everything and the merest of smears could taint your family for generations to come. If you were cheating on your spouse, you did not openly celebrate it. If there was incest in your family, you did not broadcast it to the world. You kept such things HIDDEN. *Jerry Springer* profiled people who not only did these things but also had no compunctions about talking about it, IN FRONT OF THE WHOLE WORLD.

It was as though everything I had been raised to believe and uphold all my life, everything that was drilled into me as "proper behavior" suddenly turned around on its head. It seemed like I had suddenly entered an alternate universe and was indeed out, very out of my element.

Yet, I couldn't stop watching and I eagerly tuned in at its regular time. I was hopelessly riveted. It's like Americans say, "*Watching a car crash*". You don't want to look but you can't help but look. There was always something that captivated me. Whenever I thought I had reached a point where I could no longer be shocked, no longer be horrified, a new episode will take me even lower.

It was on *Jerry Springer* that I saw my first homosexual. Even though I was well aware of the concept of homosexuality -having read more than my fair share of American novels- I had never seen such a person out and about in Nigeria. It was simply not accepted and every man or woman, regardless of their sexuality, was expected to marry and have children. On *Jerry Springer*, I saw quite a few of them and it was like being given access to something forbidden. It was also on that show that I saw my first transsexual. Up until then, I had no idea a person could undergo an operation to completely change his or her sexual organs and seeing things like this made me wonder what type of country I had ended up in...

Maury was another shocker. My most memorable episodes were the ones where a woman, usually accompanied by all the men she had slept with, came to find out which of those men was the father of her child. The host, *M*aury, who would have earlier subjected each of the men to a DNA paternity test, would then read the results and tell the woman and her past lovers, which of the men she brought was the biological father of her offspring. Sometimes the woman was lucky; one of the men would be proven to be the father. Other times, she wasn't. None of the men would be the father, meaning that she had slept with more men than she'd brought on stage, and she would dash out in shame and embarrassment because the whole world now perceived her to be promiscuous.

The fact that a woman would come onto a nationally televised show to proclaim to the world that she had slept with so many men was a shocker to me. The fact that she would also proclaim that she didn't know who the father of her child was, was also inexplicable to me. It seemed to me that you would want to keep your whoring around a secret and that if it even became necessary to determine paternity of your child, to do so privately. I mean, it just seemed so obvious to me. *Didn't she know that her reputation was at stake. Didn't she know that her family's reputation was at stake? Didn't she know that her friends, her coworkers, her BOSS would see this? Wasn't she worried that no man would ever marry her?*

I couldn't understand it. *Where was the embarrassment, the shame? Where were the thoughts that future descendants would see this? Where was the modesty?* But what was even more earth shattering was that some of these women weren't

SHIFTING ALLEGIANCES

even women. They were girls. Very young teenagers and already they had multiple children. If I had seen one of these girls walking outside, I would sincerely have thought the children were her siblings... not her offspring!!!

I remember the first time I saw a girl who was about 13 with 2 children, come to the show. I couldn't wait for Nneka to arrive from her job. Once she came back, I cornered her and told her of the terrible tragedy I had seen...

"*Yes, that's America for you*", was her nonchalant response.

"*It's no big deal....*" she continued, "*... many of my classmates have babies. It's just very different here*"

"B....B...Butttt..." It was hard for me to wrap my head around it, hard for me to understand why it wasn't a big deal for American teenagers to have their own kids outside marriage. IT WAS A BIG DEAL. I sputtered aloud, "*Don't they worry that they are now finished for life... that no man would ever marry them ... that no mother would ever allow her sons to marry them. Don't they worry about these things?*"

"*Oh, No!*" Nneka laughed hysterically "*...America is not like Nigeria in that sense. A woman can have 10 children out of wedlock and a man would STILL marry her*"

She continued "*...there's no stigma here in America. No one considers you used if you have a baby. It's just life*" she finished.

I couldn't believe it. Could not believe it.

It was contrary to everything I had been raised to believe. If I had chanced to get pregnant in Nigeria out of the confines of marriage, my life would have been OVER. First of all, my family would have disowned me. Second of all, no man would ever want to marry me. I would be considered "used goods" and the shame that would have wrought on my personhood was so odious, it was a nightmare to even contemplate.

Amaka Lily

It was a generally held sentiment in our society, in fact, many Nigerian women would rather abort than have a child out of wedlock. Even though coitus was done, it was very important for a woman to maintain the perception of purity, however hypocritical.

Later on, I found out that these shows were collectively called "thrash TV" and that it was not descriptive of the majority of the American public and more importantly, that the authenticity of some of what they showed was debatable.

At the time though, I didn't know. I thought it was all real. A 100% real

After the thrash shows, I would watch Court shows. Court shows were real cases of people being prosecuted on TV and those shows taught me invaluable lessons about how American society functioned.

For starters, I learnt that America was a very litigious society. Very, very litigious. People could sue you for anything and it was surprising how seemingly inconsequential and meritless cases were won.

If a friend visited your home, slipped and fell, he or she could sue you. What's more, you would be liable for the person's injuries because the courts consider the homeowner to be negligent.

Can you believe it? A person comes to your house, eats your food, somehow falls and hurts himself and instead of appreciating your kindness and hospitality, sues you for his injuries AND the courts SIDE with the person!!!

How in the world was that fair?

Another example, say you run a restaurant and one of your patrons eats a meal, and for whatever reason, a stone happened to be in it and he broke his teeth, you could legally get sued for monetary damages. Even though it may not have been your fault, the court will hold you negligent. I even heard about one

SHIFTING ALLEGIANCES

incident where a woman mistakenly poured hot coffee on her body and successfully sued the restaurant who sold it to her.
Can you believe it?
You buy coffee, you pour it on yourself, albeit mistakenly, and yet, you sue me for damages?
What type of nonsense was that?
American law seemed CRAZY.

It didn't stop there. Adults in America are prohibited from disciplining kids. That means, they cannot flog, beat, slap their own or anybody else's children, even for disciplinary purposes. They considered it child abuse and an organization called CPS, Child Protective Services could whisk you to jail, take your children away from you and place them permanently with other people.

It was ludicrous.

My definition of child abuse was very different from what Americans considered child abuse. Child abuse was beating a child violently, for no reason at all or for an extended period of time. The mere application of a cane, a palm or a fist did not automatically constitute child abuse and I found the total banning of all forms of punishment to be a bit excessive.

I had known many children whom words alone were not effective in curbing bad behavior and only the application of pain deterred them from continuing their wrong path. Many times, I had seen how a carefully placed slap to the cheek of a mouthy child, nipped bad behavior in the bud. I had witnessed throughout my educational career how immensely motivating a cane was and how it transformed dumb students into academic superstars. There was even a popular saying, "*Spare the rod and spoil the child*" to illustrate how corporal punishment was essential to bringing up a child with the right character. I thought that not allowing some form of discipline could cause mouthy and disrespectful kids. I thought that if these laws were applied in Nigeria that many of our parents would be in jail…

Amaka Lily

As time has passed with me living in this society, I have relaxed some of my disciplinary views. Even though I still believe that discipline is necessary, I have found that there are multiple options apart from corporal punishment to achieve corrected behavior but we are going too fast, let's return to the court shows…

There were other strange things I learnt. For example, Americans considered 18 years old to be the start of adulthood. Once you turned 18, your parents could legally push you out of the house and expect you to fend for yourself. I didn't think that was fair but perhaps with mouthy kids that could not be disciplined, the parents had no choice. In Nigeria, you lived at home until you were married off and your parents' paid for your university education -that's of course, if you managed to enter a Nigerian college- and living expenses. Here, parents were not mandated to pay your university education and many students had to take out loans. It was strange.

Americans also had a very different idea about what appropriate dating ages were. If you are 18 years or above, you are not allowed to date someone younger than 18. They consider those younger than 18 minors and dating them could cause you to be sent to jail and be labeled a sex offender for the rest of your life. They also look with revulsion at older men who date much younger women. They say it is "gross" and prefer to see people within the same age group dating each other.

I thought that was funny. Having seen men date and marry girls who were a third or a fourth of their ages in Nigeria, I thought the law was ridiculous. *How are you a sex offender if you date someone that's a year or 2 younger than you? How are you a sex offender if you date someone who is willing to date you?*

But in the end, those court shows proved instrumental in teaching me important things about American law such as what

SHIFTING ALLEGIANCES

my rights were, what to be wary of, how to protect myself - such as not lending money to anyone without signing a contract- and basically how to act in American society.

I also learnt some American vernacular. For instance, Americans call a rude person, a person with an "*attitude*". If a person, object or situation is bad, they say the person, object or situation, "*sucks*". They also call beating up a person "*kicking their arse*". The latter expression still makes me laugh till this day. The thought of someone kicking somebody else's buttocks is just hilarious.

So this is how I kept my mind occupied while I waited for my social security card to arrive. Watching show after show and gaining knowledge about American society. But after a while, I started becoming bored of it, so bored, that one day, I did something that I have been too ashamed to tell anyone.

I called 911.

I still remember that day. The usual shenanigans on *Jerry Springer and Maury* could not hold my attention and so I decided to do something different. I decided to call 911 and see how it really worked. After dialing the number, I heard an operator say "*911, what is your emergency?*" As soon as I heard that, I froze. I did not know what to say and so I hung up. I thought that was the end of it. I didn't know that in America, if you call that number and hang up, they will come to your place. They have a system which traces all calls back to the caller's home and they dispatch a police who's nearby to investigate.

5 minutes later, I heard a loud knock on our door.
BANG, BANG, BANG
"*Who... Who is it?*" I asked trembling
"*It's the police*", came a deep authoritative voice "*... someone called 911*"

Amaka Lily

Chei![20], Olopa![21]. I was scared, more than scared. I didn't expect the police to show up. *What had I done? Would they take me to jail?* Oh God.

Gingerly, I opened the door. This tall, muscular African American man stood in our doorway, examining me carefully.

"Is there a problem?" he asked

"No si… sir!" I stammered *"… it was me, I made a mistake"*

"You sure?" he asked

"Ye… Yes Sir!" I responded *"… it really was a mistake"*

"Alright…" he said *"…but I have to check around just to be sure. Can I come in?"*

It was more of an order than a request and so I allowed him in. He checked every room in our house while I stood at the door quaking. When he was done, he came over to me with a look that suggested he had been through this before.

"Maam, the 911 number is an emergency number and should only be used for emergencies. Do you understand?"

"Yes, sir" I responded. I was mortified, deeply mortified

"When you call us like that, you take us away from people who may really need us" he explained. *Do you understand?"*

"Yes sir", I responded. I felt terrible *"I am really sorry"*

"Just don't do it again" he said, then as if in afterthought, he asked *"Where are you from?"*

I couldn't lie. I said Nigeria and felt so ashamed of the bad impression I had created in this man's mind. He was going to hate all Nigerians now…

"Oh yeah?" he responded, his face breaking into a smile *"What's it like living in the motherland?"*

I told him it was nice and I had just arrived. He asked me a few more questions, and then finally bade his adieu.

I was so relieved to see him leave.

---

[20] Exclamatory shout
[21] Yoruba word for Police

SHIFTING ALLEGIANCES

I never told Nneka what happened.
I have never called the police again.

Amaka Lily

Chapter 3

An American Job

SHIFTING ALLEGIANCES

Eight weeks to the day of my application, my social security card finally arrived in the mail.

I was ecstatic.

I was now a legitimate American citizen

I could now be employed!!!!

I danced and danced and danced.

I danced from the parlour to the kitchen. I danced from the kitchen to the verandah. I flashed my card over and over again in the faces of my cousins, until Uncle had to tell me to stop. Next up, I picked up the day's newspaper and began scouring the job ads. I circled all the jobs I thought I could do, even the ones that were really a stretch. My plan was to bombard many employers with my CV.

Surely someone would bite?

Jobs circled, I cleared my youngest cousin from the family computer and began emailing my CV. I did not leave that computer until I had applied to every single job I had identified. When that was done, I went to my room to dream.

What would it feel like to actually be an American worker?
How would it feel to finally be in the system?

I didn't have to wonder long, because the next day, I got a call for a receptionist position.

The pay? $7.50 an hour.

Could I come in that Friday for an interview?

"*BUT OF COURSE!!!!*" I yelled, a tad too excitedly into the telephone -I couldn't help myself- "*…Yes, I can come. What time do you need me to be there?*" It was only after I had taken down the details and hung up the phone that I remembered I didn't have interview clothes.

The only clothes I had were the ones brought from Nigeria plus the new ones I'd bought in America… all casual, all jeans.

I had nothing to wear.

Luckily, Aunty Priscilla -God bless that woman- came to the rescue. She had some old suits, which were now too small for her frame which she graciously offered to me. I selected one that seemed closer to my size and tried it on. It was loose, but nothing that 2 large safety pins couldn't fix.

I cinched the waist and surveyed myself in the mirror.

I
LOOKED
SMASHING!!!
I looked like a lawyer!!!!
I was now ready to take on the world.

That Friday, I woke up early. Even though my interview wasn't until 2pm, I felt it necessary to be in serious mode. I didn't watch my usual *Jerry Springer* or *Maury* shows. I didn't want anything soiling my thoughts.

Mrs Rita Chelsea was the owner of the ad agency I was interviewing at. She was a mid-forties white lady with starkly red hair. She welcomed me warmly, offered me a chair and brought me coffee. I accepted everything, albeit nervously.

Then, she began to ply me with questions. One after the other, the questions kept coming. *What was my background? What did I hope to gain from this position? How long did I intend to stay? What were my future goals? My educational goals?* On and on and on. I tried to answer her questions as quickly as she threw them, while praying I didn't spill any coffee on myself. The woman was relentless. She questioned me for one hour straight.

Next she asked if I knew typing. I replied in the affirmative silently thanking God for the brutal typing class I had taken in secondary school. A class so intense that the slightest mistake caused you to be knocked on the head by the dreaded Mr. Nwosu but which at the end of the term, made all of us excellent typists. She then took me to a computer and asked me to demonstrate my skills. I did so while she stood looking over my shoulder. After that, she gave me a writing test, a comprehension test and a reading test. Today, I look back and

SHIFTING ALLEGIANCES

wonder how I kept my composure, but the gods were definitely on my side, because she offered me the job on the spot.

I could not believe it.

Everything was finally coming together in my life.

I was now going to be able to afford college.

I had learnt in the preceding weeks that I didn't need to save up the full tuition amount to start college, but that having something to contribute helped. Now, I had a job that would help me contribute something.

I was deliriously happy.

"Thank you so much Mrs Chelsea. Thank you! Thank you! Thank you".

"Great" she said. *"Now, a few ground rules"*. For starters, I was no longer to call her Mrs. Chelsea. I was only to call her Rita, just as I would call a comrade of mine. I was very uncomfortable at that request because we, Nigerians don't call people in authority by their first names. It was considered disrespectful. I tried to explain to her that I couldn't do that but she insisted I do so.

Next, she told me that I wasn't expected to wear business suits at all in the office. She said the dress code was "business casual" and in that office, that meant I could wear jeans. Now THAT was a piece of news that I readily accepted. Not only would it not be necessary for me to spend money which I didn't have buying work attire, but also, my fear of looking like a class mate's grandmother was gone.

One of the things that had concerned me was wearing work clothes to school. Since I had planned to go to school right after work, I didn't want to look older than I was. I wanted to look young, to blend in with my peers and I had wondered whether I would need to carry a change of clothes and carve out extra time to change after work.

Amaka Lily

Being able to wear jeans meant I could seamlessly go from work to school and no one would be the wiser.

She also mentioned something called health insurance which she said I'd qualify for, only after I'd worked for the company for 3 months. I remember thinking as she explained what it was, that it sounded like a waste of money. *Why pay for something that was tied to your probability of falling sick, in a country where the likelihood of illness was low?*

It didn't make sense.

Finally, she concluded by asking if I could begin work the following Monday.

My answer?

"OFCOURSE I COULD"

I went home that day in a truly joyous mood. I was so happy. I danced and danced and danced. I sang praises to God and kept a praise record running constantly in my room . This time around, Uncle Ebuka left me alone.

The following Monday, I set out to work.

I was wearing my brand new jeans. The same jeans I'd bought for $10. I was also wearing my brand new sneakers that I was really proud of. I thought I looked very good, like I could pass for an African American, which was my greatest desire.

I strutted my stuff. I wanted the whole world to see how good I looked. When I boarded the bus, I grabbed a seat that was in the aisle and stuck my legs out so that everyone would notice my shoes. I was so proud of myself. So, so proud of myself, until it dawned on me that I lacked something that every other sneaker-wearing person had. Something that was so essential to wearing sneakers.

SOCKS!

I WAS NOT WEARING SOCKS

I wanted to die!

I had never worn sneakers in Nigeria. It was either slippers or proper shoes. The last time I'd worn socks was when I was in primary school. I had no idea that you needed to wear socks with sneakers. I had no idea that socks made a difference to how your sneakers looked. I had no freaking idea.

God I was so embarrassed.

My new found bravado disappeared. This is what I get for showing off. I quickly tucked my essentially naked feet into my seat and hoped no one had noticed me. I was so so embarrassed. So so embarrassed.

Now I can laugh at myself and at how clueless I was. Apart from the absence of socks, my $10 sneakers were also not of the designer variety, the kind that really impresses Americans. So basically, what I was wearing was pretty unremarkable.

Mercifully, I didn't know that at the time.

Amaka Lily

I worked with three other people in the office, John, Sharon and Kathy. They were all white and they all welcomed me warmly into the office. They asked me where I was from, asked how I was adapting to the U.S. and after telling them my name, asked me if there was a short version of it.

"Ummm, Deka, I guess?"

It was from that moment on, that I began to be known as Deka.

Ms. Kathy and I became fast friends. Even though she was as old as my mother, she talked to me as if I was a peer. I wasn't used to that. In Nigeria there is an unbridgeable gap between adults and younger people, a gap that continues to be maintained even as you age. You don't freely discuss certain things with older people and they won't discuss certain things with you. Too much familiarity was discouraged and that was understood by everyone.

Ms. Kathy wasn't like that. She treated me like her age-mate, as though my opinion mattered. It made me feel important. She was also incredibly in tune with all things young and we spent a lot of time discussing American celebrities, a subject we were both obsessed with.

It was from Ms. Kathy's mouth that I first heard the word calories. Ms. Kathy like a lot of white American women was obsessed with her weight. Extremely obsessed. They know exactly how many calories each food item contains and monitor their meals closely lest they become fat. I discovered that the worst insult you can call a white American woman is "fat". Actually calling them "fat arse" can send them into a deep and lingering depression. They subject their bodies to countless diets and other deprivations, just to be called "skinny" and are extremely happy when they lose weight.

It was unbelievable to me.

SHIFTING ALLEGIANCES

Coming from a place where an *ikebe*[22] was a sign of great beauty, where a fat person was a positive sign of good living and a thin body an indication of starvation or worse, an incurable disease, it just did not make sense to me.

Why, in a country of plenty, would a person deliberately strive to look starved?

Why, in a country of plenty, do rich women deliberately starve themselves just to be considered beautiful?

Why? Why? Why?

It was warped.

Very warped.

But it really wasn't their fault. Their men loved really thin women and considered bones beautiful.

Anyway, Ms. Kathy was always counting calories and telling me what foods I should eat and not be eating. Whenever we went to lunch she would look at the menu and the first thing she would do is point at things saying "*Oh, that sure will pack on the pounds*"

When I was still new to the office and trying to be friendly, I would follow her and order whatever she settled on, which was usually salads, wheat bread sandwiches or other bland fare. After a while, I stopped doing that.

The foods she always wanted to eat were not only less filling but also, they were tasteless. *When did I become a herbivore? Why did I have to eat food that tasted like chalk when my body was craving greasy, carbohydrate laden and spicy foods? Why was I paying for food I was not enjoying?*

And so I began to tell Ms. Kathy -always politely of course- that I wanted to eat other things. I wanted to eat that deep fried rotisserie chicken with the side order of curried rice and baked potatoes. I wanted to have a side order of dessert, of cheesecake and ice-cream. I wanted to drink real coke, not the

---

[22] Big buttocks

diet one anymore, but the one that had all the calories. It was sweeter.

At first she said "*You gotta watch it Deka. Those things pack on the pounds. You are gonna blow up if you are not careful*". But I didn't care. I couldn't care. Yes, let my body blow up. Let it blow up. It needed to. I was still so thin and needed to look like I had been living in America. I needed those fattening, tasty foods, foods designed for a Nigerian palate. When she saw that I couldn't be swayed and that my fast metabolism, which I didn't even know I had, prevented me from gaining pounds, she gradually relented.

Speaking of food, I had to adjust to American party food. The first time I went to an office party, I expected to see things along the lines of jollof rice and fried chicken. Meaning I expected to see real dishes. Instead what I saw were chips, salsa, biscuits, cold cuts and soda. I was shocked to say the least. Those were not party food!

They also had parties they called potluck where everyone was expected to contribute food. It didn't seem like a party to me if you were bringing food with you. I thought hosts were supposed to provide everything. That's how it was in Nigerian. *Why did guests have to contribute?*

It was weird, but like many things, I adjusted.

SHIFTING ALLEGIANCES

I loved making money, loved earning money. Even though I was earning $7.50 an hour, less the taxes that is mandatory in American society, it was still a lot of money to me.

It was DOLLARS baby, DOLLARS and a dollar was a 150 times the value of our Naira.

That was real money baby and it made me feel so good.

When I first started working at Bedazzled, I tried to speak to everyone with an American accent. I especially did this while answering the phones. Like many Nigerians, I thought that by speaking with an American accent, I would sound cool. I did not want to speak with my natural Nigerian accent, I thought it was "razz"[23], ugly, and I just wanted to blend in.

My script was to say, *"Hello, thank you for calling Bedazzled agency, how can I help you?"*

But a strange thing happened. When I tried to use my new voice to speak, the callers, couldn't understand me. The sound that emanated from my throat was indecipherable to American ears.

I could not understand what was going on.

My voice sounded perfectly American to my ears and I couldn't understand why the callers kept asking me to repeat myself or sometimes, ask to be transferred to someone else.

Wasn't I speaking their language?

And so I tried even harder to speak *phonee*[24]. I raised the pitch of my voice, added a little lilt. I raised it so high that sometimes I felt like I was about to choke. Sometimes it felt like I was learning English all over again.

Still, nothing, in fact, more callers would ask to be transferred to someone else. The more I tried to not seem Nigerian, the more I sounded like something that was not American.

---

[23] Nigerian slang for ghetto
[24] Nigerian slang for a westernized accent

Amaka Lily

It was frustrating.

Finally, one day after another caller had insisted I transfer him to another person, I decided to shelve it and speak with my natural voice.

As soon as I did that, an even stranger thing happened. Not only did the callers now understand me, but they also began to compliment my voice. They would say things such as "*Oh, you have such a lovely British accent!*" or "*Your voice is so beautiful*"

I could not believe it. No one had ever said I had a "*British accent*" and certainly we Nigerians didn't think our accent was "lovely".

What were these callers drinking? But the compliments never stopped and even to this day, years later, I still continue to draw the occasional "*beautiful accent*" comment from some Americans.

It was a lesson I needed to learn. I had so imbibed the message that a Nigerian accent was inferior, and a western one much preferable, that I did not realize what I had. I did not realize that the accent I so derided was actually considered exotic by others, just as I considered their accents so. I was trying to be something else when what I already was, was okay.

But I was just beginning. There were many more lessons to come in the ensuing years.

The funny thing was, when I stopped trying so hard to speak phonee[25], American mannerisms crept into my voice, naturally.

My voice situation resolved, I threw myself into learning about our little organization. Emboldened and motivated, I asked my coworkers to teach me what they were doing, even offering to take up extra tasks. I was the first person to arrive in the office and the last to leave. Ms. Chelsea took note and

---

[25] Nigerian slang for a Westernized accent

SHIFTING ALLEGIANCES

encouraged the others to show me how to use computer software.

I learnt fast.

It was at *Bedazzled* that I first learnt to write my dates in the American way i.e. from 18/2/2005 to 2/18/2005 and that "cheques" were spelt "check" and "colour" was written "color".

I learnt to say "*Bless you*" when somebody sneezed, instead of "*Sorry*" and "*Excuse me*" instead of "*Sorry*" when I mistakenly tripped on someone.

I also carefully watched my colleagues' interactions with each other. This was the first time I had ever worked in close quarters with white people and I was curious to see how they truly behaved. I noticed that Ms. Chelsea treated all of us, her subordinates with respect. She didn't treat us like we were lower than her. She treated us as if we were all mates.

Instead of commanding you to "*Do this?*", or "*Do that*" she would say "*Could you please do this?*" or "*Would you mind doing this?*" and she was the boss!!!!

She never used a commanding tone at all. Her voice was always low and my coworkers used low tones as well.

I was amazed. In Nigeria, you always knew who the boss was and the person never made you forget that. If you came to *Bedazzled*, you would never have known who ran the place.

I found this sentiment shared in the broader society. No job was looked down upon because of its title. Particularly striking was the case of Nurses and Secretaries. I found that Nurses and Secretaries were highly regarded in America, the opposite of what obtained in Nigeria. Nurses were considered almost on par with doctors and paid significant salaries. Secretaries here were almost like business people. They wore suits, maintained calendars and even had their own special holiday called "Sccrctaries Day".

I was really impressed and thought this further underscored

Amaka Lily

how advanced America was, in that it valued people irrespective of their titles.

It seemed as though America was truly better than Nigeria. Truly better in a lot of ways.

Chapter 4

Tonsillitis

Amaka Lily

A month into my work life I got tonsillitis. *"No big deal"*, I thought. I knew the drill. I had caught tonsillitis so many times in Nigeria that I could treat myself blindfolded. Two antibiotics taken daily for a week was the solution for this condition and it worked every time. Sometimes, not taking any medication and simply riding it out would suffice which was actually my first course of action. Well, that did not work. A week later, my throat still ached. It throbbed and throbbed and throbbed. I could barely swallow food and had a headache, fever and was coughing up little splatters of blood. I knew I needed antibiotics FAST.

After work, I went straight to *Fresh Groceries* and perused the medicine aisle. I couldn't find any antibiotics there. I then went to the pharmacy which was housed at the back of the store. *Surely they would have some antibiotics?* I had about $50 with me and thought that would be sufficient. In Nigeria, antibiotics cost about 20 naira a pill. It had to be cheaper in the country that manufactured the drug...

I went up to the counter assistant and said

"Hello, do you have antibiotics and how much do they cost??"

"Huh..." she looked at me quizzically, confusion quickly spreading over her face. *"... it would depend on what type... Can I see your prescription?"*

I was confused. *What prescription?* I repeated *"I just want to buy antibiotics?"*

"Yes, but you need a prescription before you can buy antibiotics"

I was still confused. *Why was she insisting on a prescription?* I just wanted to buy antibiotics….. I mean…

SHIFTING ALLEGIANCES

wasn't this a pharmacy? *Since when did one need prescriptions to buy common medicine[26]?*

Seeing my confusion, and putting together my accent, she finally surmised I was a foreigner.

"*Are you new to America?*" she asked, her tone now kind.

"*Yes, I am*"

"*Well, in this country, pharmacies don't sell drugs to people just like that. You have to get a prescription from a doctor BEFORE we can sell you anything. It is the law*"

At that moment, the laws in America were beginning to just be absurd. It seemed that there were laws for the most mundane and meaningless of things. It was becoming really tiresome. I could understand the laws to get a social security number and to protect you in a contract. *But a law that prevented you from buying simple medicine?* Now that was just RIDICULOUS.

I persisted.

"*But what if you know what's ailing you? Do you still need a prescription for something you know what the treatment is?*"

"*Absolutely! You cannot buy any prescription medication in the U.S without a prescription.*" she reemphasized. "*No pharmacy will sell medicine to you here without a prescription*"

This did not make sense to me. In Nigeria, a person could easily walk up to any pharmacy to buy medicine and no prescription was needed. *Why did medicine require a prescription here, when in Nigeria it was available without one, and in unlimited amounts? Why was it that the country that manufactured the drugs, had so many hurdles that did not exist in other countries?*

It didn't make sense.

---

[26] Drugs, Medicine, Medication are used interchangeably in Nigeria to refer to prescription medicine.

But this was America and what's that saying again? *When in Rome, do as the Romans do?*

"So what do I do?" I asked the lady. There was no way I was going to have a good night's sleep with this pain. My throat was sore and I needed some relief. *"I really need this medication. Where can I get a prescription today??"*

"Well you can go to General Hospital which is 3 blocks away" she offered *"they have doctors there 24-7. Go to the emergency room section, and they would give you a doctor who will write you a prescription"*, she offered helpfully. She even gave me directions to the place.

I was grateful.

I went straight to General Hospital and asked to see the *"Doctor for Prescriptions"*

"What are you here for Ma'am?" an obviously overworked attendant asked of me.

I told her I had tonsillitis.

"What's your name, age & address?"

I told her

"Do you have any health insurance?"

"No", I answered.

She ushered me into another section where another nurse took my vital signs. She checked my blood pressure, temperature and heart rate.

I was okay.

I asked her when I could see the *"Doctor for prescriptions"*. She told me there was no "Doctor for prescriptions" per se but that I could get a prescription after being seen by a doctor.

She took me to the waiting room. I looked around. There were about 30 people waiting in this room. I asked her, *"How long will it take before I can see the Doctor?"*

"Oh, it would be a while" was her response

And what a diplomatic response that was, because if I had known what a *"while"* in American emergency rooms meant, I

SHIFTING ALLEGIANCES

would have gone straight home, tonsillitis be damned. But I was still new to the U.S. and I didn't know what that meant.

I took a seat and waited.

And waited

And waited

And waited.

All around me where people in various stages of illness. Some groaning loudly, others cradling a broken arm or leg. Blood spattered bandages everywhere.

It was crazy.

Every so often, a nurse would come out and call a person's name.

Jude Robinson

Carlos Henriquez

Joe Thomas

Sky Ramos

It seemed like everyone was called but me.

Twice while waiting, there was a huge ruckus. The first was an ambulance filled with people involved in a drive by shooting. Because the people being brought were either half dead or bleeding profusely, they took precedence over those of us who were "*not so sick*"

The second was a pregnant woman who was practically giving birth as she was rushed into the hospital.

Again she took precedence over those of us who were "*not so sick*"

I understood even though my patience was tried. But even if I didn't, there was nothing I could do about it.

4 hours and 30 minutes later, it was my turn.

Before the lady even called my name, I knew it was going to be me, me of the unpronounceable name. The look on her face said it all…

"*Sorry, I can't pronounce this name*, she preambled, *IN-NEE-JEE- DEK-KER*

Amaka Lily

ON-NU...."

"That's me" I answered sparing my father's name from further disrepute

"Oh I'm sorry", she beamed brightly at me *"what would you like me to call you?"*

"Just call me Deka" I said. It was an effort to talk to this woman. My throat was hurting and I had lost 4 hours of my time. Uncle didn't even know where I was as I did not have a cell phone. I was also hungry, feverish and my throat was still aching.

She took me into another room and sat me on a bed

"So what's wrong with you? She asked. I told her I had tonsillitis

She looked at me disbelievingly. *"How do you know you have tonsillitis?"*

"Look at this woman!" I thought to myself. *"Did she think this was the first time I had caught tonsillitis?* I KNEW the symptoms. Aloud, I reassured her that I had tonsillitis.

She said she needed to be sure. Asked me to open my mouth and peered into my throat with an instrument. After looking, she took another instrument to poke my throat, take a sample of God knows what and then left to do some tests.

I waited in that cold hard room for what seemed another eternity.

Then she came back with results of my tests. *"Looks like you were right. You do have tonsillitis"*.

"Duh". I thought to myself.

Are you allergic to any medication?

I told her No.

She then gave me a prescription for antibiotics.

Finally I had the blessed prescription in my hands.

I rushed back to *Fresh Groceries* pharmacy and presented the prescription to another pharmacist. I thought that was it.

SHIFTING ALLEGIANCES

Then that bloody question again, "*Do you have health insurance?*

What was it with this health insurance? This was the second time I had been asked that question, why was it so important?

I told the pharmacist no.

She said "*It might be a little bit expensive because you don't have insurance*" and went ahead to ring up the price.

It came to $20. I swallowed it quickly and rushed home, wanting to be done with what I thought had been a horrible day.

But that wasn't the end of it.

Two weeks later, I received 2 bills from General Hospital. One was for the hospital itself and the other was for the nurse practitioner who had seen me. The total was $498.52. $500 for seeing a nurse practitioner for 20 minutes!!!

I began to freak out. There was no way I was going to be able to pay this bill and also be able to contribute to my school fees. I barely made enough as it was and I didn't think an American college -which I hadn't yet selected at the time- would take me in without ANY money and I HAD TO GO TO COLLEGE.

I was scared. I thought the police would come and arrest me for non-payment. It did not occur to me that the police in America don't arrest people for hospital bills -hence the reason for my big bill since I was paying for the many people who had utilized the hospital's services but never paid-. It also did not occur to me that I could negotiate with the hospital to make little payments.

I cursed the tonsillitis that had put me in this situation. *Why oh why did it come when it did? Why oh why did it come with such intensity? Who knew that treating such a common ailment would prove so expensive?*

Luckily, Uncle Ebuka stepped in again. He didn't want me to defer college. I had come too far to stop now. He offered to

Amaka Lily

pay off my entire bill and I didn't have to pay him back. To say that I was touched to my bone would be insufficient to convey what his gesture meant to me. Nevertheless his kind act granted me peace and enabled me to focus on what was important.

Selecting an American college!

Chapter 5

An American College

Amaka Lily

When I began searching for universities, I was shocked to find out how many universities America had. America had thousands of universities, thousands and thousands of universities and it was not uncommon for one state to have as many as two hundred colleges. As I looked into their characteristics, I realized that the reason for their profusion was because America tried to cater to every need a student could possibly have…

There were universities for people who didn't have money and universities for those who had a lot of money.

There were universities for people who wanted to attend in the daytime and universities for those who wanted to attend at nighttime.

There were universities for people who liked to be in a school building and universities for those who wanted to do their school-work at home.

There were universities for people who wanted to study in the city and universities for those who wanted to stay in the suburbs.

There were universities for people who wanted to focus on a specific field and universities for others who wanted to sample multiple fields.

There were universities for men only and universities for women only.

There were universities for people of one race and universities for people of every race.

There were universities for people of a particular faith and of course universities for those who didn't serve anything…

Many universities, many choices and each one of them offering an American education, the most sought after education worldwide.

I knew what I was looking for in an American university. I wanted a university that was affordable and offered classes in

SHIFTING ALLEGIANCES

the evening. Since I worked during the day, I needed to be able to take classes at night. The college also had to be on the bus route as buses were my only mode of transportation. My search led me to Rose Titus College, a well regarded 4 year college 30miles from my home. In addition to meeting all my criteria, it also offered student payment plans, which meant I didn't have to pay the entire cost of the school fees upfront. I could pay it in installments.

I applied.

Three days later, I got an acceptance letter

It was shocking how fast it came. Whereas back home, even with connections and money, you still had to wait months before you knew whether you'd been accepted or not.

Here it took just days.

America was just great!

I showed Ms. Chelsea and all my other coworkers my acceptance letter. I was so, so happy and excited. Ms. Chelsea and Ms. Katy congratulated me but my other coworkers didn't seem as excited as I was about going to college. They said *"What's the big deal?"* which made me wonder what was wrong with them.

Didn't they realize what a gift it was to be accepted into an American college?

Much, much later, I would discover that my coworkers were not unique in their thinking. A sizeable number of Americans do not view college as a big deal and do not choose it as a career path. College is seen as one of many avenues to getting a job and not THE only avenue as far as we Nigerians are concerned. Other highly regarded avenues in the U.S. include joining the military, attending a trade school and serving as an apprentice. I also found that not having a college degree did not preclude one from getting a professional job and that many employers considered experience and ability to learn, to be far more superior to what they termed a "piece of paper". Lastly,

Amaka Lily

the society as a whole did not consider college degree holders to be the only people worthy of respect. Americans felt that as long as you had a job and paid your bills on time, that you were a worthy member of society and accorded you respect.

It was shocking to me. Having grown up where it was expected that you pursued a college degree -despite the fact that obtaining one was another matter-, it was shocking to see that in a country where such an education was easily obtainable, that not all of the populace partook of the opportunity. Coming from a country where people liked to show off their degrees, where it wasn't uncommon to see a person announced as the Honorable. Dr. Mr. Engineer Nwafor it was a mind shifting realization.

I finally understood why during the 8 weeks I had stayed at home, why I had seen so many TV ads urging people to enroll in colleges. I had not understood why anyone would need to be "encouraged" to go to college.

Now, I understood why.

SHIFTING ALLEGIANCES

A week before the semester started, I received an invitation to attend a new student orientation. I informed Ms. Chelsea in advance and she graciously allowed me to leave work early on the day of the orientation so that I would not be late

I was so grateful.

On the D day, I walked into that orientation hall with a big smile on my face.

I was ecstatic.

My dream of getting a college education was about to come to fruition.

I was seated in a large room with other new students. The college staff welcomed us warmly and offered us pizza with cold soft drinks. They also handed each of us folders that contained a *Welcome to Rose Titus* letter, school brochures, paper pads, maps and pens. I was impressed. I didn't know that schools gave students free items like that. They were not only organized, but also very generous.

After we had settled down, we were given a history of the university by one staff member. He told us what year it was founded and how it had grown to its current size of 4,000 students. He also helped us locate important buildings such as the library and financial aid office on our maps. Another showed us how to calculate our GPA and told us what building to go to receive extra coaching for our school work. I was getting more impressed. I could not believe that a school could offer free lesson teachers for their students.

Then the last staff member mentioned something which made my heart stop and prompted me to ask the speaker a question. *Did he just say that if you maintained a GPA of 3.5 and above, you would automatically get a full scholarship for the next semester?*

"*Yes, that is indeed correct*", the man replied, and I almost fell out of my chair.

Amaka Lily

"*WHAAAAAAAAT*", I screamed inwardly. This was unbelievable. This was just unbelievable.
Free tuition for getting good grades?
Like I needed any more motivation to study harder!
Oh America was such a great country! Great, Great, country. It was way more advanced and forward thinking than Nigeria could ever be. They truly supported their students. They gave you free food and free note pads. They gave you free coaching and money to go to school.
How much more wonderful could this country be?
But then I started thinking about my fellow peers. *What if they were as poor as I was and needed the money to pay their own tuition? What if the competition to get a 3.5 was fierce?*

I thought about how having free tuition would free up my salary to enable me send more money to my family. I thought about how great I'd feel to be recognized for academic achievements. And I decided at that moment that I would aim for not just a 3.5 but a 4.0. I needed to make sure that I got a score high enough to ensure I always got that money, regardless of the competition.

Soon, the orientation came to an end and they wished us well with our college careers. As we walked out, one of the speakers said that personal advisors were available to help us with registration and that if we wanted to, we could get registered immediately.

The *Effico*[27] in me did not need much prompting. I went immediately to get registered. They made us take some tests and then after that, a counselor helped me select my first set of classes. Like my parents, I had decided to pursue an Engineering path and Calculus, English and Physics were the first classes I signed up for.

---

[27] Slang term for a driven and efficient person.

SHIFTING ALLEGIANCES

When my personal advisor handed me the slip of paper that listed my college classes with their start and end times, I almost started weeping.

It had been a long time coming but finally I was now a legitimate college student.

Amaka Lily

One of the things I had looked forward to was having American friends. Having grown up in a country where everyone looked like me, I wanted to have black friends, white friends, Indian friends... you name it. I also had a list of questions that I had generated from childhood and wanted to get the answers for. I wanted to ask black Americans what it was like living in America, why they were always so cool, why they were the best singers, best dancers, best dressers, best everything. I wanted to ask white people why they always felt a need to tan themselves and why they sometimes turned pink when angry. I wanted to ask Indians why they danced so much and looked so pretty in their videos. I wanted to ask them why their ladies had a red mark in between their forehead.

I wanted to touch white people's hair and see if it was as soft as it looked.

I wanted to understand.

SHIFTING ALLEGIANCES

August 22, 2005 arrived.

I stepped into Rose Titus community college at exactly 6:30 pm. I was armed with a brand new bag bursting with brand new books. My first class, Elementary Calculus was not to start until 7pm but I couldn't wait.

Could. Not. Wait.

I took a seat in the first row and surveyed each of my classmates as they came in.

Our class was arranged in a semi-circular fashion with the Professor's podium located right in the middle. This meant that from wherever one sat, one could see every single face. I noticed that the majority of my classmates looked to be much older, like 30's and above. Very few of them looked to be younger than 25.

At 7 o'clock sharp, our professor came in. His name was Tom Carmichael and he had a PHD in Advanced Mathematics. He handed each of us a big white placard and asked us to write our names.

I wrote my name in full even though the placard could barely contain it, NJIDEKA ONUORAEGBUNAM.

Professor Carmichael then proceeded to call each one of us by name. When it came to my turn, I saw the familiar look of pain, confusion and anxiety that envelops the faces of every American who first sees my name. I quickly told him not to worry and to just call me Deka.

He smiled appreciatively, thanked me and moved on.

After the roll call, he went into the details of the course. Since it was a once-a-week class, we would cover a lot of material each time we met, which was for 3 hours. There were to be 4 quizzes, a midterm and a final. To get an A, one had to score an 89 and above. My ears perked up when he said he'd offer extra credit for participation in class. Anyone who contributed to class discussion would accumulate extra points. I didn't need to hear that twice.

Then, the lesson began.

I was focused. My mind was parched and yearning for knowledge. I could not believe I was finally studying a college course, and not just any college course, but an American college course.

But as he worked, I began to realize that I knew what he was teaching

I had done this before!!!

Even though it had been 4 years since I last sat in a math class, I realized that this professor was teaching what we had called Further-Math in secondary school.

I was stunned.

Why was my secondary school math being covered in college?

I didn't know it then, but much later I found out that the British system of education Nigerians follow, more than prepares one for college in the United States. Many of our secondary school classes are in effect 1st and 2nd year college classes in America. Furthermore, the emphasis that is placed on theoretical writing in Secondary school comes in very handy when it comes time to write the numerous college papers.

My shock soon gave way to the realization that this was a good thing. I could really participate in this class and get extra points. I could also share my knowledge with my classmates, who were looking rather stumped.

It could be a great way to make friends.

And so like I had done all those years before in secondary school, I raised my hand when the teacher posed a question. I eagerly and perhaps a tad too joyously described how certain problems should be solved. I even threw in some alternative ways of solving the problems if the professor didn't seem to be following my suggested method. I didn't think too much about what I was doing. Answering questions and supplying answers

SHIFTING ALLEGIANCES

was the accepted way of learning in Nigeria and I didn't think there was anything wrong with it.

Professor Carmichael also didn't seem to mind.

No one else was raising their hand.

After a while, I noticed that whenever I raised my hand, snickers would follow.

At first I ignored it, but soon it became louder. When I turned to where the noise was coming from, I noticed a group of African American students, chuckling to themselves.

I turned back around and continued to supply answers. I thought it was something else that was making them snicker.

Then it came, words that I will never forget...

"African Booty scratcher"
"This bitch needs to quit talking so much"
"Why won't she just SHUT THE FUCK-UP!!!"

A sea of loud laughter suddenly washed over that side of the class and I knew instantly that it was directed at me. I turned around again and was faced with the meanest set of eyes I had ever seen. A gaze so full of hate and animosity that I forgot what I was about to say.

Her placard read "Tameka Robbins"

I was puzzled.

What had I done?
What had I done?

Professor Carmichael didn't appear to have heard the insults, but by the laughter that followed, I knew my classmates had. I was embarrassed. I shut up immediately.

What had I done?
What had I done?

I didn't know how to cope with this. I had never been insulted in class and I didn't know how to cope with all the hatred that was focused on me.

My mind struggled to find answers.

What had I done?

Amaka Lily

What had I done?

At 8:30pm, Professor Carmichael announced a 15 minute break and we all dispersed to drink water or use the bathroom. I noticed Tameka off in a corner surrounded by the same people who had laughed at me. After vacillating for a while, I decided to muster up some courage and talk to them.

Surely, there had to be a reason for their behavior?
Surely, Tameka couldn't just hate me for no reason?
Surely, we could work this out?
"Hey, excuse me...." I began
"BACK OFF ME BITCH", she yelled with such hostility that I actually fell a few steps back.

I was stunned.
I was knocked speechless.
I was humiliated.
I didn't know what to do
All the people around her were laughing and whooping and I didn't know how to react.

I mustered what little pride I had left and went back to the class. Till this day, I still don't know how I found the strength to sit still for the rest of the hour. I did not answer any more questions and was effectively muted. Meanwhile my thoughts continued to race...

What had I done?
What had I done?

When I got home that night, I couldn't sleep, I kept asking myself
What had I done?
What had I done?

At work the next day, I could not concentrate. At my English class later that evening, I agonized over the previous day's event. I wracked my brain over what I could have possibly done in such a short amount of time to have made

SHIFTING ALLEGIANCES

such bitter enemies. I thought about the look of hatred Tameka had leveled at me.

Why the hatred?
Why the hatred?

Finally, I told Uncle Ebuka what had happened. I needed to make sense of it.

"*Welcome to America!*" he said strangely unsurprised "*…now you would start to see the real America*" he ended ominously.

I asked him what he meant by that and he said.

"*Many African Americans hate Africans that come to this country*". "*They feel that we come here to take their jobs and are unappreciative of the sacrifices they have made for us to be here*"

"*But…*" he continued "*…we don't take their jobs. They refuse to do the lowliest work and want the government to take care of them. WE are the ones who willingly take up those lowliest roles, yet they still hate us*"

My mind was spinning. I had to sit down. I was unprepared for that. *Why didn't we know this back home? Why wasn't this told?*

"*It is the hidden secret. Even if you were told back home, you wouldn't have understood… not until you came here.*"

"*But why Uncle? Why? Don't they know that we like them? Don't they know that we want to be their friends?*" I was unwilling to let up. All those years of watching *The Cosby show* and *A Different world* had ingrained in my mind a totally different type of African American and I was unwilling, totally unwilling to accept uncle's explanations.

"*They don't know that and frankly they don't care*" Uncle said "*the African Americans you see here are very different from what they show us back home. The ones here are extremely rude… they are not welcoming at all… You are better off just staying away from them*" he finished

Amaka Lily

I resisted, *"But Uncle..."*

"Njideka, just stay away from them and if you doubt me, go and ask Kofi them" and with that my uncle left me.

"Kofi them" were the Ghanaian family that shared the same apartment complex we lived in. Our neighborhood housed a large number of African and Caribbean families.

I called Kofi who was a few years my senior and shared what uncle had just told me. He agreed with everything uncle said. He told me that as a teenager he was regularly mocked and beaten by his African American classmates because of his clothes and accent. He said that they had called him *"African Booty Scratcher"* and stolen his money. It had gotten so bad that his parents were forced to transfer him to a private, majority white school, where he no longer suffered such treatment.

His finishing words to me were *"Just stay away from them Deka. They are not like us. They may have our skin color but that's where the similarity ends"*

I was devastated. *Did this mean I would not have any African American friends?*

How could this be?

The next couple of days, I spent my time just observing the interactions of Africans and African Americans. Since I had now been sensitized to the hidden tension that underlay these two groups, I wanted to see for myself and get confirmation. I watched them in the bus, in restaurants, everywhere. It is amazing what you see when you begin to focus on certain things. I noticed that the two groups seemed to hang out only in their own groups. There was no mixing, no hanging out, no friendship.

It appeared that there was an unspoken agreement that African and African Americans did not mix and that people in America understood that.

I persisted.

SHIFTING ALLEGIANCES

I asked some other Africans in the community what their experiences had been like with African Americans. It was similar to what Uncle and Kofi had said. Not one had a good thing to say about them. Not one. Tales of being robbed, beaten or insulted by African Americans were relayed to me. I listened to all of this news in disbelief, but like a stubborn goat still persisted. I could not believe that the friendships I had planned out in my mind, would never occur. I just couldn't accept it. And so I deliberately tried to engage some African Americans in conversation, something I had never striven to do before. I would say "*Hi, Hello*" and try to talk to them, figure out what they were all about. But it seemed like once they heard my accent, a certain veil come across their faces.

They could tell I was African and didn't want anything to do with me.

Finally, I gave up. I decided to adhere to the rules that had been established before my arrival, rules that everyone else seemed to accept.

I did not want any further trouble.

I just wanted to go to college.

The following Monday, I arrived at my calculus class. I planned not to say a word. I was just going to sit quietly and do my work. I didn't want to instigate further attacks on my personhood.

But that was not to be. Professor Carmichael kept calling on me. Calling and calling on me. I don't know whether he did it to encourage me to speak, because again, no one was speaking, and he remembered the zeal I had exhibited on the first day of class. Nevertheless he kept calling and calling my name.

At first I answered quietly, with a low voice, trying not to bring attention to myself, trying to act unwilling, but he persisted and truth be told I really, really, really, really love answering questions, that I decided to break my vow of silence.

Why did I have to be quiet?

Amaka Lily

Why did I have to shut up, just to keep from displeasing a group of people?
I wasn't doing anything wrong. I wasn't deliberately intruding in their space. *Why was speaking up in class so wrong?*
I decided *"No more"!*
I had not spent all those years yearning for a college education just to be shut up by a bully.
I had not spent hundreds of dollars in school fees just to be pushed around by a person who had a misguided hatred for me.
No more!!!
And so I went back to raising my hands and volunteering answers.
Almost as soon as I raised my hand the snickers began, but this time I did not care. If they wanted to criticize me, that was their problem. I no longer wanted their friendship anymore.
What was the worst they could do to me?
I continued.
During the break, I noticed Tameka and her clique staring at me, whispering to themselves, some rolling their eyes, while others looked on with pure hatred. I steeled my eyes, made them as hard as I could, and stared back.
I was not going to be intimidated.
I had a right to be in the class and I had a right to learn. I also had a right to participate if the professor encouraged such? *Who were they to dictate my behavior? If the professor didn't mind my talking, why should they?*
When class ended, I stood up with my head held high and confidently walked towards the bus stop. I half expected them to follow me, hurling insults or perhaps start a fight. My heart was beating furiously. I did not want to fight but I knew that if something came about that I needed to fight back. It was the only way I could prove that I was not going to be played with.

SHIFTING ALLEGIANCES

But nothing happened. Instead they all walked as a group to their cars. The next week, same thing. Apart from hateful glances, they did nothing to me after class ended. They didn't even hurl insults at me in class.

Finally, as the class got harder, even the glances stopped as everyone became focused on passing the class.

Because I knew the coursework, my standing in class grew. My other classmates looked at me as some sort of math genius, when in fact everything was just a revision for me. During breaks, some would approach me and ask me to explain certain concepts. Twice I hosted a weekend teaching session for classmates who needed extra tutelage before quizzes. I began to make friends, lots and lots of friends and the majority of those friends were foreigners. I am not sure why that was but I suspect the feeling of being new to the U.S. was an additional bond that brought us closer.

We understood the feeling of otherness.

There was Supriya who was my best friend in calculus. She was also very smart. She was the one who once when I was complaining about how corrupt Nigeria was, told me that India was much worse. That then inspired a game where we each tried to one-up the other with examples of how corrupt our governments were.

Long story short. She won that game.

There was Amina, a Senegalese girl who introduced me to the underworld of cheap African hair braiders. Braiders who braided, weaved or sewed hair in their homes because they lacked the necessary papers to do hair in a legal establishment. Braiders that not only did such beautiful work on my hair, but also saved me a fortune in hair costs.

There was Harry from Germany who was such a happy fellow but who loved to drink beer a little too much. He drank beer before class, during class -in a tiny flask that looked like a water bottle- and after class. I don't know how Professor

Amaka Lily

Carmichael never caught him because he was pretty obvious about it, unless of course, Professor Carmichael just didn't want to address it.

There were other people, but these are the ones I remember the most.

That first year was also remarkable because it was the first time I fielded a lot of questions from people about my background. When they found out I was African, they would first ask what it felt like to live in Africa -which many kept thinking was a country and not a continent-. Others would ask how I learnt to speak English so fast, how it felt to wear clothes for the first time and to live in a sturdy building.

At first I answered them gleefully, taking great pains to explain to them what Nigeria was all about. I told them that Nigeria was colonized by the British and that English was the official language. I also told them that we had similar modern buildings, just like in Britain, and in fact many of our houses were sturdier than American houses because they were built with cement. I told those that asked that I had never walked around naked and in fact could not wear a skirt without an underskirt...

But after answering questions like this for about a hundred times, I began to get annoyed. Some of these questions were just unbelievable. *Could these people really be that unknowledgeable about Nigeria? Did they really believe we lived on trees and danced naked with animals under the moonlight? Did they really believe we were all so backward?*

I would find out much later that the reason people asked some of these unbelievable questions, was because they truly believed, Africa was backward. They had been shown only certain sides of Africa from the media and not the varied, complete picture. The sides of Africa that were shown repeatedly were either of those strange remote Africans who inserted plates into their lips or piled rings on their necks to make it longer. If it wasn't that, it was the parts of Africa that were either famished or war torn. They didn't show the regular, every day sides of modern Africa and so we remained in their minds a very dark and backward concept, a continent with no redeeming value.

It was around this time that I began to be very protective about Nigeria. Whereas before I would be the first to criticize Nigeria and its deficiencies, now I became its foremost supporter. I vigorously and passionately defended Nigeria against any type of mis-information. I wouldn't allow anybody to criticize the country, especially not when it was based on erroneous information. As I defended the country, I began to realize what Nigeria had. Things that I had taken for granted and never thought meant anything, now that I was a million miles away, I realized how very precious they were. I started becoming proud of the country.

Towards the end of that semester, I discovered another piece of good news. Rose Titus allowed you to take up to 18 college credits for the price of 12 credits. They were essentially throwing in 2 extra classes for free.

2 extra classes for free!!!

My head almost exploded with joy. This meant that I could rush through my education. This meant that I could finish my schooling in less than the 4 years, the engineering program entailed. This meant that I could make up for all the time I had lost in Nigeria!!!

I was in bliss. Coupled with the thought of free scholarship that came with maintaining a 3.5 or above GPA, I was even more motivated. I studied like a lunatic with the result that I achieved a 4.0 at the end of that semester.

Just like I had planned.

The next semester, I signed up for an 18 credit course load, and the following semester did the same. I maintained an 18 credit course load for all the semesters I was enrolled at Rose Titus until the day I graduated.

My life revolved around classes. When I wasn't at work, I was at school and when I wasn't at either, I was in the library. My home was basically a place to sleep. I had classes every evening, Monday-Friday and on Saturday mornings. I also took extra classes in the summer. I had no life and I didn't care. I took advantage of commute times to study in the bus or do my homework. I studied into the wee hours of the morning. Sunday was my only day of rest. After church with the family, I went back to my studying.

When I look back to that time, I cannot believe the academic load I carried. It was grueling. I cannot do it today. But at the time, it did not feel like work. I was happy and my mind was parched for knowledge. I was proud to be in a university and proud to be taking college classes.

I also wanted to make up for lost time.

The nature of Rose Titus was such that friendships made in a particular semester rarely survived beyond that. This was because Rose Titus was targeted towards working adults, not regular, college-aged students. Meaning, it offered flexible schedules to allow the former, take classes at their convenience. So if you were a person who could only take classes in the evenings and on weekends, Rose Titus was great for you. If you were someone who had taken classes years prior, dropped out and now wanted to complete your requirements, it was also great for you.

This meant that the people in your classes ran the gamut of varying levels of college completion and the probability of not seeing them the next semester was high. For some it could be their last semester, for others, their first. For still others, who may have shared the same major and level that you were in,

SHIFTING ALLEGIANCES

they could decide to take a morning class the next semester, or just take a break from their studies. The net effect was that you wouldn't see them anymore.

Further contributing to the transient nature of friendships was the fact that Rose Titus was a commuter school, meaning there were no hostels or dorms, people just came and left and so unlike typical 4-year colleges, where you could deepen friendships after classes, here it was impossible.

At first it was hard when I realized that friendships were short-lived, but like many things, I quickly adapted to it.

Amaka Lily

Chapter 6

African Americans

SHIFTING ALLEGIANCES

One night after classes, during my second year of college, I took my usual spot at the back of the bus and began reading my homework for the next week.

At the next stop, an African American guy boarded the bus and sat right across from me.

I glanced at him briefly. He seemed vaguely familiar but I couldn't be sure. He was staring straight at me, smiling. I turned my attention back to my book. He had to be looking at something else and not me...or perhaps he was crazy. *Hadn't I learned in the last 2 years that African Americans didn't like Africans?*

Then a voice...

"*You are always studying! Don't you ever take a break?*"

I glanced up. He was not only looking at me, he was TALKING to me. *Had the world gone mad? This could not bode well...*

I answered him coldly "*I am sorry but I am very busy*". But as soon as I said those words, I felt terrible. I didn't want to be mean, but the memories of Tameka's rudeness still bubbled within my soul. I didn't want to be hurt again... not if I could help it.

"*I can see that*" he responded cheerfully, flashing me a smile with teeth so perfect that it made my suddenly treacherous heart skip a couple of beats. "*...matter of fact, you are ALWAYS busy. I always see you reading or something. What do you do?*"

"*I work and I go to school*". I responded. I was still cold to him but not as hostile. There was something about him that was very disarming. Still I couldn't be sure...

"*What type of work do you do?*" he pressed and then followed with "*I am an IT specialist*"

I told him what I did. He was in my Thermodynamics class, which was why he had seemed vaguely familiar, had some skills in Information Technology but ultimately wanted to become a mechanical engineer. He said he had been wanting to talk to me since the first day of class once he had detected my accent and wondered whether I was from Africa.

When I replied that yes I was from Africa, specifically Nigeria, he began to quiz me about the country. He asked me what the culture was like, what tribe I was from and also what languages I spoke

I dropped the coldness and answered his questions as politely as I could, giving him just the basics and not elaborating. I wasn't sure what to make of this seemingly nice guy. He was very friendly and attentive but yet he was an African American. He was the type of African American I had envisioned meeting years before, until I found out they hated my people. I couldn't let my guard down. No way. He could decide to flip and start insulting me the next minute… I had to be careful.

Just before his bus stop, he gave me his number and asked me to call him.

I did not.

At the next Thermodynamics class, he came and sat right next to me.

"So why didn't you call?" he asked, looking at me with a mischievous grin. I couldn't look him in the eyes. He had these penetrating green eyes that I had never before seen in a black person. He seemed to be looking into my soul…

"I was…"

"Busy!" he finished for me and we both laughed.

We spent most of that class time passing notes and joking with each other. By the end of that class, I was so comfortable with Malik that I decided to break my 2 year vow and take a chance of friendship with this African American guy.

He would become my first African American friend.

It would be one of my best friendships in the U.S.

SHIFTING ALLEGIANCES

Malik was what I called a *Cosby show* kid. His parents were middle class and he was nice and cultured, just like the kids on *The Cosby show*. He was exactly my age and looked a lot like the actor that played the title character in *Tshaka, King of the Zulus*. He was 6 foot 3, very dark and extremely ripped. He had the slim but cut look that I adore and carried himself like he owned the world. In addition to his green eyes, he had extremely white teeth and many times, I would stop and stare because I had never seen teeth so white in my life.

Early in our friendship, Malik had wanted to date me. I refused, even though deep down I wanted to. I stopped myself from dating him because I still harbored a few misgivings about African Americans and was scared of being hurt. I also wasn't ready for the type of backlash I expected to get from Uncle and Aunty.

It was also easy not to have a boyfriend during that period because I had plenty of things to keep me busy. I was working full-time, 5 days a week and taking classes 5 nights a week. I was also taking Saturday morning classes, going to school year round, including summers and during my spare time, was either studying or searching and applying for new scholarships. I was an over achieving, nerdtastic bookworm and I was happy with that lifestyle. Malik being the perfect gentleman did not press the issue and we maintained a friendship.

It was with Malik that I was finally able to get the African American perspective on why there was conflict between Africans and African Americans.

I still remember that conversation. It was on a night when we were waiting to catch the bus home. Since we were the only ones at the bus-stop, I decided this was as good a time as any to ask him what had bugged me for 2 years now.

"Malik why do African Americans hate Africans?"

"Why would you say that?" he asked, looking at me puzzled *"Do you think I hate you?"*

Amaka Lily

I explained to him what I had gone through my first day at Rose Titus. I also shared with him what Uncle had said, what my other African friends had experienced and what I had seen with my own eyes.

There seemed to be a trend.

After listening, he jokingly responded *"Shoot, I'd have hated you too. Why you gotta be the one showing off that you know something?"* and then when he saw that I didn't laugh, delivered this bombshell *"Yeah, some African Americans do hate Africans and that's because y'all look down on us and think you are better"*

"WHAAAAAAAAAAAT!" I screamed. This was news to me. Africans looked down on African Americans? We thought we were better? This was news to me. I asked him to explain how "we" could act superior when we were fleeing countries suffering from war, famine, dictatorships and other pestilence. *How could we feel superior when many of us were essentially beholden to America for our existence?*

He said we acted superior because we knew where we came from and they didn't. We could trace our histories back through multiple generations. We could pinpoint exactly where we originated from, and we had a language, a culture, a tribe. He, just like many African Americans did not have these things.

Also, he claimed we didn't seem appreciative of the many sacrifices African Americans had made to make the U.S. a more accepting place for all minorities. We did not acknowledge them enough and lastly, the fact that some African chiefs had participated heavily in the selling of slaves, left a bitter taste in the mouths of many African Americans. *How could brothers sell their own brothers?*

So as a preemptive move and also as a way to get back at Africans for real, imagined or perceived slights, some African Americans tried to intimidate and hurt Africans. However, he

SHIFTING ALLEGIANCES

assured me, it wasn't every African American who believed or acted in that way, just a few or as he said, "*the ignorant ones*".

I felt like my head was swimming. I was shocked, angry, upset. I felt I had been unfairly punished for something I knew nothing about. I felt I had been judged before I had even done anything.

I explained to Malik that his superiority claim was untrue. That growing up, myself and my peers had looked *up* to African Americans. We saw them as long lost relatives of ours and looked forward to meeting them. None of the Nigerians I knew thought they were superior, as a matter of fact, we had admired their style, their dancing, their singing, their music. We wanted to be as cool as them and made great strides to emulate them.

But once we got here and saw how rudely they treated us, it made us withdraw. I told him that many Africans are raised to give and expect respect and do not linger in places or with people who don't accord them that. I told him that that was why I was initially hesitant to be his friend.

As for selling them as slaves, I explained that only those with great power such as the Chiefs did so. The common person did not partake in selling slaves and it was unfair to put all of us in one bucket.

And so we went back and forth and at the end of that evening, we both had a better understanding of each other and reached the conclusion that it was all a big, big MISUNDERSTANDING and a vicious cycle.

I could see how the cycle could begin, using aspects of my experience as an example. An African comes to America expecting the warm embrace and fellowship which Africans typically afford foreigners. He comes across an African American who insults him and makes him feel inferior. He fights back in two ways. He withdraws and no longer expects friendship or he insults the African American by trying to make the latter feel inferior. He could accomplish this by mocking the latter's lack of history and culture. Years later, this same African comes across an African American that has no such issues, is open and wants to be his friend, but the former is now closed off and wary. He has been hurt by his "brothers" and does not trust the friendship offered to him. This new African American interprets the behavior of this African to be stand-offish, superiority thinking and now thinks all Africans think they are superior and so the cycle is repeated with successive participants using their experience as their only gauge of truth and hurting each other in the process.

The cycle is only broken when one person decides to risk a friendship with the other side, in spite of what he or she has heard, because only through friendship and dialogue can prejudices be corrected.

Malik's friendship and the talks we had freed me of the misconceptions I had about African Americans. I realized that not all of them hated Africans and for those that did, it was probably due to stereotypes and the aforementioned reasons.

I became more willing to open up to them and take risks and consequently, my circle of friends grew. I was not able to make deep friendships with every single one I met because some were just so steeped in their beliefs that they couldn't let me in while others were so culturally dissimilar that it seemed we communicated on different wavelengths.

Nevertheless, I achieved my goal of making friends with some of them and that was enough for me.

Malik introduced me to his close circle of friends. Ray ,whom we all called Ray Ray and Ahmad

Every Sunday evening, we would all meet up at Malik's home to hang out. Sometimes there would be food, sometimes games -I usually just watched- but mostly we talked about life.

Ray Ray was I guess one would call an "educated thug". On the outside, he was very intimidating. You would have thought

SHIFTING ALLEGIANCES

he was in a gang. He was 250 pounds of solid muscle and usually covered in all black, black shoes, black jeans, black T shirt and a skull cap. He also carried a mean scowl on his face. But even though his appearance was menacing, it was not a true reflection of his mindset. He was very soft spoken and highly, highly intelligent. He was passionate about all things black and was the first person to teach me about the black experience in America.

He taught me about racial profiling, when a person, usually black was automatically assumed to be a criminal, due to the person's race. It was the reason why American police frequently stopped black drivers if they were driving an expensive car. He said that American cops believed that blacks could not afford expensive cars and that if a black person was found in one, it was likely that he or she stole it, not owned it.

Blacks even had a name for that phenomenon. They called it *"Driving while Black"*.

He gave me tips on what to do if I was ever profiled. He said *"If you are driving and the cops stop you, leave your hands on the steering wheel… don't take it out for any reason, even to check your bag because the cops could think you were trying to grab a weapon and shoot you"*. He also said I should never, ever argue with an American cop, even if I were in the right as they could use it as a basis to haul me off to jail.

When I told him that I didn't have a car so that wouldn't be a problem for me, he said racial profiling wasn't just limited to driving, but was in every facet of American society. He said I could be judged negatively, just for being black.

That struck a chord. I realized that the reason why I was constantly being followed at a particular store I frequented was because of racial profiling. One of the attendants, an Indian lady always made a beeline for me whenever I entered the store. She followed me while the other shoppers, usually white went along their merry way. She didn't even try to hide it. She made it very apparent that she was following me and watching every single thing I did. I had quickly surmised that she thought I was a thief but why, I didn't know. After Ray Ray told me of racial profiling, I was able to put two and two together and figure out why I had been followed.

When I told Ray Ray, he tried to encourage me to stop patronizing the store. He said that I needed to "*speak with my money*" and show them that their behavior was unacceptable. That would have been a good idea except that my budget didn't give me the liberty to do so. They had a lot of items I liked and their prices were unbeatable. You couldn't get a better deal at another store. It seemed silly for me to spend more money for the same item at a more expensive store, just because someone thought I would steal things. I just couldn't justify the extra expense. However, after being enlightened on racial profiling, I felt I needed to inflict some sort of justice on that lady. I needed to salve my wound of being thought to be a thief just because I was black, so this is what I did subsequently. When I was in the area, I would make a point to stop at the store with no intention of buying anything. I would just loiter around, examining items I didn't care for and then move on to another aisle. I would do this aisle after aisle after aisle. All the while, the lady would be standing a few yards away, looking at me, her face unexpressive. Sometimes I'd ask her questions to seem as though I was really interested in purchasing something. Other times I wouldn't and then would leave without purchasing anything. I didn't do this too often because I never really had that much time to waste but it felt good to make her follow me and perhaps divert her attention from a real thief. The lady never really knew what to do with me because I could come in the next week and actually purchase some items…

Ray Ray was the first person to tell me that black men in the U.S. outnumbered all other races of men in prison and it wasn't because they had actually committed more crimes, but because

SHIFTING ALLEGIANCES

the laws were set up against them and racial profiling played a role as well. It was from him I first heard the term "3 strike rule", a rule that punishes people excessively if they have been convicted of 3 or more crimes. He said the judicial system in the U.S was set up against blacks and cautioned me to distrust anyone connected to it.

It was also Ray Ray that told me that not all white-looking people are considered white people in America. He said white-looking people such as Italians and some Hispanics were not considered "real" white people but rather minorities and that their skin color was not white, but actually "olive colored". To be honest, I couldn't tell the difference between this olive color and white colored skin. All the people he pointed out to me looked pretty white to me. I guess the differences are more apparent to a person who grew up in America, but to my Nigerian eyes, they were definitely oyibos[28].

Ray Ray also taught me the "one drop rule", the rule that states that any person that has a drop of black blood in his or her body is automatically considered a black person in the U.S. I did not readily agree with this at first. After a lifetime of seeing pure black Nigerians, I could easily spot anyone with a hint of mixed race in them and thought they should be labeled appropriately, but Ray Ray assured me that as long as they had a bit of black blood, they were considered black in America. It didn't matter if a person's great, great grandfather was the only black in a long line of ancestors and that the person in question looked as white as can be, that person was still considered black, nothing more, nothing less.

When I proclaimed that it was strange to call an obviously mixed person black, just because he or she had black blood, he responded that those were the rules in America and everyone accepted them.

---

[28] White people.

Amaka Lily

Ray Ray also taught me that the term *half caste*, which we Nigerians use to refer to mixed people and has no negative connotation whatsoever, was unacceptable in the U.S. and told me to call such people bi-racial, if I couldn't call them black, per the one drop rule. I thought these new racial constructs were very weird but since this was what it was called in America, I filed them away in the back of my mind.

Lastly, he taught me about slavery. Even though I was familiar with the concept, we had never really delved into the details of what it was really like for blacks in the U.S. It was not taught in any of my secondary school classes. All I knew was that my fellow Africans had been kidnapped, traded and taken by ship to the West. I also knew that they had been beaten, chained and made to work on farms. I had no idea that the slaves in the U.S. had been threatened with death for speaking their language. I had no idea that white men had periodically raped black women. I had no idea that blacks were made to believe they were inferior.

Ray Ray educated me on these things. He taught me about Jim Crow laws that segregated whites and blacks as recently as the 60s. He told me about how blacks were routinely lynched and that the punishment for dating a white woman was death. He told me the whole gory ordeal that at times, I felt like my heart was going to burst. It was so painful. I had no idea it had been this bad, no idea at all and I felt the pain of all African Americans.

There were times however when Ray Ray concerned me, when I was forced to question his sanity. Such occasions usually arose when a particularly heinous incident of racial profiling or mistaken identity had occurred. Like when a black person was unjustly killed or found to be innocent after spending years in jail for a crime he didn't commit. Such occasions made Ray Ray boil. He would rail and rail about "the man", his name for white people, the "racist society" and unjust system. He said white people were deeply racist and was convinced they were involved in a vast conspiracy to eliminate the black race. Nothing you could tell him could dissuade him from that belief. He claimed that AIDS and other diseases were concocted by white people and deliberately placed in Africa specifically for our destruction. He called whites "devils", "untrustworthy" and seemed to detest the whole lot of them.

On those occasions, I found it hard to believe Ray Ray. My experiences with white people up until that point did not match the claims Ray Ray was making. They had been so nice to me. Ms Kathy and Ms. Chelsea had treated me really well. They had treated me like a peer, an equal, a human being. Ms. Chelsea had been particularly accommodating of my school schedule and had let me leave early on multiple occasions when I had exams. I did not detect any sense that they wanted to harm me or loathed me. I did not detect any negativity from them at all. Sometimes I argued with him about his accusations, other times I just let him be, while holding onto the beliefs that I had within.

Once though, Ray Ray and I got into a big argument, our biggest argument ever. It was when he said that America offers no opportunities to black people. I countered by telling him that America offers free education to every single American child, including blacks, from kindergarten all the way to high school and that for those who wanted to go to college, scholarships and loans were available for that. I also pointed out that it provided free food, free housing, even job training for those that were unable to afford it. I told him that these resources were not available where I came from and that I had to pay for everything I got or rely on the kindness of relatives. I also told him how difficult it had been for me to get into college in Nigeria and told him that he should be appreciative for what he had here.

Amaka Lily

He fought back by saying that whites had us Africans "brainwashed" and that in fact, they were "looting" our continent of its resources. I fought back and said that they had developed our countries, brought us education and tried to help our poverty stricken nations. He said I was STUPID if I thought that the western brand of education was the only type of education available. He said that before western colonization, we had been civilized and had our own brand of education. He said that before colonization, we had well developed cities, empires and that it was only with the advent of the white man that we forgot our previous greatness. He insisted that we Africans are brain washed, brain washed, BRAIN WASHED and that we were dumb, dumb, DUMB.

I was boiling with anger. I was so angry, I was shaking.

Never did I think that someone with no idea of my upbringing would come out and speak authoritatively about my experiences. It seemed like everything I had been raised to believe about myself, my heritage was a lie... and I resented it.

I wanted to yell, scream, fight Ray Ray. *How dare he tell me about MY heritage? How dare he insult my people?*

Malik noting my demeanor, wisely dragged me outside and attempted to calm me.

"How dare he say that?" I asked *"HOW DARE HE SPEW THAT NONSENSE!!!!?*

"It's okay Deka. It's okay"

"He doesn't know ANYTHING about Africa or what I experienced there. How can he say that we are brainwashed? How dare he?"

"Calm down Deka" Malik urged. *"...just calm down, he didn't mean it like that"*

"What do you mean he didn't mean it?", *"He DAMN NEAR argued with me"* –Notice that my American English had been improving- *"He believes that shit!"*

"Just calm down Deka".

SHIFTING ALLEGIANCES

I went home. I didn't want to be in the same room with Ray Ray ever again. I was through with that STUPID boy. So through with him.

Malik made Ray Ray apologize to me a week later. He came to our home one evening and actually knocked on our door to ask for me. Uncle Ebuka who answered the door, looked at me with a questioning expression when he saw who it was, but he didn't say much, just told me I had a visitor. I went outside to talk to Ray Ray.

Ray Ray was contrite. He explained that he usually got upset whenever he heard Africans attribute their civilization to whites when long before colonization, we had ours. He didn't take back what he said about brainwashing but admitted he could have framed it differently.

I accepted his apology. In the days preceding this, I had thought a lot about how differently Ray Ray and I had been raised. I did not grow up in a society hating whites and viewing them as having evil intentions. I grew up in a society where whites were highly regarded, where many Nigerians treated them better than their own people. They were considered great benefactors who had colonized our nation and brought education to us. The fact that there were also very few whites in Nigeria and a sighting was so rare, put them in a special, esteemed status. It also didn't hurt that they were typically rich. I also did not share a history of slavery and could not relate to being treated differently because of the color of my skin, Indian attendant notwithstanding.

In Nigeria we were all black and no one was considered inferior because he was a shade darker. There were other ways people were discriminated against such as by tribal lines-of which I'd never personally experienced or engaged in- and by economic lines. Ray Ray had experienced the opposite. He had been demonized for his skin color his entire life!!!

Amaka Lily

Because of these differences, there was bound to be conflict between us. Nevertheless, I still needed Ray Ray. He was showing me a side I'd never heard about, a side that I'd never read about in a book. He was also making me think. I wanted to continue learning from him. If his sentiment was shared by many people, I needed to be aware.

I forgave him.

Another friend of Malik's was a guy called Ahmad
Ahmad was what Ray Ray called a *"sell-out"* or *"self-hating black"*.
His crime?
He dated only white women and also had more white friends than black friends.

Ahmad was the complete opposite of Ray Ray. He wasn't passionate about anything black and in truth, didn't know a lot about black or even African issues. The first couple of times I met him, he didn't say much to me. He just spent time looking at me. It was as though he was trying to figure out what I was all about. *Who was this African girl in their midst?* When he finally assessed that I was "okay", he opened up. Initially, I was appalled at what he had to say. He felt that Africa, which I had to remind him many times was a continent and not a country, was very backward. He believed that the majority of us lived in remote forests, parading around naked and in our spare time, played with wild animals or performed rituals on each other. For those of us who didn't live in forests, he believed we lived in great poverty and famine. He did not have one positive image about Africa, not one.

He also hated the term "African American" and didn't want to be called that. He said that America was the only country his ancestors had known and lived in for generations. "*Why*", he asked, should "*African*" be appended to his race when

SHIFTING ALLEGIANCES

Americans of Dutch or English ancestries didn't call themselves "*Dutch American*" or "*English American*" respectively? He thought that adding that extra descriptor served to divide Americans and wanted to simply be known as an American.

That was one area where Ray Ray and I united, as we couldn't understand how a person could be so dismissive of one's heritage. Ray Ray as you already know was extremely passionate about everything black and always wanted to remind everyone of his heritage. I myself had become a fiercely proud advocate, more than I ever was in Nigeria and couldn't accept another person's willful dismissal -as it felt to me- of my culture. It was funny how this change occurred. Years back, I was the one railing against the country of my youth, but once I had gained distance and had a chance to look at it with a new set of eyes, and realize all the valuable things I had taken for granted, I became its fiercest supporter.

To be honest, I couldn't really fault Ahmad for his lack of knowledge. Like my classmates, most of what he'd learned about Africa, came from the media. In addition, he was raised by white parents as his birth mother had abandoned him shortly after his birth. Consequently, he had no real idea of what being black or African, was really like.

I spent some time correcting Ahmad of his false perceptions. I explained that Nigeria had buildings, roads and infrastructure just like the U.S. and that yes, in certain areas, the infrastructure was dilapidated but it was there nonetheless. I told him that I did not start wearing clothes in the U.S and save for the moment I had been birthed into the world, had never gone around naked. I also couldn't climb a tree, would not go near a lion if they paid me, and the only rituals I performed were brushing my teeth and taking a bath…

Amaka Lily

It was interesting how different Ray Ray and Ahmad were. Even though they were American blacks, their thoughts were polar opposites.

Malik was smack in the middle. He empathized with Ray Ray when it came to racial profiling but did not rail against "the man". He preferred to see the good in people first unless he was shown otherwise. He also did not mind calling himself "African American". He said it was a lot better than being called "black" which connotes a lot of negative images. He hungered for a deeper connection to the motherland and wanted to be able to trace his roots. He had also studied quite a bit about African cultures and hoped to visit an African country one day, although he wasn't sure where to start. Many times, in the arguments our group had, he acted as the peacemaker. He usually took my side, so that I was never alone in our "battles".

Most of our meetings though, were peaceful. We didn't argue every time. Sometimes we just exchanged information about how we each grew up, the rites of passage, things like that. When I first told the guys that it was legal for a man to marry more than one wife in Nigeria and that there was no limit to how many wives, a man could marry, they all screamed, hi-fived each other and proclaimed that Nigerian men were the luckiest men on earth. In retrospect, it shouldn't have been that surprising. Men are men everywhere.

They talked about how great it would be to have one wife for each day of the week and how America needed to take heed. They also liked the idea of gender roles, how women were raised to take care of their men and how divorce did not automatically entitle a woman to half a man's property. Occasionally, they teased me about finding them a "Nigerian wife" and wanted to know when I would introduce them to my Nigerian friends.

While they were busy dreaming of a polygamous and male dominated utopia, I was getting influenced by American ideas,

SHIFTING ALLEGIANCES

particularly in the area of women's rights. American women had a lot of rights and could get away with things that would get them a beating in Nigeria. Here they were not only considered equal to men, but the laws also protected them more than men. A wife could tell her husband to sleep on the couch if he annoyed her. She could also ask him to leave their home and have the police escort him out if he resisted. If they were divorcing, the man had to pay alimony and child support otherwise, he could be sent to jail or have his wages garnished.

Women could also slap men here and the men would not strike back. American men considered it cowardly to hit a woman, not something a "real man" would do. In fact, if they saw a man beating a woman, many men would come to her aid and beat up the "beater". If the cops came, the beater will be sent to jail for good measure.

Coming from a society where men ruled, where it wasn't uncommon to hear men beating their wives, where wives were regularly kicked out of the home, where men didn't pay child support, this was mind boggling to me. I thought about poor Mrs. Hassan who lived in our quarters and who you'd occasionally hear her cries when her husband beat her and Mrs. Chukwudi who it seemed like every other day, her husband was throwing her things out of their house. The only exception to the rule was Mrs. Adeola who, bigger than her husband, fought back whenever he attacked her. She didn't take his beatings lying down and gave as good as she got. You could always hear them fighting and then on Sunday, both of them would appear together in church holding hands. Their relationship was comical, but I digress…

Marriage and children were not pushed as the ultimate goals for women in America. You could choose to pursue a career and never get married, and it was okay. If married, you could choose to delay having children or decide to NEVER have children and that was okay too. You were also not looked down upon if you chose the latter, in fact there were married couples in the U.S. called "child-free couples" who had made the decision to never have kids, despite the fact that they could do so and were married.

I must admit, when I first heard of that concept, I was floored. I couldn't believe any woman would willingly sign up for that. *Wouldn't she miss never having children? What about when she got older? Who would take care of her?*

It seemed almost sacrilegious. In Nigeria, a major purpose of a woman's life was to BREED and a woman who deliberately chose not to do so, did not exist in our consciousness. Every woman wanted to give birth. Women who couldn't for medical reasons were considered sad, pathetic figures, not a person a woman aspired to be.

But like I said, Americans didn't look down on child-free couples and the more I considered it, the more I began to see some validity in it, even though it was still not a path I would have chosen. *Is it not best not to have children, than to have them and not be able to take care of them? Wouldn't it be better to admit that one does not have the time, money or inclination for children than to go along with society's mandate and end up resenting and mistreating the poor children?*

Truth be told, some people were never meant to have kids. They neglected their children and seemed to find them an imposition. Also having kids changed some people's lives for the worst. They had less time for their partners and less time to pursue their own interests. They felt trapped, especially the women. They lost their freedom, their bodies and their entire sense of self.

All of the child-free couples I met seemed happy. They were stress free, always had the latest gadgets, travelled regularly, ate out constantly and just seemed to enjoy life. Ms. Kathy and

SHIFTING ALLEGIANCES

her husband were child-free. The Burns, another family that lived close to Malik's were also child free.

Americans also did not ostracize you if you wanted a child but couldn't give birth. You were not looked upon as inferior if you were found to be infertile. An American husband would not discard you if you could not give birth to his child. Here, giving birth was viewed as one among many options of having a child. There was surrogacy where a woman would carry a child that was biologically yours or your husband's for you. There was adoption which was also very highly regarded by Americans. Basically, you would still be accorded all the respect that was given to a natural mother even if you didn't go through the birth process.

I thought about how freeing this was and how having these options probably removed a great deal of stress from American women's minds. I thought about how a Nigerian woman would consider it a great shame if she could not give birth to a child and how easily such women would be replaced by their men. I wondered how they'd feel if the American options were acceptable in our culture...

There were other things. A mother in America did not look like a mother in Nigeria. In Nigeria, mothers looked a certain way. They dressed like mature women, in dresses, skirts or traditional attire, very conservative and never revealing. In America, mothers wore jeans and young, hip clothes. They looked just like young girls. Also fathers in America did not behave like typical Nigerian fathers.

American fathers played sports, videogames, went to clubs and lived a very active life. They didn't just work and pay bills and on the rare occasion, go out drinking with their buddies. They still maintained their interests. They also didn't dress up in "daddy-attire". They wore young, hip clothes. Like their wives, you couldn't tell who was a father based on his dressing.

Amaka Lily

Also, a woman didn't need to know how to cook to get married. It was not a requirement here. Ordering food from outside or preparing micro-waved meals, was a perfectly acceptable way for a mother to feed her children and she wasn't considered inferior for lacking homemaking skills.

My notion of gender roles was dissolving before my eyes. The definition of what it meant to be a family was expanding before my eyes.

But there were some things that seemed to go way beyond what I thought was normal. Like the concept of househusbands, men that took care of the home while their wives worked. The men cleaned, cooked and took care of the children. It seemed unmanly to me, for a man to do a woman's work. It seemed unnatural to me for a woman to be the sole breadwinner. But this was America, things were different here.

Uncle never stopped giving me quizzical looks when the guys walked me back to our apartment. I know he felt that I should not be associating with them, but the fact that I seemed happy and was doing well in my studies, reassured him that I wasn't making the wrong decision.

So, he let me be.

This was basically how I spent my final college years, taking classes, hanging out with the guys and learning about America.

It was a happy life.

I had everything I wanted, a college education and friends of every race. I had a good job where I was learning and my coworkers loved me.

My family in Nigeria was also doing well. I had paid off my loan and was sending money to them every month.

Life was good.

I had no problems at all.

SHIFTING ALLEGIANCES

Amaka Lily

Chapter 7

Lawrenceville

SHIFTING ALLEGIANCES

May 24, 2008, 3 years after I had arrived in the states, I graduated with a Bachelor of Science degree in mechanical engineering. I had finished that 4 year program in just under 3 years.

Magna cum laude...

Ms. Chelsea threw me a party.

Uncle Ebuka threw me a party.

I was feted as if I had just found the cure for cancer and I was happy, immeasurably happy

In 3 years, I had gone from dreaming of a college education to gaining one in engineering.

In 3 years, I had gone from being a hopeless sack to one who believed anything was possible.

In 3 years, I had accomplished the American dream.

My future stretched before me brimming with possibilities. There was nothing I couldn't accomplish in this great country.

Absolutely nothing

Amaka Lily

I was offered a position with Pluto Engineering Associates, the premier engineering firm in our state. They gave me a sign-on bonus of $500 and a $500 clothing allowance.

I was in bliss.

$1,000 was a lot of money.

Two weeks before I was to start, I received a call from their HR representative informing me that I had been posted to Lawrenceville, 3 hours away. Lawrenceville was their newest site and they needed to ramp up personnel ASAP. She said I'd be given an extra $1,000 for relocation expenses if I accepted the new posting.

An extra thousand dollars?

It seemed like a no brainer. I said yes, but as soon as I hung up, the magnitude of what I had agreed to, dawned on me.

I did not know a single person in Lawrenceville, not a single person and I had never moved to a place where I didn't know a single soul. The thought of being alone in a new city was scary.

Very scary.

For the first time in my life, I would truly and utterly be alone.

Who was going to help me cope?

Who was going to help me assimilate?

But then the more I thought about it, the more I realized how silly I was being.

This was America for goodness sake, not a village in a remote forest. *What was there to be scared of?*

Not knowing anyone could actually be a good thing! I would be free to do what I wanted, go wherever I pleased and wouldn't have to answer to anyone.

This would actually be my first chance to truly be an adult in America and the freedom that came with no oversight was intoxicating.

I informed Uncle Ebuka of the good news and he praised my decision. The next couple of days, we went through the

SHIFTING ALLEGIANCES

Lawrenceville yellow pages and identified apartments. Within a week, Uncle Ebuka had helped me secure an apartment over the phone, sight unseen.

On the day of my move, he rented a U-Haul truck, gathered some furniture that they hadn't used in a while, my bed, dresser plus a few pots and pans and drove me, Aunty, Ebuka Jr and Chinedu, two of my junior boy cousins to Lawrenceville.

They accompanied me to sign my lease and set up my new place. After they were done, we all held hands and prayed. Uncle Ebuka blessed my new home and asked that God protect me in this new town. We all said Amen.

Up until that moment, I had been the picture of calm, cool confidence but once they started to leave, I began to freak out. Fear and anxiety filled me. My nearest family was now going to be 3 hours away. *How was I going to survive on my own?*

But as soon as that thought came, I reminded myself that I was about to embark on a very exciting journey.

There was no need for fear.

When they left, I surveyed my new home for the first time.

My apartment was beautiful, very very beautiful. It was spacious and had really nice hardwood floors. It had also come with a free refrigerator and gas stove which Uncle told me was standard in American apartments.

I was proud of it.

This was a long way from the boys quarters I had inhabited less than 4 years ago. Mosquitoes were a distant memory and now I had own room, my own bathroom, my own space.

I spent the next couple of days getting to know the area. I discovered where the grocery stores were, where the mall and library were and what buses came to my area.

I could not wait to start working, to start earning some real money.

I could not wait for my adult American life to officially start.

Amaka Lily

July 21st 2008, I began work.

There were 10 of us recent engineering graduates who started working at the same time. 8 males and 2 females.

I was the only black person.

I didn't think much of this distribution at the time.

I had worked with whites before, schooled with whites before... I didn't anticipate any problems.

Within days, I noticed a problem. The men seemed very uncomfortable around me, very very uncomfortable. It was as though they had never been in such close proximity with a black person before and did not know how to act.

We were all stuck in training for 6 hours each day, so I had plenty of opportunities to observe them. They answered my questions perfunctorily and did not laugh when I joked with them. Some actually looked alarmed when I approached them as if they feared I would bite their head off.

This was new territory for me. I had never before experienced any type of odd behavior from white people. All the whites I had encountered prior to this had been nice, open and kind. They had never seemed uncomfortable around me.

These men, though polite, were very uncomfortable. They were also not friendly. One of them, Ryan was actually hostile. He glared at me when I spoke to him and his body language screamed "*What the hell are you doing here?*" and "*How dare you talk to me?!*" It was as though he resented the fact that we occupied the same space, like he felt that I was undeserving to be in the same job as him, despite my grade point average- which he didn't know about- or my willingness to work- which he hadn't observed yet.

It was a weird vibe.

Stephanie Lieberman, the other woman, did not seem to engender the same feelings that I did. The guys LOVED her. Every morning, she would be greeted enthusiastically by them. The guys would congregate by her cubicle after we were done training, trade jokes with her and invite her for drinks after work.

I got the "run away" treatment.

It was hard not to take it personally, very hard.

I felt invisible, unwanted and somehow inferior. It was as if I wasn't even there, like I wasn't a human being.

I confided in Stephanie about the men's treatment of me and her response was that I was over thinking it, that the men were not like that. She said I was mistaking shyness for rudeness and that it was all in my imagination. But when I began to cite examples of how the men treated me, the curt way they answered me and the fear and hostility some seemed to have towards me, she reconsidered. She said they probably felt uncomfortable around me because they weren't used to me and invited me to tag along with her to their next happy hour.

I told her I did not drink and she said it wasn't about drinking, that in America, happy hours are ways people got to know each other and that participating in that would help the guys be comfortable around me. She assured me that they would see me as "cool" and "one of them" and I wouldn't have any more problems.

It seemed like a good idea.

I agreed to go.

That Friday, when Stephanie announced that I would be tagging along for their happy hour, I saw a look of shock quickly pass through the men's faces. Ryan as usual, looked pissed off, but outwardly, they all said it was okay. I made no mention of what I'd seen and just hoped that the guys would change as Stephanie had promised.

Wishful thinking.

At the bar, it was business as usual. Nothing changed, even as more and more pitchers of beer disappeared before my eyes. The guys never relaxed nor loosened up when it came to me. When I asked questions, it was the barest of responses I got.

Amaka Lily

When I tried to make eye contact, they averted their eyes. It was as if I were a bother. It was obvious they didn't want me there.

They just wanted to hang out with Stephanie.

There are not enough words to describe how I felt sitting there.

I felt hurt, humiliated, discounted.

I felt like a fifth wheel.

The way they treated me, made me feel like a strange, mutant creature, suddenly set free to the dismay of normal, better people. I felt like a form of life that did not deserve to be accorded the basic respect that all living things should get.

How could they sit there and treat me like that?

How could they be so rude?

Didn't they think I had feelings and that I was a human being?

But outwardly, I acted like nothing was bothering me. I pasted a smile on my face even though inwardly I was dying.

After an hour of enduring this behavior, I politely excused myself and left, my coca-cola barely touched.

As I left the bar, I promised myself, "*Never again*". No longer would I try to force a friendship on these people. I knew now that it was an exercise in futility. I would take whatever treatment they gave to me, no longer expecting or asking for more. There were millions of other people, who would be happy to be my friend. Millions.

These men were nuts.

The following Monday Stephanie came around to my cubicle saying it was too bad I had retired early. She said that they had had a "*ton of fun*" and that we all needed to "*do it again*".

It dawned on me that Stephanie, as dear as she was, was incapable of seeing how differently we were treated. Since I had promised myself never to be subjected to that type of

SHIFTING ALLEGIANCES

humiliation again, I knew I would never accompany her. Outwardly I said "*No problem*", but every Friday, I made myself disappear when happy hour time came …

Amaka Lily

On our first day of work, we, the new engineers, were informed that secretaries were to support us with administrative tasks. We were encouraged to delegate as much of such tasks to the secretaries so that we could focus the majority of our time on engineering issues, our first priority.

Admin tasks were fax and copy jobs. If you needed to have one of those done, you filled out a slip of paper with your name and a description of what you wanted done. You affixed the impacted documents to the slip and deposited the entire package into a box titled "New Jobs" which the secretaries managed. Once they had completed your request, they would transfer it into another box titled "Finished jobs".

This was the process of requesting assistance for admin tasks and such requests were to be completed within 3 hours.

In practice, that wasn't what occurred for me. Whenever I placed a request for either a fax or copy job, my request was either done late or completed in a very shoddy manner.

Every single time.

Once, I tried to ask one of the secretaries why a fax I had placed at 9 am, was still not done by 3pm, and she answered me in such an angry and defensive manner, that I regretted asking the question in the first place. It was as though she were trying to tell me that I had the nerve to ask to have anything done or to expect anything done for me.

I apologized.

But when it came to Stephanie or the guys' jobs, it was done promptly.

How did I know?

Well, all the entry level engineers sat in the same aisle and you could hear the secretaries when they came by to deposit their jobs. Yes, the secretaries –who were all white by the way- made personal deliveries for my peers and I knew this because I would hear Stephanie or one of the guy's thanking them for their promptness and I never heard them once complain about the quality of the secretaries work.

Aaah, the cruelty of people in this world, is amazing.

The disparate treatment I received in that work place was amazing.

But what could I do? I didn't want to complain. If I did so, I could be perceived as a whiner and I didn't want that. I didn't want to jeopardize the great job that I had. The money helped me live well and also assist my family.

I didn't want to ruin that.

So I swallowed my feelings of marginalization and disrespect and didn't say a word. I just did my jobs myself and never asked for help again.

Amaka Lily

After 3 weeks of training, my peers and I were assigned to project teams. A project team at Pluto consisted of a cross-functional group of people assembled to solve a specific problem or deliver a specific deliverable. A junior engineer was usually part of several teams, working on different projects. In addition to project teams, we were also assigned a manager to report to and do occasional work for. My peers and I shared the same manager but since each person did individualized work for him, we never crossed paths.

I was excited about the project teams. Finally, I'd be around a different set of people. Maybe now, I could actually develop a proper working relationship with my colleagues and perhaps even make some friends.

But that wasn't to be. I was never able to develop a proper working relationship with my white colleagues and in fact found myself being constantly on edge, never knowing what to expect or what would happen to me.

Let me explain. There were some groups I worked in where I came away with the feeling that I was hated or that the participants wondered what the heck I was doing there. It was apparent from the way they squeezed their faces or rolled their eyes when I spoke.

There were other groups were I felt simply tolerated. Where I was allowed to speak the ideas I had in my head but came away feeling like the group had already decided what direction the project was going to take. I remember one where, whenever I made my recommendations, they would keep quiet staring at each other, and once I was done, thank me for my contribution, but then continue as if I'd not even spoken. No feedback, no acknowledgement. Nothing.

At first I'd asked myself, *Was it something I said? Was my voice too loud? Did my breath stink?* I'd analyze and over-analyze everything I had said, trying to figure out what the reason was. But no matter how much I tried, I couldn't seem to

SHIFTING ALLEGIANCES

determine what I did wrong. Then I thought "*Hmmh, maybe it was the way I said it*" and then would take great pains to keep my voice very soft, very friendly, even prefacing my comments with "*If I may add...*" but the behavior did not end. Later, I started noticing that other participants would incorporate my ideas into their feedback without giving me credit and when they did so, they were received with great enthusiasm and acknowledgement.

Soon, I put two and two together.

Their behavior had nothing to do with my delivery or the content of my suggestions.

They just didn't want to hear from me and so I learnt in those groups to just keep quiet.

Still there were other "normal groups" where everyone seemed to get along and respect me, where I felt like a normal, contributing member of the office, but where the sentiment did not extend beyond the meeting. There were no extensions of friendship, no invitations to visit, no deeper conversations encouraged aside from work. Sometimes I would see some of these team members in the hallway and they'd acknowledge me with a hello. Other times, I would see the exact same team members and they would act as though they did not see me.

Once I thought I'd finally broken through this barrier. I was in the cafeteria buying lunch when Jim, our financial analyst lined up behind me. I said hello, he said hello back. Then he asked: "*Did you say you were from Nigeria again?*" I replied in the affirmative and it turned out he had actually visited Nigeria in the past. He used to be in the military and had travelled to a lot of African countries in his prime. He knew a lot about Nigerian history, the tribes, customs, even food. We were having a good discussion, until Cindy, our IT analyst, came into the cafeteria.

That was when I experienced something, I had never previously experienced.

Jim did a complete 180. He turned his back on me and started talking to Cindy.

He acted like I wasn't even there.

At first I stood there, waiting for him to turn around and at least end the conversation we had been having, but nope he did not do that.

He did not turn around to talk to me again.

It was like I did not exist.

It was like the conversation we had been having, never occurred.

I bought my food and continued on.

So consequently I was always on edge. I never knew what to expect or what type of behavior I'd be a recipient to. I could never feel really secure in that organization. Working in those groups was an exercise in pretending my eyes were not seeing what they were seeing and acting like all was well with the world, even though my heart was breaking.

Sometimes I felt like a participant in an elaborate mind game, except that it was a game where I didn't know the rules. Again, no outright hostility was meted to me, no scathing rudeness, nothing tangible that I could really hold on to. Just silence, dismissal and the sinking feeling that I wasn't acceptable.

It hurt.

I felt unable to trust anyone there, as their behavior was so inconsistent.

The only person that was consistent was Stephanie. She still made time to talk to me. Even though these were mostly superficial conversations, I appreciated them. In that increasingly lonely workplace, it was a very important lifeline.

SHIFTING ALLEGIANCES

Outside of work, my problems persisted.

When I would use the bus to go to work, I started noticing even more strange treatment. Our company was located in the middle of a downtown, a densely populated white environment. I noticed that when I entered the bus, some of the white people flinched as I approached their seats. Some would get up and move away if I sat near them while others remained seated but glared at me or shifted in their seats nervously.

At first I thought I was seeing double. *Surely it couldn't be me?*

Surely, my personhood could not be inspiring such a negative reaction?

But I wasn't seeing double. It happened so often and so blatantly that I knew it wasn't double vision.

The feeling of being a mutant, leprous creature now began to follow me everywhere. It wasn't just in the office now, but also out of the office.

There was more.

Being followed around in stores became a much more frequent occurrence. If I visited 3 stores, I would be sure to be followed in at least 2 of them.

Finally, I acknowledged the fat elephant in the room.

It was because I was black.

There was no other reason why I was treated differently at work and outside of work. Blackness in Lawrenceville was unacceptable, not respectable and charged with negative stereotypes. There was no other logical reason.

It was from that moment that I began to pay attention to my skin color. Whereas before, I never even considered what I looked like or what my color was like, now I realized that it affected people, whether I wanted it to or not. I had to keep it at the forefront of my mind to explain away odd reactions and prepare me for anything.

Amaka Lily

I began to see myself as a black person first, not Njideka anymore, but a black person.

It was also from that moment that I began to expect to be treated differently. When I went into a restaurant and the waiter was condescending to me, I knew it was because of my skin color. If I walked into a group of people and they clammed up once I arrived, I knew it was due to my skin color. I also started noticing other people's color. I'd scan the bus once I entered and look for an isolated seat. If that wasn't possible, I'd look for a seat that was next to people that didn't look mean. I remembered the stories Ray Ray had told me of what they did to blacks in the fifties. I didn't want to end up dead.

But even though I expected bad treatment, a part of me quietly hoped to be proved wrong. And each time I was treated badly, a hole deepened in my heart. It hurts to be profiled, hurts to be treated negatively, and no matter how many times, I experienced racist behavior, it still stung like it was the first time.

I once went into a Chinese restaurant where the waiter refused to serve me. It was one of those places where you had to order your food over a counter and then pay and wait for them to give it to you. The lady taking orders just acted like I wasn't even there, even though she had watched me come in and our eyes had locked once I got into the "ordering area". I stood there for a good 3 minutes, standing, saying *"Excuse me"*, *"Excuse me"* to no avail. Then a white man came in and she immediately became energized, the picture of pleasant customer service.

It was another server who came in from behind her that took my order.

I felt so distraught and hurt by that lady's behavior, but as usual, didn't say anything. In retrospect I should have walked away but I didn't. I went ahead and placed my order and collected my food.

SHIFTING ALLEGIANCES

One night I had to work late at the office and didn't get home until 11pm. It was dark all around and my apartment building was a long walk from the bus-stop. When I got off the bus, I noticed a white girl, about 20 or 21, walking a few yards ahead of me. When she heard my footsteps, she turned around. Once she saw me, she picked up her pace and hurried towards the main entrance. Our building was such that to get in, you needed a badge, otherwise, you couldn't get through. It was typical for renters to hold the door open for other renters if they noticed them following. I had watched this occur many times and had held the door open myself many times.

But once this girl got to the main entrance, she swiped her badge, got in and slammed the door after her

She did not hold the door open for me.

I didn't blame her.

All she had seen was a black person which to her meant the epitome of evil. She could not accord me the dignity that "normal" people were given because to her I was dangerous, not a fellow vulnerable female.

Amaka Lily

Any hopes I'd had about friendships outside of work being comparatively easier to make, were also dashed.

In Nigeria, you made friends just as you went about your life. You didn't have to do anything special or join groups to make a friend. In America, it was just the opposite. Because of the fear, suspicions, different cultural values and stereotyping that taints American relations, many Americans don't just approach strangers. Everyone keeps to themselves and minds their own business. This behavior also filters into the home place. You can live in a place for 10 years and never talk to your neighbors; in fact people have died all alone in their homes only to be discovered months later because no one bothered to check in on them.

At first, I'd carried the same mindset I'd had in Nigeria, of expecting friendships to just happen, but when time passed and it wasn't happening, I realized I needed to be proactive.

Specifically, I needed to join groups.

At Rose Titus, friendships, albeit transient ones, had been easy, but now that I thought about it, I realized I had been in a giant academic group. That's why it had been easy. I needed to be a part of something before I could make friends and so I set upon the process of looking for a group to join.

I looked up some professional groups and discovered that Lawrenceville had a young engineering professionals group near my job. I signed up but when I visited, I found the same sentiment from my job, mirrored in the group. The people I met were polite but not open. Some seemed uncomfortable and apart from answering the requisite *"Where did you go to school?"* or *"Where do you work?"* did not volunteer anything more about themselves.

Other races I met there, like the Indians and Hispanics, were not friendly at all. They acted like they were better than me and that whites were the only people worth befriending. Unfortunately, I did not find many blacks in these professional

SHIFTING ALLEGIANCES

groups. Many of the blacks in Lawrenceville occupied lower level positions such as janitors, cleaners, security guards and so consequently, were not in the same work circles I was in.

But I kept trying, kept trying. I desperately wanted to connect, wanted to have friends. I wasn't used to not having a social network and felt a compulsion to continue seeking. I told myself that somewhere, there had to be a group that would accept me, a group where color did not matter. I thought about the 3 years I had known Ms. Chelsea and Ms. Kathy. These had actually been nice, genuinely friendly white people, albeit in another city. I thought about my former Asian and Hispanic friends.

These people had not been a figment of my imagination.

There had to be more people like that.

I joined more groups, went to all sorts of events, yet nothing panned out. I joined even more groups, Chess, Salsa dancing, you name it. Groups I never thought I'd join, groups that I had no skill for, or any real desire to be a part of, save for the possibility that I'd be able to make friends. I signed up for so many groups, each time hoping that one of them would be the jackpot, that in one of them, I would meet kind, open people who would accept me and make all this effort worth it.

After all, wasn't persistence supposed to be the key to success?

But the more I tried, the more it didn't work.

It was discouraging

One day, I came across a newly started social group. The ad read

"Young couple in their mid 20s looking to make new friends to go ice skating. Scott's Ice skating is offering a special discount for 8 people. Beginners welcome. Must be in your 20s. Contact Jennifer via this email"

I emailed the Jennifer and introduced myself. I did not tell her I was black but told her I was female and 23 years old. I told her I had never skated before but was willing to join because I wanted to make some new friends. She said I didn't have to worry about anything and that skating was easy and that if I had any problems with it, she would personally show me how to do it. In addition, she sent me directions to the skating rink, including her phone number. She asked me to contact her if I had any more questions and ended with the line that she looked forward to meeting me.

I was happy. I thought this was finally it. I was going to make friends with ice skaters and probably become an ice skater myself.

This particular ice skating rink was located 45 minutes from my workplace. Because I used the bus, it was an hour away in the opposite direction, making my total return time, about 2 hours. I got there on the appointed day at 7pm. Skating wasn't to start until 7:30pm but Jennifer had said to arrive early to acquaint myself with other new people. When I got there, I found 7 people, 5 men and 2 women, all white. The lady I had been talking to, Jennifer, was dating one of the guys. All the other people were new like me.

As I introduced myself, I immediately had the sinking feeling that Jennifer had thought she had been corresponding with a non-black person because she looked shocked. I could also see the now familiar tensing of faces, rigidity and discomfort settle on all their features.

As usual, I pretended not to notice. I put a smile on my face, introduced myself while extending my hand for a handshake. I thanked Jennifer for organizing this outing and tried to talk to the others, you know, asking them if they were expert skaters, if they had any tips, if the skating rink was hard, stuff like that.

If I were an actor, I would have won an award.

But alas, my efforts were in vain. All I got back were terse responses.

SHIFTING ALLEGIANCES

I swear, if I was in Nigeria, I wouldn't have remained in that situation for a second, but since I wasn't and I was desperate, I persevered. Finally, it was time for skating. I went to rent skates and joined the group at the entrance of the rink.

At the very least, I was going to make the night a fun night regardless of what they thought of me. I was going to skate. It wasn't until I got on the ice that I realized that no type of skating would happen… at least not from me.

For starters, I could not control my legs.

Each leg was going in the opposite direction and try as much as I could, I could not "direct" them.

It was a terrifying sensation.

My legs were twisting in weird angles and I felt certain, horribly certain that my legs were going to break.

"*Chineke meeeh!!!*"[29]

"*Who send me so oh?*"[30]

I looked around wildly for my group mates to see if any of them could help me, if one of them could show me how to control my legs. But none of them were nearby. They were all skating away.

I grasped at the wall of the rink, trying to hold on to something solid, something that was not slippery but my legs kept moving. By this time, I don't need to tell you that I was done "skating". I just wanted to get out of that rink and far, far away from that ice. But I couldn't get out. My legs were doing their own thing and I could not get out, could not get back to solid ground. All around me were people of all ages, including children a third of my age, skating around with wild abandon, going round and round in circles. Finally, I saw a gentleman who looked to be skating out of the rink and I begged him to help me, explaining that I was a new skater and that I was

---

[29] God Ohhh!!! Igbo Exclamation
[30] Who sent me?

going to be seriously hurt if I didn't get off the rink immediately.

Maybe it was the look of fear on my face that made him decide to help me. Maybe he thought *"This black girl shouldn't be in the ice rink anyway"* and was doing his fellow whites a favor, I don't know. All I know is that this white guy gave me his hand, one of the nicest things a white person had done for me since I moved to Lawrenceville.

Unfortunately, he probably, instantly regretted his decision, because as soon as my hand found his, it clamped down immediately, in a vice grip. I would not let go and I could not help it. It didn't matter that the man kept saying, *"Relax my hand. Please relax my hand"*, I could not relax his hand. It was as if my body, having found something solid, had decided it was never going to let go, not until I had been deposited onto solid ground

Thankfully, he did lead me out of that rink. I thanked him profusely but he did not stay to listen. I took off those terrible skates and went to return them. There was still 25 minutes of skating time remaining but I didn't care that I was losing money, a first of its kind, because I hate to waste money. I didn't want to see those skates ever again. I went over to the little corner where Jennifer had asked us to reconvene once the set was done and just waited for it to be over. I was so embarrassed. Shame, mortification all washed through me and I just wanted the day to be over.

Finally, the set ended and my team mates returned. But the difficult interaction or its lack thereof, continued. I was expecting some sort of *"Hey, I noticed you didn't' skate much"* or *"Sorry you had to leave the rink early"* acknowledgement from my peers, but that never came. It was like they hadn't noticed my absence from the rink which I knew couldn't be possible as I was the only black person in that rink.

How could they have missed me?

SHIFTING ALLEGIANCES

I could not understand it, could not understand this lack of empathy and indifference. It seemed like I was in an alternate universe, a universe where people just didn't know what to say to a different person.

I had had enough. I bid my adieu and told them to have fun.

As soon as I stepped out of the building into the dark starry night, I burst into tears. The combination of having survived a near calamitous incident plus the pain of experiencing yet another night of unfulfilled expectations and not making friends, overpowered me.

I cried and cried and cried.

I felt so horrible, unlovable, and terrible.

I had never worked so hard for friendship in my life and I had also never failed so miserably at it. "*It was no use*", I choked, swallowing back bitter, bile filled tears.

Oh, I was so hurt that day. So so hurt. All the pain and frustrations I had been carrying since I began at Pluto, came out that night. Deep, heavy sobs, racked my body. I shook and shook and shook.

How much more rejection could a person take?

When would people just treat me like a human being?

Mercifully, no one saw me breakdown. The night was still early and everyone was at the rink, waiting for the next round of skating to begin

I walked to the bus stop and waited for my bus.

It would be a long time before I joined another social group.

Amaka Lily

Those first few months were tough.

Far away from friends and family, facing constant rejection and unable to make new connections, I was incredibly sad, but I could not tell anyone. I could not bring myself to tell Uncle Ebuka because he was so proud of me and thought I was doing well.

How could I tell him I was depressed?

I also couldn't tell my family in Nigeria what I was experiencing because I didn't think they would understand. *How could I be sad in America, the land of milk and honey, the land of 24/7 electricity, the land they all aspired to come to? How could I be so sad when I had dollars and an American college degree?*

How could I be sad?

How could I be sad?

I could just hear my mother saying *"However bad America is, it is still better than Nigeria"* and *"Would you want to come back and live in darkness, poverty and corruption?"*

I could only confide to my journal.

Once in a while, Malik would call me and ask how I was doing. Sometimes I told him that I was having difficulty making friends, never elaborating, to which he would always respond *"It takes time"*.

I would ask after the others. Ahmad had gotten engaged and Ray Ray was still arguing with people about his beliefs.

I began to look forward to Malik's calls. His calls reminded me of a better time in my life, a time when I wasn't really bothered by racism, a time when I felt accepted. I'd even try to prolong his calls because I didn't want him to hang up because I knew that when he did, I'd come right back to darkness and extreme loneliness and I didn't want to be there.

I could not understand it.

SHIFTING ALLEGIANCES

This U.S. I was experiencing was very different from what I had initially known. I could not reconcile the sudden change in the country I had loved so much.

Why was it so cold?

Just when I was ready to start enjoying my hard won life, *why did racism have to affect me?*

I finally understood some of what Ray Ray had tried to tell me, that America was very different for a black person. Since I had never seen myself as a black person, but as Njideka the person, I had never fully related to what he had said. Now, I was feeling the impact of what it meant to be black in America.

And it was not fun.

Not fun at all.

I walked around like a person with an interminable disease, feeling like I had a big stamp of REJECT on my forehead, wanting closeness but fearing to take another chance, not wanting to face the harsh sting of rejection again.

Amaka Lily

Seven months into my job at Pluto, a ray of light came into my life in the shape of Lamar.

Lamar was a security guard that had been hired to work on our floor. When I saw him for the first time, I was overcome with joy. I had been so starved of people like me that seeing a black person now gave me joy. I just knew he would understand what I was going through.

I just knew it.

And I was right.

Lamar understood exactly what I was going through and validated all the feelings I had had about my workplace. He told me that my experience with the cross-functional groups was a common one, shared by many minorities. He said that basically, the whites in my group were racist but since they couldn't be outwardly racist –because it is illegal- tried to show their disapproval in subtle ways such as playing mind games or giving me the silent treatment so that in that way, you didn't have a tangible case against them if you chose to complain.

When I ran Ryan's behavior by him, he said it was probably because Ryan thought I was an "*affirmative action candidate*" who had gotten her position by being black. I asked him what that meant and he said affirmative action was a policy the government had instituted to try to ensure there was equal representation by all races in the workplace. Unfortunately, to meet this policy, some employers hired people that were not as qualified, leading well-qualified people to view all affirmative action candidates as suspicious and ill-equipped for their job.

The secretaries in turn, did not respect me because not only was I a black professional -which was a rare sight in Lawrenceville-, but also because their attitudes towards blacks were still in the 18th century.

He said "*You can't expect the same type of treatment that a white person will get... You just can't. Expecting that is just asking for abuse. You will never be considered equal to them*

SHIFTING ALLEGIANCES

and it doesn't matter how high up the career ladder you go. You are black. You will always be considered inferior to your white counterparts"

I found that hard to accept. Yes, even though I'd been having difficulties since I started in that office, I didn't want to believe that for all of my American life, I would always be considered inferior to my white colleagues. I told Lamar about Mrs. Chelsea and my previous coworkers. *Why hadn't they treated me terribly when I worked for them?*

His response, "*You were never a threat as a receptionist. A receptionist is a low level position and it is not uncommon to see blacks in such roles. However, once you enter a real, professional role, their true colors come out. They start feeling like you are encroaching their God given turf, and they will resent you"*

The world suddenly seemed unsafe to me.

How was I going to succeed in America if the higher I advanced, the more people hated me?

How was I ever going to feel secure?

Lamar saw the look of alarm on my face and quickly tried to assuage my fears "*Don't worry Deka, you will be okay. Like I said earlier, you are not the first person to experience this and you sure won't be the last. This is just how America is. Just smile, put up a good front and do an excellent job. Also, try not to give them any fodder against you cause they will use it"*

My alarm lessened but it didn't totally dissipate.

I thought long and hard about what Lamar told me. The reasons he gave about how whites saw blacks in Lawrenceville seemed plausible. It explained a lot of things I had experienced. I realized that in the years prior to Lawrenceville, I had inhabited a very sheltered world, a bubble if you will. My life had revolved around school and school connections, and I was finding that as a result, I had no real sense of how America truly operated. I had also changed cities to one that was more conservative and less diverse.

Things were bound to be very different.

In the past, I had dismissed some of what Ray Ray had told me, not wanting to take sides in the white versus black debate and also because I believed some of those claims to be preposterous.

Now I was starting to see some validity in his claims. I realized that I better start paying attention to those who knew the country better than I did.

I started hanging out more with Lamar. I know there were some raised eyebrows as to why I, an engineer, was hanging out with a lower level staff, but I didn't care. Status no longer mattered to me. I cared more for friendship and understanding and Lamar more than fit the bill. He introduced me to his family, friends and church and those connections helped jumpstart my social life by introducing me to more black people. All of Lamar's friends and family were working class, blue collar people but I appreciated them. They treated me well, invited me to events like BBQs and church events, so I had things to look forward to.

I now understood why new transplants preferred to live in a place where similar people lived. Going out in the world, on your own is not that easy. Having people who accepted and understood you made the process much, much easier.

I didn't feel so alone anymore.

Chapter 8

Strange developments

Amaka Lily

My life at Pluto was proceeding normally, at least as normally as one could under those circumstances. I still did not feel fully comfortable in that organization but I had formulated a way to make my work life more palatable. I put a smile on my face and went about my duties as cheerfully as I could. I no longer expected to make deep friendships with my colleagues; neither did I expect them to do anything for me. As long as I had a job and got paid, that was all I cared about.

Things seemed to work quite well with that decision. An amicable, albeit superficial relationship persevered.

June 8th 2009, New Products Day. New Products Day was a once a year event where the different engineering teams showcased their latest designs to top management. I was going to be presenting. It was a rite of passage for the most junior engineers to present projects on behalf of their team and I was excited, very excited. If there's anything I love more than life itself, it is presenting.

On the day of the presentation, word spread that Jacob Serb was in the office. This was cause for concern. Jacob Serb was our Vice President of Operations, who had risen to the ranks of Chief Engineering officer, by the tender age of 30. He was a smart, ambitious man who was also very intimidating. He also had a reputation for quizzing people and tearing down anyone he thought was spouting shaky facts. Basically, he wasn't a nice man and worse, he had a penchant for visiting branches unannounced.

Not surprisingly, people didn't relish his surprise visits but since he was a VP, there was nothing anyone could do about it. I silently hoped he would not be at the New Products presentation, but that was wishful thinking. When I walked into the meeting room, I found him seated at the head table calmly going through the slides that I was to present.

I went up to him and introduced myself, explaining that I would be the one speaking about Prototype 604. He looked at

SHIFTING ALLEGIANCES

me and uttered what sounded like a cross between a grunt and a snort... I couldn't be sure. But I was used by now to strange treatment from white people so I didn't let it bother me.

As people filed in, I reflected on how lonely corporate America could be, particularly if you were black. There was not another black person in that room, not one. It would have been nice to see another black face, to feel like I was one among many. It was particularly acute in this environment where the other races were not welcoming, where one felt totally clueless about their social customs, where no one seemed to care that you were not happy or not fitting in. It would have been nice, but alas I was the only black person, and I felt alone, vulnerable and like I stuck out like a sore thumb. I wondered what it had been like decades ago, when there were even fewer black professionals in corporate America. ..

The presentations went quickly. Apart from answering a few clarifying questions from top management, there was really not much for a junior engineer to say except to follow the PowerPoint.

When it came to my turn, I began. *"Good morning Ladies and Gentlemen. My name is Deka and I'm really appreciative of you all coming today. Today I will be presenting Prototype 604, which bar none, is our best car engine yet, with....."*

Someone piped up *"What do you mean the best? We are not a company of mere words... Explain what you mean by our best car engine!!!"*

I turned around, it was Jacob Serb. I swallowed. *"Well by the best Sir, I mean that we have found a way to exceed the performance of our current series 6 products. This one is more efficient, has more power and we believe our customers will buy it because it can actually be priced same as our current Prototype 603 product"*

He interjected *"How do you know that? All our series 6 products perform as expected. Why should we invest in this?*

Also, how do you suggest we sell this product if we decide to produce it?"

Okay what was going on? Was this a fight or something? I didn't understand. I had worked on this product, so of course I knew how it performed, but it was strange that he was asking me all these questions? Typically, these would have been answered way before the project was prioritized for development and way before I came into the picture.

What the hell was going on?

"Well sir, we have added more enhancements such as improved torque delivery. Also, the fact that we can manufacture it without significantly raising the cost to our current consumers, means that we'd be providing more value for them"

"BUT DID THEY ASK FOR IT? Jacob Serb continued to press. *"Did the research indicate that our customers are in any way dissatisfied with our current offerings?"*

"Not exactly... Bbbuuttt"

"BUT WHAT???" *"We don't have time to be making vanity products... you engineers have a tendency to run wild with your ideas... we have to be practical... yes, it may be a valuable product, but we just don't give value just for value sake and we also don't manufacture products just because we can. We are in business to make money, NOT LOSE MONEY "* he was yelling now *"SO TELL ME, WHY SHOULD WE OFFER THIS PRODUCT?"*

Now I was really concerned, actually worried at the way things were going. I wasn't prepared for this. I wasn't prepared for this barrage of questions that deviated from the script. I wondered if this was deliberate, if this was a way of hazing unsuspecting junior engineers. I looked around at my colleagues but everyone seemed to be averting their eyes, I thought I could even detect a smirk in some, but I wasn't sure. I needed help. I needed to get away from this situation as gracefully as I could. But there was no running away. Jacob Serb was looking at me expectantly, awaiting an answer to his question

I went with what came to my head.

"Well Sir, I don't believe we can continue maintaining our position as the leading engineering company in America if we do not continue to innovate and offer more value than our competitors. Yes, the research did not indicate that our customers specifically requested these extra enhancements, but that is not to say they would not be impressed with the latest design. Preliminary surveys done with our customers indicate there is a lot of excitement about this engine. It is just that much better. Also, what does it hurt if we give more for the same price? As long as it's not costing us significantly more to produce, and it isn't, I think it's ok".

It was all I had.

Jacob Serb looked at me for one long moment and then asked *"What's your name again?"*

Oh God, why was he asking? *"Deka"*, I responded.

"Great work!".

Great work? Me! Great work*???* Did he just say *"Great Work"* to me?

"You may go back to your seat Deka.... Who's next?" and just like that, my interrogation ended

I went back to my seat feeling like I had just been through an alternate reality.

What just happened?

It had been a weird discourse. *Why did Jacob Serb not allow me to go through my presentation like the others? Why had he peppered me with questions? Why did he switch from harsh interrogator to sudden "complimenter"? Why? Why? Why? Was he just bored? Was he just trying to rattle me? Was he ensuring I knew what I was talking about?*

So many questions, no answers.

Amaka Lily

After the meeting, I went back to my cubicle. As I was preparing to go to lunch, Jacob Serb appeared by my desk and in front of everyone, asked me to join him for lunch. I was concerned. *Why was he asking me, the social outcast, out to lunch? Why did he not ask the other junior engineers? What was going to happen to me?* But I needn't have worried. Jacob Serb turned out to be a nice guy, a really, really nice guy.

He started out by asking me a lot of questions, inquiring into my background, Nigeria and how I was adapting to the United States. I answered warily, saying everything was nice, wondering why the sudden interest in my life. It turned out that he had actually had some experience in Africa. As a college student, he had travelled to Kenya on a volunteer mission and had lived there for 5 months. He knew a lot about the tribes, culture and even a little Swahili. I was impressed. I would never have expected someone like Jacob Serb to be able to locate Kenya on a map, not to mention knowing some of the language.

He asked how I was doing at Pluto and wanted to know in great detail about my work and projects. I told him, leaving out the parts about feeling lonely and excluded. It just didn't feel appropriate to bring up all that stuff.

He told me he saw a lot of promise in me, that I thought quickly on my feet and gave good answers. He encouraged me to reach out to him if I ever needed help and gave me his business card with his cell phone number added to it. I was appreciative. It had been so long since I'd received any type of professional acknowledgement from anyone. So so long. It felt nice to be treated like a human being again. It felt nice to be a person, not a color.

The lunch went on for 2 hours and after it was done, he paid for both of our meals.

I was in heaven.

SHIFTING ALLEGIANCES

He walked me back to my desk and I could see some people trying to peep out of their cubicles at us. I imagined they wondered why I of all people was walking side by side with the great Jacob Serb.

I walked with my head high. For once, I felt special, acceptable.

I mattered.

I hoped that Jacob Serb's friendship would encourage the others to start treating me better. Perhaps now, they would deem me as "safe" and just a normal human being.

Amaka Lily

Two days after my lunch with Jacob Serb, I was called into my boss's office.

He said that people had reported me, that I had not locked up every single drawer in my cubicle the day before. He said that our company required all employees to lock up every drawer before they went home and that leaving drawer's open was a big no-no and he was officially giving me notice. He also said that I'd not turned off my cubicle light after work which was in violation of the company's green policy

I was surprised. I didn't know our company required us to lock every single locker. I usually locked the ones that contained confidential files but left the empty ones unlocked since it didn't make sense to me to lock them. I also didn't know that we had a green policy. Our company usually left its lights on 24 hours, 7 days a week. *When did they start insisting that the lights be turned off?*

When I inquired as to when this became mandatory, my boss cut me off, "*Just turn off your cubicle lights and ensure that your drawers are locked. That's all Deka*" and with that I was waved out of the office.

It was odd. *Why hadn't there been this insistence on locking drawers and turning off lights? Why all of a sudden?*

Lamar told me not to worry. He said there were worse things than being reported for not locking drawers. In the grand scheme of things, this was minor. He reminded me that as long as I had a job and was getting paid, that was all that mattered.

I agreed and from that day onwards, never left a light on or locker unlocked, even though I noticed that people still continued to leave the lights on overnight.

I didn't want to be reported ever again.

Days passed.

I came to work another day, sat down and immediately sat up.

SHIFTING ALLEGIANCES

My chair was wet, soaking wet. I had a wet stain on my skirt as if I had just peed on myself. I looked up at the ceiling to see if it was leaking.

Nothing. It was as dry as the Sahara.

I asked around my area to see whether anyone had any information as to why my seat was wet.

Nothing. No one had any idea.

I brushed it off.

Another day, I found all the pens in my coffer leaking. Furthermore, my stapler, note pads, file holder and regular office supplies were all overturned. Everything was in complete disarray. "*It was probably the maintenance staff*", my boss informed me, "*perhaps they just hired someone new... don't think too much about it*".

It seemed a bit of a stretch, but it was plausible. I left it at that.

But things steadily became worse. Grammatical errors began to appear in my work, a chart I'd slaved over would come out wonky or a simulation would be missing parts.

When it first started, I thought it was odd. I am usually anal, severely anal about the quality of my work. If there was something I derived immeasurable pride from, it was my work and my identity was inextricably tied to it. I didn't think I was capable of making careless mistakes like what was appearing, yet when I checked the records of who last accessed my files - they were all saved on a shared drive, per department policy- it was my name that consistently came up.

At first I chalked it up to oversight. Since the system was incontrovertible proof of who had last accessed a file, and since I was the only one who had access to my computer, it meant that I WAS the one who made the mistakes. Yet it wouldn't stop. Mistakes kept appearing and they kept getting bigger and bigger. I became alarmed. "*What was happening to me?*", "*Had

I developed some sort of dementia?", "Why was I making lots of mistakes?"

I couldn't tell anyone. That would put my job on the line!!!

I began checking and rechecking my work. Multiple times a day, I would check. Before I left work I would check and first thing when I arrived, would check again. But the mistakes kept appearing, nothing I did could make it stop.

What was happening to me?

Then one day, buried within the text of a PowerPoint presentation I had been working on, directly under the agenda bullet were the words.

PLUTO SUCK MY DICK

"*Whatttt!*" my eyes almost popped out of their sockets "*What is this?*" Now I knew that no amount of dementia, tiredness or oversight would have made me type that. No amount of temporary brain insanity could have made me type that nonsense. It was at that point that it finally dawned on me:

Somebody was sabotaging my work.

Somebody was playing a cruel joke on me!

I became alarmed. *Why would someone do that? Why would someone want to make me look bad?* And worse, *What would have happened if I had not caught this error in time?*

The more I thought about it, and the more I thought about all the earlier strange incidences, the more I became convinced that I was indeed, the pawn in a cruel joke.

I had to let my boss know this.

I had to let my boss know before it got out of hand!!!

I went to him. I actually said to him "*I think there's a conspiracy about me in this firm. Someone has been tampering with my work files and I have proof today that it isn't me*"

Big mistake.

If I had known then, that a black person using the word "conspiracy" in an American work place automatically relegates you to a paranoid and laughable status, I would never have said a word. But I didn't know and just came out with what I was truly feeling.

My boss did not take too kindly to my "*accusations*". He actually yelled at me. I was shocked. He said no such thing could be happening at Pluto, a company where everyone was "*forthright*" and "*committed to teamwork and the success of the company*". He asked me to show him proof that someone else had accessed my files. I replied that even though the computer appeared to show that no one else, except me, had accessed it, I would never write something like PLUTO SUCK MY DICK in a presentation. It wasn't me. I also tried to convince him that the strange occurrences of my chair being wet and my pens leaking were proof that someone was trying to make me look bad.

But it was a wasteful attempt. Everything fell on deaf ears.

My boss's response was that I should try to be more vigilant about my work rather than accusing my coworkers of something that low. He was so empathetic that I was somehow to blame that I began to even doubt myself. I apologized and left his office.

I felt embarrassed, mortified and humiliated. I had gone to my boss hoping for some help but instead had looked like a fool. I tried to replay the incidents that had occurred.

Could I really have written that?

Could I really have written something that bad?

But I knew the answer was No. Despite what the computer said, I knew I did not write that.

I thought about telling Jacob Serb, but if my boss's reaction to my claims was any indication, Jacob would probably deny my claims as well. Besides this wasn't something that should be brought up to someone that high up in the organization anyway.

Amaka Lily

I scratched the thought. I was going to deal with this situation on my own. I was going to salvage my name even though no one believed me.

First I would protect myself. I decided to password protect every work I saved so that no one could ever tamper with my files again. Second, I would ignore the pranks played around my desk. I would act like it didn't bother me so that whoever was playing the game quit, eventually.

I began my vow. The password protecting worked for a while but soon, even that work began to be tampered with. I switched to emailing final copies of my projects to my personal email and emailing them back to my work email in the morning. It was only in this way that I was able to successfully protect my work.

The other pranks however, continued unabated. Sometimes my computer would suddenly blackout while I was working and I would find it to be unplugged. Other times, it was my internet connection or phone. Once, after a long holiday weekend, I smelt a dead rat in my thrash can. Another time, it was vomitus. Those last two incidents forced me to begin checking my thrash first thing when I came to work. I would also leave it overturned the rest of the day, just to be sure nothing was ever put in.

Outwardly I didn't complain but inside I was dying. I was hurt and angry. I was hurt that something was happening to me, yet I couldn't complain about it. I also couldn't provide substantial proof that it was being orchestrated by someone. I was being hurt and there was no one to direct my anger to.

It was a strange type of war. I had never before faced a situation where I didn't know the enemy, where I didn't know who was trying to hurt me. This was different. This consisted of shapeless, faceless creatures, who though invisible, inflicted real pain.

It was mind games. It was mental cruelty.

SHIFTING ALLEGIANCES

The preoccupation with protecting myself and anticipating an attack, led to me having sleeping difficulties. My mind would race at night wondering if I had covered my tracks, wondering if I had sent every important email to my personal email account and whether somehow, those had been intercepted. I would toss and turn thinking about potential problems, wondering if something on my desk would be stolen or rigged to hurt me. I also developed panic attacks. My heart would beat rapidly whenever I approached my job and continue beating until I left work. I began to dread coming to work. I no longer knew what to make of my work place. It became a big, scary place that I no longer felt safe in.

This went on for months.

Amaka Lily

Chapter 9

An unexpected turn

SHIFTING ALLEGIANCES

October 16th 2009.

My boss and I went on a site visit. We finished early and my boss gave me the rest of the day off. I was ecstatic until I got home and realized that I had not emailed copies of my files as I usually did to my personal email, each evening. "*Oh God*", I thought, but I knew I had to go back. *Who knew what the perpetrators would do to my work if I left it for just one night?*

I boarded the bus back to my job.

I noticed that when I got onto my floor, that it was very quiet. But then I thought that since it was the middle of the day, it probably wasn't unusual. People were deep at work. You could hear the clickety clack of typing fingers. I planned to go into my cube, email my stuff to myself and then quietly dash out.

What was unusual was that when I crossed the corner to enter my cubicle, Stephanie Lieberman was sitting on my chair and my computer was unlocked.

What was Stephanie Lieberman doing on my computer?
"*Stephanie?*"

She turned around, and when she did, I saw that she had open a flowchart I had recently completed, one that I was going to give to my boss the next day.

In the few seconds that I stared at her, it all came together. She was the one. She was the cause of all my pain. She was the one who had been modifying my documents all this while and trying to make me look bad.

Stephanie oh Stephanie.

Words cannot describe the anger, disbelief, pain and betrayal I felt. Perhaps it is similar to what a wife feels, when she catches her husband in bed with her best friend, or what a child feels when his parents leave him for someone who is not blood. I don't know, all I know is that the last person I would have suspected of doing this to me was Stephanie. I thought she was a friend. Even though we had not been as close since

Lamar came into the picture, I had still greeted her and made small talk with her. *Why did she do this? Why would she do a thing like that to me?*

"*SO YOU ARE THE ONE!*" I screamed "*YOU ARE THE ONE WHO HAS BEEN TAMPERING WITH MY WORK ALL THIS WHILE???*"

Stephanie didn't say a word, she just looked at me with a guilty look on her face.

I felt my anger rising.

"*GET OUT!!! GET OUT NOW!!! GET THE HECK OUT OF MY COMPUTER!*" and with that last statement, I pushed her away from my computer and she fell.

Before I knew it, strong hands had lifted me away and people had appeared between us. I was screaming, Stephanie was screaming. Everyone was screaming.

My boss came out and asked what the ruckus was all about.

I told him, the words quickly escaping my lips. I told him of how I'd caught her modifying the flowchart I was preparing for him and how she'd been the one sabotaging my work all this while. I reminded him of when I came to his office months prior to report that someone had been tampering with my files and how he had waved me away telling me I was wrong. Well, Sir, here was the proof. The flowchart, a pass-worded file was now on display for everyone to see. *How could Stephanie explain being on my computer without my permission? How could she explain having access to my pass-worded file?*

My boss turned to Stephanie who was whimpering. He asked her to explain what she was doing on my computer. Rather than answer the question my boss posed, Stephanie just kept repeating that I had pushed her. She also kept rubbing a part of her arm, saying it hurt and that I had dislocated it.

I rolled my eyes. She was lying. I hadn't pushed her that hard. *What was she doing IN MY FILES?*

SHIFTING ALLEGIANCES

My boss asked the other people what had happened. They all said I pushed her, that I came in screaming and pushed her. The way they said it, you'd think I just lost my mind and pushed her, like I did it without any justification. No one talked about the fact that she was IN MY COMPUTER.

Stephanie's whimpering got louder, next thing you know, it went to full blown wailing. She said I had broken her arm and that it hurt so badly. The girl was trying to be an actress. Even a blind person could see that she was trying to divert attention from what she'd done. WHAT WAS SHE DOING ON MY COMPUTER? But then the wailing got louder and louder. Next thing you know, an ambulance was called and Stephanie was taken to the hospital.

My boss asked me to wait for him in his office.

I paced all over my boss's office. I could not sit. I was anxious, wired and fired up.

15 minutes later, my boss came and delivered the most startling news of my life

"Deka, I am sorry to say this, but..." he sighed *"... you have to leave!"*

I was stunned. I felt like I had just been punched in the stomach. *Did I just hear what I thought I just heard?*

"I don't understand"

"Deka, I am sorry but you have to leave. You have been terminated"

"What do you mean Sir?!" my voice was a little higher than normal *"...What do you mean I have to leave? Why do I have to leave? What about Stephanie? SHE tampered with my work. SHE'S BEEN TAMPERING WITH MY WORK?"*

"It doesn't matter Deka, you cannot go about pushing people in the workplace... it is not allowed... we could get sued"

"But Mr. Wilson, you know you haven't heard me do that to anybody before... You know that's not my character... This WAS JUSTIFIED SIR... it was very justified. My voice was cracking. I was desperate. I could not believe this was happening.

I COULD NOT BELIEVE MY JOB WAS ON THE LINE.

"I am sorry Deka, but by pushing her, you violated our assault policy ... and we have zero tolerance for that... I am sorry, but you have to leave"

"But she tampered with my work...Sir, she tampered with my work!"

He did not respond

"Sir, SHE TAMPERED WITH MY WORK. WHAT HAPPENS TO HER?"

He did not answer, and that was when it dawned on me that my job was truly gone.

SHIFTING ALLEGIANCES

Pffffft, just like that.

I looked at my supervisor for what seemed like a long time but probably was just a few seconds. I wanted to ask him how he could do this, how he could leave me out in the cold. I WAS the person that was wronged here. I WAS the person who had been consistently wronged for months!!!

But there was no use pleading my case, his decision had been made and I did not have a leg to stand on.

"I would need to collect your badge from you and your keys"

I handed them to him

"Please remain in this room. We will pack your things for you and bring them here"

I wanted to cry, my heart was breaking and I felt unfairly treated, but I did not let on.

I did not show what I truly felt inside.

Fifteen minutes later, a box of my pictures and little mementoes were handed to me and I was escorted out of the building by a security guard.

I repeat, I was escorted out of the building by a security guard, as if I were an unwanted guest, as if I wasn't the person who had worked there for over a year!!!

It hurt.

It hurt like hell.

As I walked past my now former cubicle, I saw people straining to look at me. I gritted my teeth and held my head high.

I refused to give them the pleasure of seeing me broken.

I had to hold on to the last shred of dignity I had.

Once out, I crossed the street to wait for my bus, still holding my head high.

When the bus came, I walked in with my carton, still holding my head high.

It wasn't until I was safely ensconced in the back of the bus that I lowered my head and gave myself to tears.

I cried and cried and cried

I could not believe I had just lost my job.

It was not fair. It was so unfair.

My body shook with great sobs and the tears poured freely, blinding me at times. I could not swallow. My throat felt like a huge ball of bile was lodged in it. I thought I was going to choke.

It was not fair. It was so unfair

I went over the day's events, over and over again

I could not believe what had happened. I could not believe that I WAS THE ONE REMOVED from the company.

THIS WAS NOT RIGHT.

THIS WAS NOT RIGHT.

Luckily, since it was still before rush hour, I was the only passenger in the bus. Just like on that ice skating day, no one else saw my pain.

I reached home, turned off my phone and went straight to bed.

I didn't eat. I couldn't eat. I wept again.

Why did Stephanie do that to me? Why?

I tried to think of what I might have done to make her angry but couldn't come up with anything. It was true that since Lamar had come into the picture, I had focused most of my time with him but that was because I didn't have a choice. Stephanie hung out with my other coworkers and the latter didn't want to hang out with me. *What was I to do?*

Still I had not forgotten her. I'd still greeted and made small talk with her.

Why would she do a thing like that?

I couldn't find answers.

I thought about my boss and how he had been so quick to fire me? *Why wasn't I given some sort of due process, a way to*

SHIFTING ALLEGIANCES

have both mine and Stephanie's side aired? Why was I cut off so suddenly and so unceremoniously?

It was unfair.

It was so unfair.

The pain I felt was deep, very deep. I felt betrayed, discarded and when I finally fell asleep, it was a troubled sleep. Visions of wild animals chased me with Stephanie and Mr. Wilson, egging them on. They clawed at me, tearing at my flesh and I couldn't scream. I woke up 3 times bathed in sweat.

The next morning, the financial implications of losing my job sank in.

What was I going to do?

What was going to happen to my family?

I had not been without a job since I came to the U.S. *What was I going to do with myself now?*

I had to find a job. I had to find a job fast.

I picked up my phone, realized it was turned off, turned it on, and almost immediately it began to ring.

It was Lamar

"*Hey Deka, where you been? Been trying to reach you since yesterday... Are you okay?*"

Hearing his last question, made me start bawling again.

"*Not good, I .... I... don't know what to do*"

"*Where are you*"

"*I... I... am at home*"

"*I am coming over*" he said, and with that he hung up.

I felt immediately better. Lamar would know what to do. Lamar would know what to tell me.

When he arrived, the first thing he did was to give me a big long hug.

We don't hug like that in Nigeria, but God, it felt so good.

His touch said he cared, he understood and that he had my back. It was exactly what I needed at that moment.

Then he sat me down.

"*What happened?*" he asked and it all came pouring out. I told him about the pranks, the tampering of my documents and how at first, I'd thought I was the one at fault. I told him of how I'd discovered it wasn't me and the attempt I had made to tell my boss and how he had made me feel like I was lying. I told him about the stress I had undergone in the last couple of months trying to protect myself, the fact that I saw Stephanie on my computer modifying my document and how I'd pushed her away and subsequently gotten fired.

He was silent for a moment, then he asked "*When did you first notice your documents were being tampered with?*". I told him it had started months ago. He said "*Specifically, when did you notice the pranks and odd behavior?*" I thought back and I realized it had begun soon after the New Product's presentation. He asked me if anything unusual had happened at that presentation and I recalled the relentless way Jacob Serb had asked me questions, questions that were unrelated to what I was presenting. I also remembered that he'd later taken me out to lunch and spoken to me.

"*Back up*", Lamar said "*did you say Jacob Serb took you out to lunch?*" I replied in the affirmative and as soon as I said that, it was as if something clicked in our heads at the same time.

Jacob Serb's taking me out to lunch was what had caused my problems. The fact that one of the most respected leaders in our company had taken a liking to me, a black woman, the lowest of the low, had enraged certain members of my group.

"*They set you up Deka.... They set you up to fail*"

Wow, it was worse, much worse than I thought. I would never have imagined that a person -or people- could be that threatened, just because a senior VP took a liking to me. I would never have imagined that a person -or people- could stoop that low to make an innocent person look bad?

SHIFTING ALLEGIANCES

Was being black that hateful?
Was being black that despised?
It seemed to me that there had to have been more people in cahoots with Stephanie. She couldn't have been able to pull everything off without some complicity. *But why her? What had I done specifically to her? Why was she the hatchet man? Was it because they -whoever they were- thought -rightfully so- that I would never suspect her? Was Mr. Wilson involved?*
Questions upon questions with no forthcoming answers.
How had Stephanie been able to log onto my computer? How had she been able to get my password? Then I remembered Stephanie was dating Rodney, who was in charge of our IT department. *Could Rodney have decrypted my password for Stephanie?*
"*Oh My God*"!!! So when I had mentioned to my boss that there was a conspiracy against me, I really had no idea, how right I was. Neither did I know the extent of the conspiracy. It was scary to finally realize how big it had been. It was scary to realize how well executed it was.
"*So what do I do?*" I asked Lamar. "*What are my options*"? I thought I had a case for a lawsuit actually, a pretty good case…
"*Not a lot Deka*", Lamar replied sadly "*The fact that you pushed Stephanie, even though it was justifiable, puts you in the wrong. There a'int no way a judge would be sympathetic to you, a black woman for pushing someone at work. They already think all black women are angry and troublesome. No one's gonna side with you*", he finished

I was devastated.
I had unwittingly given them the power to hurt me.
I had played into their hands.
I started weeping again.
My life was finished.
My life was finished in America.

"*Calm down Deka, calm down*" he urged "*it's not the end of the world... calm down*"

But IT WAS THE END OF THE WORLD. My life was finished. It was completely finished in this country

"*Girl, it's okay, stop crying. Look, at least you were not sentenced to jail for a crime you did not commit? At least you were not framed for a crime you did not commit?*"

"*What are you talking about? I WAS FRAMED! I was made to feel like I WAS LOSING MY MIND*"

"*Girl, get a grip, you only lost a job*"

"*But the job was EVERYTHING I HAD. It meant EVERYTHING to me. How am I going to help my family?*"

"*Well, hold on. Have you filed for unemployment insurance?*"

"*What is that?*"

"*It's a government agency that gives you money when you are fired. The government pays you if you are unemployed... well, it's not a lot, but enough to tide you over while you look for work*"

I was shocked. I did not understand this country. One minute I felt the country had it in for me, the next minute it was extending out a hand to help me. But the prospect of getting free money sounded good and a flicker of hope was ignited in my heart...

"*The first thing you need to do is call them and see if you qualify... these things are tricky... sometimes an employer would try to contest it...*"

And just like that, my hope dimmed. Pluto would surely contest this.

"*You don't know that Deka. Stop being negative. First call them and see what they tell you. In the meantime, start updating your resume. You will be fine*"

He was so certain. I started to feel that way too. Maybe life wasn't so bad afterall...

SHIFTING ALLEGIANCES

We talked for a long time. He told me stories of how some blacks had been framed by white people and spent decades in jail for crimes they did not commit. He told me of how some black men had been falsely accused of rape or stealing and how fake "eye witnesses" had placed them on the scene. He told me of how evidence had been planted on some black people and how they were assigned bad or ineffective lawyers due to their poverty, which led to them being imprisoned. I know he was trying to comfort me, by showing me how my problems were minor compared to others, but as I listened, all I could think was "How *can I ever trust a white person again?*"

He said that I really needed to learn how to survive in America and that the first step was to never forget what color I was. He said whites would always feel threatened if they felt a black person was going to get something they wanted-which in my case was recognition from a top level executive - and that they would stoop to any level to remove that threat. It all went along with their perception that certain things were theirs -and theirs only- and that blacks and other minorities did not deserve them. We the minorities would always be considered second class citizens.

It was just the way America was

He said every minority has to play a role in the workplace and the role meant you couldn't be too assertive and definitely not aggressive. To be successful, YOU HAD to be viewed as harmless.

The world seemed darker after he left. *How could I ever trust a white person again?*

The following Monday, I called the unemployment office and was told I qualified for assistance. I was grateful. I updated my resume and began applying for jobs.

But inside I had changed. Something had died inside me. COMPLETELY.

Amaka Lily

I no longer felt I had unlimited potential in America. I no longer felt the sky was the limit because if my skin color continued to pose problems for me, I would never succeed. I applied for jobs, but unlike my first year in the U.S., I could not seem to close the deal. I would get interviews because of my association with Pluto, but I would subsequently get a *"Sorry, we have chosen to go with another candidate..."* letter, after they had seen me in person.

I persisted, but as the rejection letters piled up, I sank into depression. This was worse than the kind of depression I'd suffered when I'd struggled to make friends. The world seemed dark and scary, and I could not see the light at the end of the tunnel. I felt useless. I didn't know who I was without a job, and at the rate I was going, *would I ever find a job?*

It became harder and harder to motivate myself to apply for jobs and go for interviews. I found it harder and harder to be optimistic about my job prospects.

Some days I cursed myself. I rued the day I had pushed Stephanie. If only I had just held myself back, I would still have a job. Other days, I justified pushing Stephanie. *"She deserved it for tampering with MY files"*. But as I vacillated between emotions, I never wavered on the fact that something had been fundamentally wrong with the way I had been treated. *How come Stephanie wasn't made to answer what she was doing on my computer? Why was I the one quickly sent home that day?*

When I wasn't applying for jobs, I spent time in the library researching the treatment of blacks in the U.S. I was searching for some comfort, some way to understand what had happened to me, and explain why I had been so ganged up on. I read articles upon articles of racial profiling, beginning from slavery days, to the Jim Crow era, to the modern era. I devoured real life stories of people who had been injured, imprisoned or suffered some sort of harm due to being black.

SHIFTING ALLEGIANCES

I would go to black oriented sites and read their stories and tips on how to survive in corporate America. It was amazing how many blacks shared the same experiences I'd had in Pluto, of feeling left out, cut off and unwanted. It was comforting to know I wasn't alone. From these sites, it was further underscored that there was a code of behavior expected of blacks in corporate America, a code of behavior that was non-threatening to whites. Among them were that you could never raise your voice and never show that you were angry. If one did so, not only would the person be kicked out of a job, but if female, would also be labeled an "Angry Black Woman", a death sentence for a professional black woman. You could never advance if you ever displayed angry behavior. Never, ever advance. It didn't matter if you'd only done it once and it was due to having a bad day. It didn't matter that other races could get angry whenever it suited them. There were no allowances for a black person to be angry. Zero. None.

I learnt that I could never expect to be treated the same way as a white person and that there were two interpretations of laws in the U.S, one for whites, and the other for minorities and that harsh sanctions were leveled against people like me. I learnt that I would encounter situations which I could never complain about and would have to turn a blind eye to because to complain could relegate me to outcast status via expulsion or exclusion and I couldn't afford to have that happen to me ever again.

Some of what I was reading were things I had already suspected on my own. Others were brand new concepts. All of them were carefully filed at the back of my mind, never to be forgotten.

For some reason, the black sites attracted white supremacists who would regularly leave insults and racial slurs on the boards. These supremacist writers also wrote the names of their websites in their signature line, so that it was easy to tell where they came from. One day, I decided on a whim to go check out one of those sites to see if they were as bad as I thought they'd be. What I found would throw me into a deeper well of depression and paranoia that would take me years to overcome. Now it is one thing to suspect that some whites harbor ill will towards black people. It is quite another to see proof, real, incontrovertible proof of the palpable hatred some of them felt towards people like me. They talked about how lazy black people were, how crime ridden our societies were and how all we wanted was a handout. They described black women as being whores, ugly, monkey-like and stinky. Some shared tales of how they had tricked some black women, slept with them and then dumped them. Others shared stories of how they had ganged up on and beaten black boys.

And what was worse was that these people seemed intelligent. They were not hicks from a racist town, uneducated and inarticulate. No, these people were very articulate and they defended with great passion, their belief that blacks were an inferior, lower race. It made me wonder if most of the whites I encountered in my daily errands thought this way.

How would I ever know which ones thought all blacks were affirmative action recipients and second class citizens?

How would I know which ones thoroughly despised blacks and which ones could potentially sabotage or hurt me?

How could I ever trust a white person again?

It hurt. It hurt greatly.

But, like a person watching a train-wreck, I could not help but return to these sites again and again.

The vitriol wasn't just limited to white supremacist sites. Even on mainstream sites, I would see a negative comment directed towards blacks. It didn't matter what the topic was about. It could be a topic about a war in Africa and someone would comment that it was typical for blacks to act like savage

SHIFTING ALLEGIANCES

animals. It could be about women and someone would throw in a comment that black women were the ugliest race of women

As you would imagine, reading all of this was not good for my mental state, particularly since I continued to interview. It made me wary and when I thought about all the experiences I'd had with white people since the moment I moved to Lawrenceville, the scorn, the fear, the evil way Stephanie and co had treated me, it made sense. When I went on interviews, I started fearing that my interviewer was one of those racist commenters and would not give me the job.

And for the longest time, it seemed like I was right.

I was not getting any offers!

Months passed.

I exhausted my savings sending money to my family, who still didn't know I didn't have a job. The money I got from unemployment, a quarter of what I used to earn, allowed me to continue to live, albeit, a very bare bones existence.

I sank deeper. Soon, I gave up applying to jobs and just stayed home watching TV. I was in such a funk that for the first time in my life, I missed paying my rent. That is until I got a call from my apartment company threatening me with eviction

I had 30 days to pay before I would be kicked out of my home.

I was roused. I checked my bank account, I only had $75.

I called Uncle and told him everything.

"*Njideka, why didn't you tell me since?*"

"*I thought I could manage it Uncle... I didn't want you to worry?*"

"*Worry? Why wouldn't I worry? You are my responsibility here! What would have happened if your mother had found out that you were evicted and I was here in this country?*"

"*Well, I was hoping I would have found a job before then...*"

"*How much do you need?*" I told him. He sent me double the amount by western union. I was grateful, but felt a bit like a failure and a disappointment. I wasn't supposed to be asking for money at this stage of my American career.

I was a veteran for Christ sake.

Uncle made me call him every evening giving him an update of my job search. I am forever grateful for that directive, because it gave me the needed motivation to go back to applying to jobs.

Finally, 4 months after getting fired from Pluto, I got a job offer from Tech Engineering. I accepted, but I wasn't the same.

I was no longer the enthusiastic, hopeful person that had started work at Pluto. I was now a closed off, untrusting person, a person who now realized how expendable she was. A person who realized that her color was a net negative in America. A person devoid of hope and happiness but who put on the right amount of façade to get through without anyone noticing.

Pluto, Lawrenceville and the internet had clearly left their mark on me.

I had lost my faith in America.

Chapter 10

A new Deka

Amaka Lily

It was a markedly different individual who began working at Tech Engineering. The hopeful, optimistic, enthusiastic person that began at Pluto, had been replaced by an extremely guarded, fearful and paranoid individual. I arrived with no illusions about the people I was going to be working with. No illusions at all. They were all mean, hated blacks and only wanted to cause us harm.

I could not trust them.

But I also could not show that side of me. To succeed in the workplace, I had to at least appear happy to be there. There was no way I'd last a week if I showed how I really felt. And so I put on the requisite persona, the happy, go lucky, blind, non demanding façade that was acceptable of people like me. I did not ask for anything, did not demand anything, and tried to make myself as unobtrusive as possible.

I particularly did not want to risk being fired again. I could not have the source of my livelihood and my family's livelihood threatened again.

My carefully cultivated persona, was very acceptable to the new whites I encountered, so much so that I began to have "friends", as much as it's possible to have friends with a fake persona. Occasionally, I was even tempted to trust them and let down my guard, but something would happen to remind me why I had put them on in the first place.

For example, the director of the department I worked in, invited the whole office to his house for an annual get-together event he hosted.

At his home, the food was kept in the kitchen while we all ate outside, in a covered tent. He went around making sure everyone was comfortable, asking if anyone wanted more food and if so, to *"feel free to go into the kitchen and get some"*. He was the perfect host, that is, until I got up to get a refill. Now, I was about the 13th person who had stood up to get more food. I had sat and watched other people, all white, get up periodically

SHIFTING ALLEGIANCES

to refill their plates with no incident, but had delayed till that point so I wouldn't feel like an "Oliver Twist[31]". As soon as I stood up, the director immediately started following me. He followed me all the way back to the kitchen and hovered around, watching me while I refilled my plate.

He stared at me while I took food.

He did not even bother to hide it.

It was, needless to say, very uncomfortable.

Why did he feel the need to watch me like that?

It was obvious. He did not trust his home to be safe with me in it.

It hurt. Even at a celebratory occasion, I was still being profiled. I put a smile on my face, acted like nothing was amiss, filled my plate and went outside. But I could not even eat the food anymore. I had lost my appetite.

It was incidents like this that made me not feel too comfortable in a white person's presence. I could never be sure what they thought about me or when they would do something that would make me feel bad, or signify I was different and so I was always on my toes, always expecting something harmful or negative from them.

I started to limit my participation in events I knew white people would attend. It was for my peace of mind. I was never so happy as when I was away from them. My anxiety went down and I could relax a lot more.

But sometimes, it was unavoidable. Every month, there was some sort of event happening at Tech engineering. A floor might be having a potluck, someone might be celebrating a birthday or a department might throw a party to celebrate the successful release of an order. For those events, you had to "show your face". The powers that be monitored who attended

---

[31] Used derogatively to mean someone who was always asking for more. A hungry person.

company events and if you missed several, would be termed a "non team player". I would attend those events but wouldn't stay long. I would just "show face", make some mindless banter and excuse myself to work.

My life now consisted of going to work, coming home, watching TV or researching race relations until I fell asleep.

It was a lonely life.

It was also an unhappy life and the more I lived like this, the unhappier I became.

Sometimes, I thought back to those early years and how naïve I had been. I would think about the initial desires I'd had as a fresh export from Nigeria, to make friends with everyone, white, black, green or yellow and how it had subsequently been thwarted.

If only I had known how hard it would be… but then again, I don't think knowing would have dissuaded me from coming to America. I wouldn't have understood it until I had lived it.

I thought back to those early conversations with Ray Ray and how I hadn't wanted to take sides with any race and how I'd fought him over his assertions. Well Ray Ray had been right as I'd now discovered. White people were all racist and they did not think a black person had any redeeming qualities. The only people who treated me like a human being were other African Americans. As people of the same hue in America, they could understand what I was going through and provide some sort of succor for me.

But the succor was not entirely sufficient. I could never get my needs fully satisfied by African Americans. No matter how friendly they were, how open they were, inevitably, we would come across an impasse, a wall we couldn't climb over. We were black but we were different. Our norms were different, our values were different. They understood what it meant to be black in America, but cultural references I would make about my values and my upbringing, were not always shared by them, least of all understood by them. They didn't understand why I religiously sent money home to my family and why I disagreed with having children out of wedlock. I didn't understand why they, and truthfully many Americans as a whole, didn't feel as obligated to their family members and why single motherhood was acceptable, amongst other things.

Amaka Lily

My identity as a woman and as a sexual being suffered the biggest blow. America made me feel like an ugly, undesirable, repulsive and at the same time, invisible woman. I alternated between not getting any attention from men for long stretches of time, to rare occasions where I'd be hit on by guys who were not my type that is uneducated, unambitious, thuggish or ghetto, basically, not acceptable for marriage. All I wanted was a guy I was raised to desire in Nigeria, a clean cut guy who was ambitious, chivalrous and appreciated education. A guy who could take care of a family.

A guy like me.

But those were not the type of guys I encountered on those few occasions I was hit on. The vast majority of the time, I wasn't hit on by anyone. Compared to Nigeria, where I was daily inundated with catcalls and all sorts of attention from acceptable, professional, men, in America, I was invincible.

I hadn't really noticed this when I was in college, since I'd only had eyes for my studies, but when I was done and was ready to date, and realized nothing was happening, I was shocked. It was not what I'd have expected. I dressed a lot better than I'd ever done in Nigeria. I also had at my disposal, the most beautiful hair extensions that made me even prettier, but still nothing. It took me a long time, a lot of research and a lot of painful self reflection, before I understood what was going on and the reasons, again, seemed to be tied to the color of my skin.

In America, dating was difficult for black women. For starters, there were not enough black men to go around. Black women outnumbered black men. In colleges, they outnumbered them even more, in some cases, in the hundreds of thousands. Secondly, when you factored out black men that were in jail- and there were a lot-, black men that were homosexuals and black men that had been murdered, it left an even smaller population to date from.

SHIFTING ALLEGIANCES

But this wouldn't even be a problem if black women could choose from other races of men, but not surprisingly, black women were considered the least attractive race of women to marry by other races. There was a color complex in America where the lighter and more European-looking your features were, the more attractive you were considered. White women were considered the most beautiful of all women and white men and other non-black races wanted them. So even if as a black woman, you were open to dating other races, it would not happen since other men would not toast you.

To make matters worse, not only were black women considered unattractive by other races, but they were also considered unattractive by many black men in the U.S. There was a social phenomenon in America, called the "trophy wife" syndrome, where a black man, as soon as he became financially successful, immediately married a white or other fairer skinned race of woman or if he already had a black wife, traded her in for a white woman or other fairer skinned race of woman. White and other fair skinned women were the ultimate "trophies" black men sought to achieve. It didn't matter if those women were fat, uneducated or unhealthy. All that mattered was that these women were white which by itself gave these men an ego boost and increased their status.

This phenomenon happened so frequently and so blatantly, that it became, like I said, a well recognized social phenomenon. The underlying message was that a black woman was not good enough.

I found all of this information through my continued research on race relations in America. It actually wasn't that hard to find. Black forums, women's forums, even the mainstream media carried lots of articles and programs discussing why black women were the least married demographic in the U.S.

Some cited that as much as 70% of educated black women never got married. Also, when you read articles online about what women were considered beautiful women, you rarely saw a black woman featured.

Once I came across a website that listed all ethnicities of women by beauty.

Guess who came last on the list?

It explained a lot to me. It explained why when I was hell bent on expanding my social network, and was joining groups left and right, why I had not been approached by any of the men I'd seen. At that time, I didn't know the extent of racism in Lawrenceville and like many Nigerian girls, had no hang-ups about dating foreigners. But when I saw that I was getting no action, I began to feel bad about myself. It explained why in the few instances I had seen of black interracial dating in Lawrenceville, that it was only of the black men, white women variety and why the men seemed so proud to be walking these women on their arms, even though many of those women were obese.

It made me wonder how black women in the United States could maintain their self esteem.

How could one hold her head high in this society?

It seemed like everywhere a black woman turned, she was buffeted with messages of inferiority. Features that I had been raised to believe were beautiful, were not considered so here.

It was devastating and soul-crushing. Even though I knew all the reasons why I was left dateless, it did not stop my desire for a relationship, and the longer I went without having a relationship, the more my self esteem plummeted.

This was not what I expected my twenties to be like.

I was supposed to be enjoying life, going on dates, having fun until I eventually found the one to settle with. I wasn't supposed to be sitting home, day in day out, month after month.

SHIFTING ALLEGIANCES

This was not how it was supposed to be. *Where was the freedom, the excitement, the adventure?* Time was running out. My 20s were passing me by before my very own eyes!!!

My depression intensified.

I felt hopeless, helpless. My skin color prevented me from having the same dating opportunities as women of other races. I didn't have the same access that they had. I didn't have the same options. By being black I was automatically undesirable.

Once in a while, I'd get an email from one of my friends in Nigeria, asking me how my dating life was going. When I told them I was not dating, they did not believe me. I wouldn't have believed it myself if I wasn't the one experiencing it. Like I said before, in Nigeria, I had never wanted for guys. I was inundated with them. I knew I was beautiful there.

Here, it wasn't the same.

I started to feel ashamed.

In addition to feeling undesirable, I felt sort of left behind and stunted in the relationship department.

There are no words to describe the type of loneliness I felt, loneliness so terrible, I felt I could drink. I cried many nights, asking God why. It nearly drove me to madness.

It made me desperate, made me settle, but I won't go into that.

I won't go into details of what lack of love did to me.

I will not.

I will not.

Time continued to pass, and I remained in the same state.

I had a hole in my heart that couldn't be filled by anybody. A hole that continued to deepen with each day I spent in America. A hole that could not be stuffed.

I was miserable. I walked around feeling loveless and unwanted. I walked around on tiptoes expecting something bad to happen to me while putting on a false front. I walked around knowing I wasn't understood by 99% of the people I came across. And I did all of this while still encountering the standard racist stuff, of being followed around in stores and getting subpar service.

It was exhausting. I felt like my head was going to burst. All the thoughts in my head, the pretence I was making, the bad treatment, all of them was like a daily assault on my brain.

How could one ever be happy or feel free in this type of environment?

Many nights when I lay in bed, I questioned the price I had paid to live in American society.

Was it really worth coming to the U.S.?

Was trading my long-term happiness for an education really worth it in the end?

And the answer ringing at the back of my mind was "*NO, IT WAS NOT!!!*"

But I didn't want to hear that.

Going back to Nigeria was not an option.

SHIFTING ALLEGIANCES

Chapter 11

The scales fall off

Amaka Lily

Before I had moved to Lawrenceville, I had eagerly adopted the attitudes and behaviors' of Americans that I thought were better than Nigerians. I was dressing like them, thinking like them- particularly in terms of women and children's rights-, marveling at how much freedom America offered and enumerating the many ways it was more advanced than Nigeria.

I truly believed that America was fundamentally a fair country and in many ways, had the best interests of its citizens at heart.

Now that I'd realized that the justice and fairness did not apply equally to people like me, I started looking at America with new eyes. I began to see a lot of fault in America and I wondered how I'd ever thought it was a great country.

For starters, the American court system was a very unforgiving system. It kept a record of every mistake you'd ever done in your life, even if it was done in your youth and you had since changed. If you ever broke a law, fought in your youth, stole something and got arrested, it went on your record. If you ever beat a child, committed fraud, or did anything that caused you to go to prison -and being that Americans were highly litigious and an invariably high number of minor incidents could get you sent to jail.-, it also went on your record. This was important, because your record was tied to your social security number, the same number that was necessary to find work and potential employers could use it to look up your past and deny you employment.

Also, access to this information wasn't limited to just employers. Anyone who wanted to dig up information about you could do so. That meant a random person you just met could find out a lot about you. All, they just needed was a computer and your name and voila, details of your past would be brought to light.

It didn't make sense that there was no privacy.

SHIFTING ALLEGIANCES

It didn't make sense that something you may have done in your youth could continue to have far reaching effects on your adult life. It didn't make sense that something you may have already paid the price for, by going to jail, could continue to haunt your job prospects and your general reputation. This was not even counting the fact that the system was error prone. There could be mistakes in your record that other people could use to judge you.

Also, the legal system wasn't fool proof. Many people had been sent to prison for crimes they did not commit. I found that a lot of black people had been sent to jail for crimes that they didn't commit or which the evidence used to convict them was fabricated and it wasn't until decades later that they were found to be innocent.

It didn't make sense, but that was how America was.

Secondly, America had a high suicide rate. When I was in Nigeria, I used to wonder why American people killed themselves. I couldn't understand how a country that had everything, money, technology, 24-7 electricity and numerous opportunities, had so much suicides, whereas in Nigeria where we lived in deep and unimaginable poverty, I never heard of one suicide. Not one.

Now, I knew the primary reason why. Loneliness. Even though I had my own loneliness problems due to racist attitudes, I found that America is inherently a lonely country which was kind of comforting to me in a sadistic way. People kept to themselves and did not go out of their way to get to know their neighbors or establish connections with people they considered different. Part of the reason was fear, prejudices and distrust of other people. The other part was due to the individualistic nature of Americans. Americans focused on the self first rather than family, and if they considered family at all, it was their own individual unit first rather than the extended family. They were not community oriented like Nigerians were. They focused on being independent, achieving an individual's, versus a group's goal, not realizing that working for a group and having more people interested in your welfare is what keeps you balanced.

In addition, they lacked coping skills. When an American comes across a problem, they break down or start taking antidepressants or an illegal drug. Many drink to cope or turn to gambling or shopping. The country had millions of drug addicts, alcohol addicts and other types of addictive people. It was interesting to note that a country where you needed a prescription to buy simple antibiotics and needed to be 21 before you could drink any alcohol, had more problems than countries were these items were easily available. They also had higher incidents of mental health issues, depression, anxiety, eating disorders you name it. Basically, all types of illnesses reigned supreme in this country despite the fact that they had a lot of money.

I also started thinking about the lack of morals in this country. Even though I'd known prior to coming to America, that they were a lot less conservative than we were, and it hadn't bothered me in my early years, now, as I thought seriously about what life meant to me here, it became problematic.

People made sex tapes and went on to become popular and rich. People would meet a guy in one day and sleep with him later on that evening. A woman could be a whore and still find many men willing to marry her. There was no shame. There were no consequences for bad behavior, no punishment for having loose morals. All the things that had been drummed into my head about ways to behave and the consequences if those behaviors were not followed, did not seem to affect people here. Instead they seemed to get away with even worse behavior. It didn't seem right. It was like the world had turned backwards on its head.

SHIFTING ALLEGIANCES

I also didn't like the way age was looked at in America. People did not value seniority or respect old age here. A grey head was not looked upon with reverence nor was their wisdom sought after. In fact, old people were derided and were usually the first people to get fired in a bad economy. Youth was instead revered and many people resorted to plastic surgery, not just to look beautiful, but to look younger than their years. Adults put their parents into a nursing home when the latter could no longer take care of themselves and sometimes, they willfully abandoned their parents.

It was counter to how I was raised.

It was an abomination.

In Nigeria, you respected your elders and taking care of your parents was your responsibility. But here it wasn't the case.

I cannot tell you how many times I saw younger kids talking back to older people here. I cannot tell you how many times, I saw an older person struggling to do something while younger people stood around, ignoring that person. Once I saw a gang of young kids cursing out an old man and no one said anything. *Why would they?* Videos of students beating their teachers filled the internet. If I had intervened, they probably would have cursed me out and beaten me for good measure.

It wasn't a paranoid thought!!!

I also noticed that some of the same problems I had seen in Nigeria were also reflected here. Poverty, homelessness and violence existed in America. There was not one day, where you didn't hear of someone getting killed. It could be a gang fighting another gang, a husband killing his wife and vice versa, children killing parents, boy friend killing girlfriend, coworker killing coworker or something else. EVERY. SINGLE. DAY.

And so the more I looked at America, the more I saw how flawed it was.

Amaka Lily

The more the years passed, the more I saw the rotten underbelly
How had I ever thought this racist, drug infested, morally bankrupt society was ever better than Nigeria?

SHIFTING ALLEGIANCES

I began to long for the simple life, a prescribed way of being and behaving. A life that I understood.

A life that had strong community ties, respect for old age, morals, a forgiving justice system and of course no racism. The more I longed for that life, the more I began to see that that life resided in Nigeria. I thought about how in Nigeria, you could not be lonely, even if you tried. Mingling was encouraged and dropping by unannounced to a person's home was not considered rude or a nuisance but was in fact, the norm. You were expected to hold family first, the whole extended family unit and you did not operate in a vacuum. A lot of people were vested in your welfare.

There were no suicides, no addictions, hell, we couldn't afford to eat, not to mention, paying for an addiction and morally loose behavior was not acceptable in Nigeria. You couldn't flaunt a sex tape and expect to be married ever in life. You couldn't sleep around and expect any man to want you. No. You were done for life.

Old age was also respected. You knew to respect your elders and you knew who was considered your "mate" there. Also, people looked forward to getting older instead of considering it a curse like they did in America. Lastly, the court system did not continue to punish you for crimes of your youth, long after you had changed your life. We didn't have social security numbers so nothing could be linked to you.

But more than that, there was no racism. My skin color had never mattered in Nigeria, I hadn't even been aware of the concept. I was a human being first. I was not assumed to be dumb, useless or unattractive just because I was black. I was just Njideka.

For all its warts and issues, Nigeria had been a better place for me.

I began to long deeply for Nigeria. I thought about all the family members I'd left behind. Not just my sisters, but

Amaka Lily

cousins, aunties, uncles and extended relatives. People that I now realized, had made my life so much better and had staved off loneliness. I now looked upon Nigeria with much fondness and became even prouder of my Nigerian identity, prouder than I was my first semester in America.
    I wanted to revel in it. I wanted to hold on to Nigeria and not let it go.
    I did not want to forget.
    I regressed into Nigerian-hood. I began to buy Nigerian books and rent Nigerian films. I'd never sat down to watch a Nigerian movie in Nigeria, now I was becoming a pro at recognizing all the actors. I bought books that I hadn't cared for growing up in Nigeria, but now, took me back to a time when I was happy.
    I became creative. I wrote a poem, something I'd never done and have been unable to repeat since then, citing my longing for the country I had run away from and regretting the fact that I had not appreciated it.
    Nigeria was now the lover I'd run away from, the one I thought I could do better than.

7 years ago
You were the fly in my ointment
The carcass in my pool
7 years ago
I could not wait to leave you
Could not be paid to be with you
Our partnership of 20 years
Had been fraught with lies
Misery and pain
I wanted out
Prayed for an out
And the gods answered my request
In the form of my lover, West
West beckoned

SHIFTING ALLEGIANCES

With promises of riches
An education
Freedom from pain
And like a cat that had been starved for 10 days
I responded eagerly
Cut the ties to our union decisively
7 years ago
I fled our home
In the dead of the night
Not looking back
Never to return ... or so I thought
7 years later
  I think of you, wondering how I could have ever been so blind
  West turned out to be a wolf in sheep's clothing
And my salvation
Barely a reprieve
In the ensuing years, I have witnessed a "love"
In the arms of my new lover that made your abuse
Seem like tender loving kisses
Daily he reminds me of my mediocrity
Daily, he tramples on my dignity
In exchange for a few trinkets of silver
He has destroyed my soul
My personhood
My humanity.
7 years later, I think of you
Thoughts of you keep me going
And keep me from losing my sanity
7 years later
I long to be reunited with you.

Amaka Lily

But my Nigerian renaissance did not stave off the pain in my heart.

The hole continued to get bigger and my misery felt bottomless. I struggled to find a cure, to find something to lift me out of the depths I had sunk into. I read all sorts of books on happiness and positive thinking, but nothing worked. I prayed to God but he seemed so far away.

I was very bitter around this time and I alienated the few friends that I had. I couldn't control myself. I talked and talked and talked and talked about how bad America was until Lamar stopped calling. But did I stop? No! I couldn't help myself. I needed to vent. My heart was full and I had so much pain, anger and resentment and could not, NOT talk. Malik still called me, but only rarely.

Now that I think about it, I must have been very attractive girl during this period. A bitter girl railing about the world and her life, about white people, black people, racism and everything, that was REALLY attractive. But I could not help myself. I was steeped in negativity and stuck in a vicious cycle. I needed people to vent to, yet the more I vented to them, the more they didn't want to stay, which made me want more people to vent to.

It was not a good time at all.

Not a good time.

SHIFTING ALLEGIANCES

One morning, I was sitting in front of my computer at work when it suddenly occurred to me that I could not continue to remain in the U.S.

I had to leave.

Two years had passed since I began working at Tech Engineering and my situation had not changed.

My personhood would never be respected. For as long as I lived here, my skin color would be a constant impediment to a happy life. I most likely would never get married. If by some stroke of luck, I did get married, I would bear kids who would not respect me and not know their culture. If I tried to discipline said kids, they would call the police on me and have me sent to jail. Those same kids would probably send me to a nursing home in my old age and leave me there to die alone.

I had to get out. I had to get out fast.

I called my mother and told her I would be making my first trip back to Nigeria.

My family was excited

Unknown to then, this was not a regular vacation trip.

This was a fact finding mission to assess the feasibility of returning home…

FOREVER.

Amaka Lily

When I told Malik of my plans to leave America, his response was not the comforting reaction I had expected

"*WHY DO YOU WANT TO LEAVE????*" he exploded

"*Because I am not happy here! I don't think I can ever be happy*"

"BUT YOU ARE NOT THE ONLY ONE EXPERIENCING RACISM HERE!!!!"

"*Yes, but it's not the only thing bothering me about America...*" I was resolute "*... I don't want to live here anymore, I have a choice*"

"YOU HAVE A CHOICE? YOU HAVE A CHOICE? Okay then, GO BACK TO YOUR FUCKING COUNTRY"

And he hung up.

WHAT. JUST. HAPPENED.

I was in shock. I could not believe what had just transpired.

Malik had never raised his voice at me. He had also never insulted me.

Why was he so angry with me?

Ring, Ring.

It was Malik calling me back

"*Deka, I am sorry. I... I...*"

'"How dare you call my country a FUCKING COUNTRY? You stupid, piece of shi*t*"

I was angry, Malik had insulted my darling country and given me a reason to direct all the anger and frustration I'd been carrying at him. I cursed him with all the bad American words I knew.

"*I said I'm sorry Deka, please let's not go there.... I didn't mean it that way*"

"But you started it. You called my country a FUCKING COUNTRY. Listen, YOU PIECE OF SHIT, *my country is still better than yours... we don't have to worry about racism or being profiled you son of a bitch. Why don't you go eat rocks, LOSER...*"

SHIFTING ALLEGIANCES

"Deka... I..."

I hung up on him. The nerve of him. *How dare he curse my beautiful country? How dare he curse my darling country?*

He called about 10 more times, but I didn't pick up.

I was done with him.

It would take awhile to realize why his initial reaction to my leaving was the way it was and why he had been so resentful and it was because, unlike me, Malik had no option. I could leave the country and go to another place.

He could not leave America, because it was the only country he knew. No matter how bad or racist it got, it was still his home, his only home. He would never be able to escape.

Chapter 12

Nigeria again

SHIFTING ALLEGIANCES

December 14, 2012 I arrived at Atlanta airport

It was from there I would begin my 11 hour direct flight to Lagos.

I was excited.

All around me I could hear *Igbo, Yoruba, Hausa and Pidgin.* Nigerians in typical fashion were returning home for the holidays. I was happy to see them. I could not remember ever being that happy to see so many Nigerians.

But God I had missed them and it felt so good to be around my kinfolk, people who were like me, people who understood me, people who would never take my skin color to indicate inferiority.

Four hours later, we boarded the plane bound for Murtala Mohammed airport. An hour after that we took off.

I was seated behind a computer screen that tracked the plane's proximity to Murtala Mohammed airport. Every so often I would check to see how close we were.

It seemed like we were never close enough.

I busied myself with my thoughts.

I thought back to the person I was, that first time I had departed for the U.S. and how I could not wait to leave. *How young and very clueless I was...*

I thought about the person I was now, older and wiser. Much, much wiser.

I wondered what had changed in Nigeria.

I thought about all my friends. *Would I be able to locate all of them on this trip? Would they look different? Would they think I had changed? Would they consider me an ajebo [32] now?*

I thought about all the foods I was going to eat. Oh how I would savour *ewedu* soup and *edikankong*. And of course, I had to visit Ghana House, if it was still there…

---

[32] A westernized, sophisticated Nigerian

Amaka Lily

I took a nap two hours in. I woke up to watch the featured movie. I ate all the meals they served.

I continually looked up at that tracker to see how close we were.

We were still too far.

I got up to walk around. Hours of sitting had made my legs numb.

I checked the computer tracker.

Still too far away

I made friends with a lady who was also from Enugu state. We talked about our village and things we knew about

Still too far away.

Finally, the pilot announced

"The plane is about to land, all passengers please return to your seats and affix your seatbelt"

I ran back to my seat to prepare for landing. As I buckled my seat belt, my excitement began to build.

In a few minutes I would see Nigerian sights.

In a few minutes I would breathe Nigerian air.

NIGERIA, NIGERIA, NIGERIA

When the first peak of Nigerian landscape came into view, I almost knocked over my neighbor in my haste to see.

NIGERIA, NIGERIA, NIGERIA

Finally we landed.

As we took our turns leaving the plane, my heart was beating FAST.

I could not wait. I was HOME.

When I took that first step out of the airplane and beheld Murtala Mohammed airport, my eyes instantly moistened.

I could not believe I was finally back in Nigeria.

I had missed the country so much!!!

I smiled as I walked down those steps, peering into everyone's eyes. I wanted all of them to know I was happy to be back.

SHIFTING ALLEGIANCES

I was still smiling until a familiar but unwelcome smell hit my nose.

Feces!

How in the world was an international airport smelling of feces? Just to confirm, I stopped an official passing by.

"*Abeg oga, Wetin dey smell*[33]?"

"*We are having problems with our toilet*" he responded.

I could not believe it ... a whole international airport had a broken toilet? This was unacceptable.

This was terrible.

Then I started laughing.

What did I expect? This was good old Nigeria, the land where things did not work *quite* as properly. I had been in the states too long and now had forgotten how things really were.

What was I thinking?

I laughed and laughed and laughed.

It would take more than feces to rid me of my high. I did not care if the airport stank of dead bodies and rotten eggs mixed together. There was no place like home and I was happy to be home.

I went through customs . No problems.

I went through baggage claim. No problems.

As I headed out to the arrival area where relatives had gathered, my heart began to beat faster and faster.

I had not seen my family in 7 years. *Would I be able to recognize them?*

Would they be able to recognize me?

Suddenly...

"*NJIDEKA! NJIDEKA!*" and I felt the pressure of warm bodies, arms encircling my neck, my hands being pulled and my sisters covering me.

---

[33] Please Sir, What is that smell?

Amaka Lily

I cannot remember ever laughing and crying at the same time as I did at that moment.
"NJIDEKA!"
My sisters looked so big now.
"NJIDEKA!"
My sisters looked so adult now.
They were hugging, crying and touching my body.
"Njideka you are so fresh now oh"
"Njideka you are so much fairer now"
"Njideka you don become oyibo[34]!"
"Njideka did you buy what I asked you for?"
On and on until I heard a calm voice…
"Njideka, so you are not going to greet your mother?"
I turned around. I had completely forgotten about my mother and rushed to greet her. I held her for a long time.
I had missed her so much.
Soon it was time to go home. Some of my sisters took my luggage from me while others held my hand.
As we stepped outside, I immediately put on my shades. It was blindingly bright and I couldn't see. My sisters commented that I had become an "*Americana*" now for wearing shades and all my protests of being unable to see were met with loud hoots.
As we made our way home, I was peppered with questions.
"Njideka so how is America now?"
"Njideka is it the winter that makes you so fair!"
"Njideka, what did you buy for me!"
"Njideka did you make any black American friend?"
"Njideka, do you have any oyibo[35] friends?"
"Njideka, do white people purge[36]?"

---

[34] Njideka, you have become a white person!
[35] White person
[36] Do white people suffer from a running stomach?

SHIFTING ALLEGIANCES

"*America is a good place!*" I responded, not wanting to go into details of what it was really like. Time will come for much explanation but now wasn't the time. I just wanted to look outside, to remember the sights again.

I was so happy.

As our packed car made its way down to Surulere, I kept swiveling my head to look around.

I was so happy to be back in my country

I wanted to shout "I LOVE YOU, I LOVE YOU, I LOVE YOU" to every Nigerian face I saw.

And I really meant that.

Really, really meant that.

But I couldn't do that. My family would have thought I had lost it. I had to maintain my composure.

This was time to just savour the moment.

We got home. My mother had prepared an elaborate meal

Jollof rice with plantain and moi moi, salad, pounded yam and egusi. She filled my plate with generous portions and gave me huge chunks of meat.

I ate and ate and ate.

Sated, I let my sisters show me around our new home. It was a 3 bedroom apartment, located in a nice part of Surulere. It was much better than the "home" we had inhabited seven years before.

We went outside and walked down the street.

I was so glad to be back home.

So so glad.

Nigeria, Oh how I've missed thee!

Chapter 13

Diary

SHIFTING ALLEGIANCES

Day 2

Mood: Sick

I was rushed to the hospital today.

I developed a bad case of diarrhea, so bad that even ORT[37] couldn't cure it. I was even given a drip for loss of fluids. The doctor who treated me told me that my diarrhea was due to the regular water I'd drank, tap water that had been boiled and refrigerated. He said that Nigerians who had lived in the West for a long time were no longer able to tolerate our local tap water because their body had changed. He said that it was typical for those who'd returned and drank such water to suffer from diarrhea and recommended that I use only purified, bottled water from here on out. He said I should even use it to brush my teeth!!!

If I didn't, he claimed, I'd get a recurrence of the diarrhea. When he told me that I had to use bottled water to brush my teeth, I couldn't help but laugh. *Who did he think I was? An oyibo*[38]*?* I had grown up drinking Nigerian water, sometimes straight from the roof when it rained and nothing had happened to me. *How could my body have changed that dramatically?*

---

[37] ORT stands for Oral Rehydration Therapy.
[38] Oyibo stands for White Person.

And even if that were the case, surely if I drank more tap water, my body would readjust to what it previously was, right?

"No", he replied. *"Your body would not readjust and you'd probably die of diarrhea before you even knew what was happening."* He told me of 3 people who had died from diarrhea within days of their return to Nigeria. Two of them had been from London and one had come from the US. He said that his professional recommendation was for me to just abstain from tap water but that if I wanted to play Russian roulette with my life, I was free to do so as well.

I didn't laugh again. This was serious. *Death*? No way. I didn't come to Nigeria to die. It was actually the opposite. I quickly gave my sisters money to buy me cartons of bottled water. The only time Nigerian tap water would ever touch my body again, would be when I am taking a bath.

It is not my portion to die in this country.

SHIFTING ALLEGIANCES

<u>Day 4</u>

Mood: Happiness

I am very happy to be back in Nigeria, exceedingly happy. Here I am a human being first, not a black person, but a person, Njideka Onuoraegbunam. I am among my people. I am back in a place where being smart or articulate is not deemed to be odd for a black person. I am back in a place where the mere sight of me does not inspire fright, fear, condescension or condemnation. I am finally, where I belong.

I feel lighter. I have no stereotypes to burden me.

I feel understood. I know what is expected of me and what the little practices and customs we do mean. I don't have to worry that I might say the wrong thing, make the wrong joke or find myself in the wrong place. I also don't have to put up a front, to fake being anything but what I am and that is just blissful, blissful, freedom.

I am especially happy to be reunited with my family. I had missed them so much and there was so much to catch up on. Ifunaya them were gisting me of their universities. Ifunaya, Amara and Chiamaka were at the University of Lagos, while Nonye, Obioma and Adaobi go to LASU. They told me of all the fun adventures they'd had, things that they'd never mentioned over the phone, lest mommy heard. I have to admit, I felt a pang of jealousy for having missed all of those events because it sounded like fun. But I reminded myself that the money I'd sent had helped make those things possible. None of them had had to suffer the indignity of having their college education postponed due to lack of money to "ensure" their entry. Each one had entered college in the same year of their graduation from secondary school. Also, my mother was now able to rent a spacious, 3 bed, 2 bath apartment which was a far cry from the boys-quarter where we'd all lived in years ago.

I still cannot believe how big my sisters are now. Whenever I'd thought of them in the U.S., the images that came up were the last ones I'd seen as we'd said our goodbyes at the airport. In my mind, they were stuck being little girls. Seeing them now all big and sophisticated did not match what my mind had of them and I have been pinching myself to remind me that they were real and live before my eyes.

Today we also talked about Nigeria, and all they did was complain. They said it was the same old corrupt place where nothing worked unless you had money. They complained about the lack of electricity, bad roads and just general difficulty with everything. They said they couldn't wait to come to the U.S. where they wouldn't have to deal with those things anymore. I laughed at them. I told them they didn't know what they were talking about, that America wasn't perfect and that I am trying to leave. They thought I was joking, *"Aaah Njideka, You wan leave place wey others dey run to[39]? You no serious jare![40]"*. They laughed. I tried to explain to them what racism was and how dehumanizing and painful it could be but they did not get it.

They could not fathom the depth of how one's color could have so many implications. One said *"If somebody doesn't like you, why don't you just ignore them and find someone else?"* They didn't understand that it wasn't just one person but a lot of people who didn't like you. They didn't understand that it wasn't just one race, but a lot of races who did not like you. They did not understand that racism was not infrequent but rather a daily assault on one's mind, which affected one's social, economic and personal life. They did not know that racism had destroyed my self esteem, that I hadn't had a date in years, that I'd been reduced to a pathetic, desperate human being and that I'd been exceedingly lonely and depressed. They did not understand that this repeated treatment threw you into such a state of agitation, paranoia and fear that you could

---

[39] Ah Njideka. You want to leave a place where others are running towards?
[40] You are not serious at all.

never truly relax because you knew that it was only a matter of time before you experienced a hurtful act.

I tried to explain these things to them but it was futile. *How bad could racism be if I lived in a place that was beautiful, modern, where food was aplenty, electricity abounded and everything worked?* They reminded me of the stories that I'd told them years before, when I was still so amazed by America, of how much better the American transportation system was and the availability of 24/7 electricity.

They pointed to me to illustrate how great my life had become. To them, I was an American success story. I had gone to an American college and finished in record time. I was now a professional, an engineer and had returned to Nigeria with "*lots of money*". My skin was now "*Fresh*" and my clothes were "*Designer*". They could not be dissuaded that America was as bad as I described and told me they would gladly accept racism just to have a chance at my now "great" life.

Truth is, they are not the only ones who share this sentiment. Everyone who has come to visit has said something similar. Just yesterday, Alero said I looked "*Yankerized*" and was now

SHIFTING ALLEGIANCES

"*a real AJEBO*[41]". There is an attitude that I'm sort of special, delicate, like royalty.

I have decided that going forward, I would no longer explain to them how America really is. It's a lost cause and besides they wouldn't understand. *How can you understand racism if you've never experienced it*? It's impossible. They sounded like me 7 years prior.

It wasn't their fault.

I will keep a smile on my face while knowing deep down the truth. Regardless of what my sisters or anyone said, I KNEW the two countries and as far as corruption, I knew it was not endemic to Nigeria but rather, an international phenomenon that even the great U.S.A was not immune to. But like I said, I'd keep that to myself.

I feel like I have changed. I am more accepting of Nigeria's flaws. After looking at the latest cars and modern architecture for years, I am seeing a quaintness to the older Nigerian models. They have a stuck-in-time quality which reminds me of old times. I took photos of them. My sisters called me an "*Americana*" when I did that. They said I am acting like an American tourist. They don't know that I am not acting, that

---

[41] Someone who lives a privileged, pampered life.

Amaka Lily

these images mean so much to me and I want to save them, to remind me of Nigeria when I return to the U.S.

Most gratifying of all is the fact that I am no longer an invisible woman. Men are chasing me left and right. It feels good, even though I know it won't go anywhere. I have not lived in America that long to believe that they really like me. They probably sense that I am from abroad, and want a chance to get a VISA. Still, I won't lie, I am reveling in the attention. It feels so good to be asked out and to be desired again. I feel like a woman, a beautiful woman and it has been a long, long long, long time since I felt that way. It is nice to feel like I am wanted. It is nice to be asked out on dates again. It is nice to know the dating norms and what to expect. It is nice to be in a place where men automatically pay, where it is an insult to their manhood for you to even think of splitting the bill.

I love Nigeria. It took going to America to make me appreciate how wonderful this country was.

I am happy here.

I have been woken up, been made alive.

I feel recharged

My soul is here.

My essence is here.

I love this country.

SHIFTING ALLEGIANCES

<u>Day 6</u>

Mood: Indeterminable

I took my sisters to Mr. Biggs today. They had been pressuring me to take them there since I arrived and no amount of telling them that Americans consider fast food low quality would make them budge. In fact, they said America was so great that a "gourmet", status item like Mr. Biggs is considered low quality.

I didn't know how to respond to that.

Amaka Lily

Day 7

Mood: Sadness

A strange type of sadness overcame me today.

I felt out of the loop, like a stranger in Nigeria.

When my sisters were singing the latest Nigerian songs, I couldn't join them. When they were discussing the latest pop culture, I couldn't relate.

I felt like a tourist, like I was observing them.

I felt like I didn't belong.

It made me sad.

Nigeria had moved on without me. People had grown up, gotten jobs, gotten married, had children. There were new musicians that I didn't know about and new songs on the radio. While I had been trying unsuccessfully to figure out America, Nigeria had "progressed".

I felt sad.

This wasn't how it was supposed to be.

Nigeria was supposed to have remained the same.

Everyone was supposed to have remained the same.

They were supposed to have waited for me.

SHIFTING ALLEGIANCES

<u>Day 10</u>

Mood: Realization that I have changed

It occurred to me that if I were ever to come back to Nigeria, I would not be able to live as I'd previously done. I have changed. Irrevocably. I now consider some things which I hadn't in the past to be basic, essential and non-negotiable and if they are not readily available, am willing to pay a lot of money to get them.

For starters, I cannot do without air-conditioning. Nigeria seems hotter than I'd ever remembered. Red, smoking, hot. I don't know whether the increased heat is due to global warming, or whether my body has changed, the result of living in a cooler climate. All I know is that whenever I step out of our home, sweat pours out of my pores like little rivulets. I am drenched before I have completed 10 steps. My body starts feeling overheated and breathing becomes laborious. I cannot wait until I have entered a cooler space, which as soon as I do, the symptoms lessen.

For the first time in my life, I now understand how someone can die of heat. Before I had always regarded with scorn, stories of people who it was reported died of heat. *How could a person EVER die of heat*? I'd always believed that something else , most likely AIDS, was the real cause of death. Now, I am a believer. I am now insisting on always being in an air conditioned place. If I have to travel to see friends, I am using a taxi and I always insist that my sisters pick one with a working air conditioner. Of course, this means that I am paying a lot of money for my transportation, but since A-Cs have now become essential to my life, I can't really complain.

I HAVE TO HAVE A.C!!!

I especially cannot do without air-conditioning at night, not just to ward of mosquitoes –which I'd come very prepared to battle with cans of insect spray, bug repellant and impenetrable netting- but because I cannot sleep without it. Two nights ago, NEPA "took light". My God, it was BAD!!!!

I could not sleep. I tossed and turned and tossed and turned. I felt like I was in an oven. Add to the fact that I'd plastered my body from head to toe with pungent bug repellant, I felt like a sticky, sweaty, greasy, mess. I thought I was going to suffocate, right there on that bed and could not wait for daylight to come. As soon as light broke, I accompanied Ifunaya to rent a generator. Renting a generator plus the attendant fuel is costing me quite a bit of money but I don't care.

I don't ever want to experience that hell again.

SHIFTING ALLEGIANCES

I don't ever want to sleep in a hot home again.

I also now require a comfortable means of transportation. Just before I'd arrived, I'd promised myself that I'd enter a local bus or *okada*[42] a couple of times while in Nigeria. I'd thought it'd be nice to relieve some of my previous experiences in those vehicles, to ride with the populace and feel like a real Nigerian once more.

I must have been out of my mind

I cannot imagine using any of the buses or bikes I have seen. Both of them seem like stressful, dangerous options and I cannot believe I'd entertained the thought of riding in one of them. Not only are the buses death traps with their non-working windows, uncomfortable seats crammed with way too many people , but their drivers drive recklessly and certainly illegally for vehicles of their size. The conductors also yelled the bus stops at the top of their lungs.

I had FORGOTTEN about that.

How could one have a peaceful ride in these types of conditions? The okada drivers were even worse. They rode like maniacs, leaning dangerously, zig zagging in between cars at top speeds, driving through areas that were never meant to be

---

[42] Motorcycle.

ridden in at all while simultaneously shouting, honking and sometimes physically fighting other drivers on their bikes. I am certain that if I rode an *okada*, I will end up in a ditch.

Not a good look for an "*Americana*".

Convenience and comfort have now become important to me and wasting time, anathema. I even hate haggling, the major form of setting prices in Nigeria. It seemed like such a hassle. *Why should I waste time, arguing with someone under the hot sun, trying to bring down the price of something that was already cheap to me?* The first time I went to the market and priced some native cloth, my sisters looked at me in horror when I readily agreed on the second price the seller offered. They protested that it was too much money and jumped into my conversation to haggle for me. They were able to bring it down to a third of the price beyond which the seller would not budge, partly because he knew I could afford it. For the rest of that day, they kept saying that if I weren't there, they could have gotten a much better deal and that I had spoilt it and I was such an *AJEBO*.

I wasn't trying to be one. The truth was that the initial price the seller had quoted had seemed reasonable to me. My mind converts all my purchases to American currency and the second price was to me a bargain. But more than that, while my

SHIFTING ALLEGIANCES

sisters were bringing down the cost to a third of the price, I felt ashamed.

It was embarrassing to be haggling.

Ofcourse, I know that when I come back to live permanently in Nigeria, I would have to go back to my bargaining ways, but for this trip, it just didn't seem worth it to me.

But that aside, I HAVE been spending a lot of money in Nigeria. In addition to the extra money for conveniences and comforts, plus mandatory bottled water and cell phone credit for myself and my family, I have been giving away a lot of money to relatives. People have been coming out of the woodwork to *"greet me"* and *"welcome me back from America"*. I didn't know them, but my mother did and as is customary, I have to leave something in their hands.

This is adding up.

Still, I am not complaining. I am happy, exceedingly happy to be back and if I have to spend more money than I budgeted so be it. Nigeria is still a thousand times better than America. My family of course is benefitting from my newly acquired *"Ajebo"* status while also teasing me about it. They are enjoying the 24/7 electricity, the air-conditioned taxis and of course the bottled water that my being here provides, but it's all good.

Amaka Lily

You cannot enjoy something while your family suffers. Without them I am nothing.

SHIFTING ALLEGIANCES

<u>Day 12</u>

Mood: Disappointment

The scales fell off today.

Nigeria was not the utopian paradise I'd imagined it to be.

It was a devastating, soul crushing, painful realization.

It was a realization that I'd fought against with all my might because I wanted Nigeria to be perfect, needed Nigeria to be perfect. Afterall, this was the country I had yearned so much for, the country I had missed so much.

This was MY HOME.

If it wasn't paradise, where else could I go?

But the problems that had pushed me away years back still remained, and in some instances were worse than before and no amount of looking at it from the bright side, could change that.

It was a realization that I have now come to accept.

Thieves came to our neighborhood last night. We were woken up around 3am by the sounds of gun shots and screaming. It was scary. We all hunched down on the floor, teeth chattering, praying to God that they didn't come near our home. It was nerve wracking. When day broke , we found out that they had robbed the Babatunde family, our neighbor three doors down.

Amaka Lily

They had beaten Mr. Babatunde, stripped him and his sons of all their clothing and left with their television, money and some jewelry. Thankfully, no lives were lost. The shots we'd heard had been shots fired in the air.

I had known that thieves were still a problem in Nigeria. In the papers recently, there had been a story about a Nigerian man just returned from Britain who had been robbed while travelling to his village for Christmas. His body was found by the side of the road with his car and valuables nowhere to be seen. In Lagos, there was one particular road in *Oshodi* which I'd been informed, was very notorious for armed robbery. As soon as you approached, you started noticing other drivers rolling up their windows, locking their doors and increasing their speed. The reason was that the robbers who patronized this road had no problem ambushing cars in broad daylight. With AK-47s in tow, they stopped cars, ordered everyone out while simultaneously kicking and beating them until the victims had given them every single kobo they had.

No one stopped to help the drivers when it occurred. *How do you compete with an AK-47?* And of course our "police" were never seen on these roads.

SHIFTING ALLEGIANCES

So I had known thieves were a problem, but I'd never expected them to come this close to me. I had not expected them to muddy up my Nigerian dream.

But come close they did and now, I had no choice. I could no longer continue to live in denial. Doing so, was at my own peril.

I had to face reality.

The first thing I had to do was to reactivate a sensitivity that had lain dormant for the last 7 years, a sensitivity of heightened awareness of my surroundings and not doing or wearing anything to attract attention. My Nigerian sense if you will. Thieves in Nigeria, typically targeted people like me, recent returnees from the West because they believed-and rightly so- that we usually had lots of foreign currency -dollars and pounds- which because of the exchange rate, was more valuable than our Naira. Ofcourse it never occurred to them that perhaps those of us who were returning, had starved and saved all year for this trip. It never occurred to them that perhaps the money we spent was not a true indicator of our financial standing in the West.

Basically, I could no longer continue to live as I'd been doing, acting like everything was okay. These people needed money and they had nothing to lose. I had to be aware of what was going on around me and take note of suspicious behavior. I also had to downplay my recent connection to the West and take pains to blend in. I don't want to stick out like an "*Americana*". I don't want my family to be targeted for armed robbery.

This made me wonder, *What if my family had been the real target? What if the thieves had heard that an Americana was in town? What if they'd gone to the wrong house? What if they came back? What if we were robbed?*

God forbid bad thing.

The second thing I needed to do was to accept the fact that even though Nigeria's social and infrastructural problems were not unique to the country, they still caused major difficulties for everyone and there was nothing funny or romantic about that.

Poverty was rampant and Nigerian people were still struggling. When you looked at the faces of ordinary people walking about, you saw suffering written all over them. Their brows were furrowed with worry and stress. Paramount on their minds was survival and just making it day to day.

I had been mistaken.

Nigeria still was a difficult and hard place to live in.

SHIFTING ALLEGIANCES

Corruption was still rampant and the country still lacked a sense of accountability. Our government officials still demanded bribes to get their work done. Our policemen still demanded bribes from the struggling populace. Newspapers continued to be chock full of stories of politicians who had absconded with our oil wealth. Politicians whom everyone knew where they lived, but inexplicably, were never brought to justice.

Oil prices still jumped erratically. NEPA still jumped erratically. The buildings were not quaint, they were terrible and in need of serious rehabbing. The cars were not quaint, they were damaged and old. The roads were bad. A lot of things were bad.

What kind of country was this?

It had not seemed that bad when I had tried to recall it in the U.S. *Had my long stay in America caused me to idealize my country and forget the bad parts?*

I still loved Nigeria but I couldn't continue to live in *la la* land

Amaka Lily

<u>Day 13</u>

Mood: Better

I feel a lot better today.

I have realized that my recent dissatisfaction with Nigeria had to do with memory, my selective memory.

I had forgotten how harsh Nigeria could be. I had been gone from the country for far too long and the rougher aspects had dimmed to the point where I no longer remembered their acuteness… until now.

But despite my disappointment, I still wanted to return. It was simple really, I am happier here. Despite all the annoyances and all the adjustments it required, it was still better than living in a place where I was the lowest of the low, where my color meant I was an inferior being, where daily, I was assaulted by messages that I was unworthy, undesirable, inferior, where people like me were subject to racial profiling and inhumane treatment, where I was wracked with loneliness and anxiety.

I didn't have to worry about any of that here and with my family, life was even better. There was also the fact that whereas the problems I had with Nigeria could easily be mitigated with money, the problems with America could not be so easily solved. I could inoculate myself from the grimmer

SHIFTING ALLEGIANCES

aspects of Nigeria with money. I could move my family into a safer, gated neighborhood, where we'd never have to worry about thieves again. I could buy a generator and a car and the problems of electricity and transportation would be instantly solved.

But in regards to America, how do you eradicate racism? *How do you fight against a mental enemy?*

The more I think about this, the more I realize that this had always been my issue with Nigeria. MONEY, MONEY, MONEY. It was the lack of money that had caused us to live in a boy's quarter. It was the lack of money that had slowed my academic progress. It was the lack of money that had caused me so much frustration and grief all those years back and it seemed that again, it was going to be money that determined how soon I was to return to Nigeria.

To quote the late great Tupac.

Some things just never change.

The question was, "*How much money would it require to return to Nigeria in the littlest time possible?*"

That amount was crucial. The right amount of money would mean a seamless transition back to Nigeria. It would mean the ability to afford a safer home, basic necessities and a comfortable life. More importantly, the right amount of money would garner my family's acceptance of my decision.

I do not expect them to happily agree to my returning from the U.S. just like that. Returning from the U.S. would mean no more dollars and that would mean that the money they'd come to depend on for their schooling and feeding would immediately disappear.

That was definitely not acceptable.

If I could show them that leaving America was not going to impact them, detrimentally, that they could continue to maintain the lifestyle that they'd become accustomed to, then I expected them to accept my decision.

I have drawn up a list, labeled "Things I need to be able to return to Nigeria"

1. New home
2. Car
3. Generator
4. School fees for my sisters
5. Food allowance
6. Extra pocket money

Now all that was needed was to figure out how much I needed to save for each one…

SHIFTING ALLEGIANCES

<u>Day 15</u>

Mood: Depressed

I am depressed.

My research findings are depressing me. I have spent the last couple of days inquiring from my family and friends about safer neighborhoods, rental prices and housing prices and the amount of money that is necessary for me to come back to Nigeria is becoming an impossible sum.

First, to get an apartment or a house for myself and family- where I would also live because single girls do not live alone in Nigeria- I had to gather at a minimum hundreds of thousands of Naira and this was just for a regular, run of the mill apartment, not anything exclusive or safe. If I wanted something in a better, safer neighborhood, I would have to cough up a couple millions of Naira, minimum.

The reason?

Lagos landlords did not accept rent on a monthly basis. You had to pay 2-3 years in advance. I needed at least $2,000 (300,000 Naira) saved up for a bare apartment meaning, no stove, no refrigerator or furniture in a sketchy neighborhood all the way to about $15,000 (2,250,000 Naira) to rent an unfurnished house in a better neighborhood. Since safety was very important to me, I estimated I needed at least $10,000 to start.

For a used car, I needed another $3,000 (450,000 Naira) saved up. So to even begin contemplating moving to Nigeria, I needed at least $14,000. This amount did not even include the cost of fuel for the car, generator etc. It did not include food, clothing and my new found essential items.

This was just the beginning amount.

The problem was that saving this amount of money would not be easy for the fact that I sent my family $500 a month from my $40,000 a year salary. I was already living on a tight budget after taxes, rent and other bills came out of my paycheck. Having to now deduct even more money for this new "project", would leave me destitute. I would be working and not living, not that I was living much anyway...

What about a second job?

Same thing. I would be working and not living and even if I did get one, it would still take a couple of years before I gathered enough money to come home.

Now, THAT was a problem.

I did not want to remain in America for even a year!!!

There was another complication. Even if I miraculously managed to save all the money I needed in a short time and

SHIFTING ALLEGIANCES

returned to Nigeria, I could not begin working right away. I needed to have completed the National Youth Service, a yearlong service that every Nigerian college graduate must complete to be considered employable.

It entailed working for the government for a year, in a state they posted you to, which could be anywhere in the country. Since I hadn't gone to college in Nigeria it meant that I couldn't get a job until I had completed this service. In addition, this mandatory service wasn't paid well which meant that for a year, I would not be able to support my family.

How could I go from supporting my family to becoming a drain?

The thought is unpalatable to me and to avoid that, I have to save up for the year I wouldn't be able to work so that my family won't have to suffer. That meant another $6,000 tacked onto my budget and that did not include food, transportation or living expenses for myself!

How was I going to afford that?

I couldn't cut off my family's allowance? It was my duty to take care of them. I could see how much better my sisters had fared because of that money. They had not had to suffer like I had. They had not missed a beat in continuing their education. Sleeping on the floor was a distant memory. They all had beds,

good clothes and extra pocket money and I couldn't imagine taking all of that away. It just wasn't going to happen.
If they are not happy, I cannot be happy.
But what can I do about the money?
Going back to how I'd lived 7 years before was out of the question. I couldn't live like that anymore, I absolutely could not. And even if I could, there was also the issue of expectations. Nigerian people expected that if one returned from living in the West, that he or she returned with at least some riches. *How could one live in America and then go back to living in penury?* It just wasn't done. Not having any money would be disgraceful, shameful. Nigerian people don't respect you if you don't have money.
I wouldn't even have respect for myself.
But this amount of money meant that my return date was somewhere in the unidentifiable future, a date that was truly, truly unacceptable to me.
Why was it so difficult to come back?
It has not escaped my notice that all the things I require to live a comfortable life in Nigeria are easily obtainable in the U.S. You do not have to put down two to three years rent before you can get an apartment in America. You do not have to pay so much to live in a safe neighborhood. Apartments came

standard with a fridge and working stove. Cars also do not require an upfront sum of thousands of dollars. Leases and monthly payments were available and affordable. Also electricity was 24/7, food was cheap and things were so much easier.

What should I do?

What should I do?

All I know is that I have to find a way out.

I am not staying in that country.

Day 16

Mood: Thinking outside of the box

I have been thinking of alternative ways to get the money I need to return.

I have thought about playing the lottery, of contacting Oprah Winfrey.

I have even thought about writing a letter to the president of Nigeria, telling him that one of his people wishes to return and asking him to help me.

Basically, I am slowly becoming mad.

SHIFTING ALLEGIANCES

Day 18

Mood: Sadness mixed with Anger

I have not been sleeping well.

The last few nights have been torturous, filled with me tossing and turning, wracking my brain, trying to figure out how to get the money I need, dreading the day I would go back to the states, wanting to hold on to Nigeria and feeling powerless to do so.

I am full of despair. I can't seem to come up with a fast way to get the money.

I am full of envy. I am feeling jealous of the Nigerians who live in Nigeria and those who otherwise, have the resources to return. They don't know how lucky they are. They don't know how I wish I was them.

I am feeling resentful. I am angry at all the responsibilities I am shouldering. *Why oh why did my father have to die at a young age?*

I feel guilty, I feel torn. *What am I going to do? Do I just,* as African Americans would say, *do me? Do I say "Screw my family" and for once in my life do something that is just for me?* But even if I ignored my family's comfort and returned quickly to Nigeria, how long would that last? I didn't have the savings to ride out a year of not working. My savings were already shot. My ticket alone for this trip had cost me $1,500 dollars and I wasn't so naïve as to think I could enjoy Nigeria without money.

Life would quickly become harsh and I definitely did not want that.

But I did not want to go back to America. The more I stayed in Nigeria, the more I wanted to remain here. I did not want to go back to that racist, lonely place. I did not want to go back to that country that made me feel like a lesser human being. I didn't want to remain in a country where I felt so despised, a country where I never felt at ease, a country where I was dehumanized, simultaneously ignored and invisible, vilified, where being black was a curse, where loneliness was my constant companion, where I was desperately unhappy.

I wanted to be back in my own country, a country where I was a human being first and not a race.

A country where I belonged.

Why was it so hard to return?

God was punishing me. He was punishing me for vowing never to return to Nigeria, years ago.

Or maybe it was the gods sabotaging me… I don't know.

SHIFTING ALLEGIANCES

All I know is that I've been cursing a lot. I curse the day I stepped into America, the cause for why I have become unable to live the way I had previously done.

I curse the fact that Nigeria, with its vast amount of resources, still hasn't figured out a way to distribute its earnings to the benefit of its populace. *Why was electricity so costly, when we provided oil to the rest of the world? Why was corruption still rampant? Why did one have to pay so much for basic human necessities? Why was security not guaranteed? Why do you have to pay so much for housing?*

I cursed the gods for taking my father too prematurely, causing me to become a financial provider to my family at an age when many of my unmarried mates still depended on their parents, because it made me too responsible and relinquishing it would cause far reaching, detrimental effects to not just my family, but to me.

I am falling into a hole.

This wasn't how my trip was supposed to go. This wasn't how my homecoming was supposed to feel. I was supposed to be happy here. I wasn't supposed to be miserable and wracking my brain in Nigeria.

What in the world was happening to me?

Amaka Lily

I wanted to scream, to weep, to stomp my feet like a two year old child. I wanted to shout so that all could hear that "*I DID NOT WANT TO GO BACK TO AMERICA*", but that was unthinkable for the first born child of a Nigerian family. I needed to get a grip. But I didn't want to get a grip. I didn't want to go back to that bloody country.

My family members are unaware of the emotions that are waging war inside my brain. I haven't told them anything. I am not telling them anything. They won't understand anyway. Even if by some miracle, they did understand, I don't think they'd be ready for the intensity of my feelings. It scares even me.

I am acting like everything is okay, but the truth is that I'm barely holding it together. The first born child usually has things together.

I hope I don't crack.

SHIFTING ALLEGIANCES

<u>Day 19</u>

Mood: Relief

I woke my mother up very early this morning. I couldn't take it anymore. I felt like my head was going to burst.

"*Njideka what is it?*" My mother was alarmed. To wake a Nigerian up in the middle of the night meant that something bad had occurred.

I told her I just needed to talk to her and we slowly made our way to the verandah.

It was about 2am in the morning. The whole of Lagos was asleep, still we spoke in low tones. We didn't want to wake up my sisters and you never knew if thieves were lurking.

I told her everything. In between sobs, I poured my heart out to her. I told her of how miserable I'd been in America and how I hadn't fit in socially. I told her of the time I got fired from Pluto and how racist Americans could be. I told her I was excruciatingly lonely and that I wanted to come back to Nigeria. I told her of my plan to use this trip to assess how soon I could return to Nigeria and that my findings so far had depressed me. I told her I wasn't looking forward to my impending departure and that the prospect of leaving without a plan was killing me.

"*I understand*", my mother softly replied

"*No you don't understand. You can't possibly understand what it is to be treated like you are a scary, unlovable human being! You can't possibly understand what it means to feel invisible around men, to not have a man toast you, to feel yourself dying everyday*"

"*I understand*"

"*No, mommy, I don't think you do. I am not living in that county. I am just existing, actually slowly dying each day*"

"*I said I UNDERSTAND, Njideka*". My mother's voice had a hint of irritation.

I kept quiet. There was silence for a good long minute. Then she continued…

"*When I first arrived in the U.S., my room-mate refused to sleep in the same room as me*"

"*What do you mean?*"

"*The woman who was assigned to be my roommate in my first year in America was white. She would cry and cry. She would refuse to sleep in our room. I overhead her multiple times on the phone telling her parents that she didn't understand why she was placed with this African girl and that she was so terrified*"

SHIFTING ALLEGIANCES

She continued *"Anytime I woke up, this girl would already be wide awake, staring at me with frightened eyes. It wasn't long before she was moved to another room"*

"I felt horrible" she continued *"... it made me feel bad about myself.... Like as if I was a mutant person. I didn't understand how someone could be so terrified of me... it made me cry a few times"*

I could not believe it. My mother had just uttered similar feelings I'd had. She had even used the same words I'd used, of feeling like a mutant and of being terrifying to people.

It meant so much to me. Not only was she validating my feelings, but she was also showing vulnerability. Nigerian parents don't usually do that. They typically portray a strong, tough love persona, except in the case of especially difficult circumstances, like when my father died. For her to tell me that she had cried due to the pain that was inflicted on her by her useless room-mate, really meant a lot.

"There were some other things..." She continued *"... racial epithets hurled in my face and your father's face. They even threw bags of dog shit in the last house we lived in..."*

"But why didn't you ever tell us these stories?" I interrupted

"Because I didn't want to taint your minds. I wanted you guys to draw your own conclusions about America". Besides it was the 70s and I thought that by now, America would be less racist"

"So Njideka" she continued "*I know exactly how you feel when you say you were treated like a second class citizen. I know the pain of being treated as if you were a dangerous person, not the innocent, harmless person you are. I know the pain of being seen as a color and not a human being. I know*"

"*I just wish you had told me this earlier and not kept it inside for so long. But if you want to come back, come back. Don't allow the fact that we rely on your money to stop you. If you are not happy there, come back. Yes it will be tight, but once your sisters graduate, do their youth service and find jobs, it should be better*"

I wasn't prepared for that one. I wasn't prepared for my mother to support my decision to return this readily. I'd expected some tough love, some encouragement to stick it out and be stronger. This was unexpected. My confusion must have been reflected in my face because she said:

"*I am serious, come back if you are not happy. Settle your affairs there and return home. You deserve a break... You have done so much for us and have made me proud. We will manage... just come back if you are not happy*"

SHIFTING ALLEGIANCES

For the first time in at least a week, happiness flooded my heart. I had the backing of my mother to return to Nigeria. Even though I didn't know how exactly we'd manage without my money, all the fears I'd had about not being able to return quickly dissipated.

It will be all right.

It will be all right.

Amaka Lily

Day 21

Mood: Contemplation

I have been thinking about America.

Now that I have been given the green light to return to Nigeria, my anxiety towards the U.S has greatly lessened.

There is still some trepidation, but it is not all consuming. I am no longer viewing America as the scary, monstrous entity it had come to represent, but rather, as a place I had once really loved.

How had it gone so wrong?

I remember how I had hoped and prayed to come to America, and when it finally happened, how happy I was.

How had it gone so wrong?

I thought about what I'd expected from America all those years back. I'd expected to be freed from all my problems. I'd expected that once I'd obtained a college education and financial security that everything would fall into place.

I had not expected racism to affect me.

I had not expected stereotypes to burden me.

I thought about my then expectations of white people, the way that I'd viewed them and the way all Nigerians viewed them. I had not expected them to hurt me. Whites were not supposed to have the same baser natures that we black people had. They were supposed to be better than us, smarter than us, wiser, more benevolent. They donated food and money to African nations. They donated medicine. They had brought us civilization and freed our minds from the grip of idol worship. They even ruled their countries better as anyone who had observed the steady decline that occurred in our infrastructure, economy and quality of life once the "pure" Nigerians had taken over from British rule could attest to.

I am realizing now that those expectations had been nurtured in Nigeria. Nigerians thought that white people were better than themselves. If a Nigerian had to choose between a Nigerian doctor and a white doctor, a Nigerian would choose the white doctor, even if both were equally skilled. They treated foreigners with awe, respect, better than they treated their own fellow Nigerians and the closer a Nigerian obtained westernized characteristics, the better and more sophisticated he or she was perceived.

If you traveled to a western country, you automatically obtained cool points. If you spoke with an American or English accent, you obtained even more points and snagging a white significant other was a big deal.

In every way, the message that whites were better than us was constantly reinforced by the culture and the people. It continues to this day and it was those expectations that I'd unknowingly carried until I found out that whites could be flawed and that the America I had longed to come to was also flawed.

If someone had asked me if I thought whites were better than Nigerians, I'd have denied it, vehemently. I had argued with Ray Ray when he had indicated that we Africans were brainwashed not knowing that he had been exactly right. We had been brainwashed and we, not whites, were the ones continuing the brainwashing.

I have met the enemy and he is us...

I had no idea that that's what I'd secretly believed. I had no idea that that was what lay within my mind. But having now lived in the two cultures and observed the behaviors of the people within those cultures, clarity had mercifully sank in.

Was my depression a result of being rejected from people I'd secretly lauded all my life? Was it the fact that the people I had been raised to see as perfect, flawless beings, were revealed to be very flawed? Was it the realization that dreams I'd carried since childhood were nothing but air? What part did racism play in my depression? What part did trying to adapt to a new

SHIFTING ALLEGIANCES

city play into it? What part did leaving home or homesickness play into it?

Questions upon questions. No easy answers.

All I know is that we Nigerians have a long way to go, in cultivating self pride, loving ourselves and recognizing our achievements, both past and present. We need to revel in our Africanness, to stop trying to be something we are not. We need to stop putting ourselves down, in favor of other, lighter, races. We need to realize that we are great just as we are, that civilization did not start with white people, and that prior to whites ever discovering Africa we had empires, traditions, rules, religious and political processes. We had our own form of education. We made great works of art, passed on histories orally and maintained elaborate customs, hallmarks of a civilized society. We need to appreciate the skills that we have in traditional medicine and the healing arts. We need to love ourselves. We need to realize that white people were human just as we were, with the full range of human behaviors that human beings had. They could be good, bad, jealous, catty, vindictive, sweet, nice, forgiving. Every single emotion a Nigerian or black person could feel, they could also feel. Believing otherwise was a recipe for disappointment as I could surely attest to.

Amaka Lily

But how does one start? How does one eke out deeply rooted convictions that one doesn't even know one harbors? How did we even start believing this in the first place? How had we made it a self-fulfilling prophecy?

It was complicated, overwhelming, daunting. It was made even worse because even as I rejected the falsity of the stereotypes, I recognized some validity to it. Whites had indeed helped African nations just as they had taken away from those same nations. Nigeria had also become worse since Nigerians had taken over from the British, although the blame –truth be told- wasn't solely due to Nigerians hands, but rather, a complex, network of international hands. Shadowy hands that pulled at the strings of our elected leaders, hands that owned most of our industries and orchestrated the way things were REALLY run. It was messy, complicated and I wasn't equipped to solve all of those problems today...

Let me go back to thinking about America. There were many things that had caused my unhappiness in the U.S. apart from my expectations of white people and the reality of racism. Being far away from home, moving to another state without having a single relative, being lonely, not having as many friends, not being able to make friends, feeling cut off, being stereotyped, being hurt and reading all those hateful blog. All had contributed to my depression. I still had to work through a lot of my feelings. I had a lot of pain, hurt, resentment, bad memories.

How was I going to solve all of these issues?

Day 22

Mood: Bittersweet

I leave for America tomorrow.

It is bittersweet.

I hate the fact that I'm leaving my family but a tiny part of me is also looking forward to going back

The reason?

I am broke. The amount of money I continue to spend in this country is ridiculous. I need a break. I love Nigeria, but I need a break

SHIFTING ALLEGIANCES

<u>Day 23</u>

Mood: Sadness

I left Nigeria today.

I didn't cry, but the American in me wept.

Chapter 14

Return to America

SHIFTING ALLEGIANCES

A grateful sense of relief washed over me once I arrived in America.

From the cold winter air that welcomed me, to the order and efficiency at the airport, I was so glad to be back. I did not miss the heat and the chaos that characterized daily Nigerian life. When I boarded my bus, I was grateful for the quiet, the spaciousness, and relative affordability of this mode of transportation. When I got to my apartment and turned on the light, I was grateful for the electricity. I was grateful for the clean water and the safety of my surroundings.

I also couldn't help but feel like a traitor and somewhat disloyal to Nigeria for having these feelings.

Wasn't this the same country I'd recently dissed? Wasn't this the same country I was planning to leave?

The constant vacillating from loving and hating a country bothered me? I didn't understand how I could feel so many contrary emotions at the same time. *Why couldn't I just have one dominant emotion towards a country? Why was I so confused?*

I loved and hated some things about Nigeria. I loved and hated some things about America.

Would I ever be in a place where I was completely happy?

I put away my things and thought back to my recent trip. Now THAT had been an emotional rollercoaster, something I hadn't anticipated. It was meant to be a simple trip, a fact finding mission to Nigeria and a chance to break away from all the negativity of America. I had not expected to find that I had changed. I had not expected to feel atimes like a tourist.

I had not expected to cry.

Still I missed that country and felt very homesick. Nigeria was still home to me. It had reminded me of who I was, what I'd forgotten about myself. It had given me a freedom that I lacked in America, a mental freedom of not having to worry about my skin colour. I was not looking forward to the racism that was bound to occur. I was not looking forward to the loneliness and depression. Even though I'd been sad in Nigeria, it hadn't been to the depth I'd felt in America, and, I'd never been lonely.

Sigh

Maybe I was asking for too much. Maybe there was no Nirvana available for me in the world.

Still I needed to be happy, not 100% happy, but happier than I'd been in the last few years.

But how could I be happy here? I never felt like I belonged. I never felt like I truly fit. I never felt like I was really understood, and it didn't matter whether it was with black, white or orange people. I never felt a 100% understood.

I didn't see how that could ever change, particularly since I no longer had the desire to try again for friendship.

Not with anyone.

SHIFTING ALLEGIANCES

A couple of days after I resumed work, I noticed I felt a bit different. I was no longer walking around weighed down with the fear and paranoia that had characterized my daily life, prior to my trip to Nigeria. I also did not feel as loveless and as unwanted as I'd felt before and it wasn't like I had suddenly been inundated with people loving me.

I had a deeper sense of my worth. I knew that there were people out there who loved me, even though I didn't always feel loved in the states. I knew that out there, there were people who accepted me and that deep down, I was a person, even though living in America had made me feel less than.

I had been "fortified" so to speak and I knew that these feelings were a direct result of my trip to Nigeria.

There were other feelings I couldn't fully specify. The bottom-line was that I felt a lot lighter and I hoped these feelings would last.

Amaka Lily

It took a couple more days before I was finally able to articulate why I hadn't been feeling as fearful and as paranoid as before.

I was no longer scared of racism. I mean, there was still some trepidation, but it was tempered, not all consuming.

Something had shifted during my time in Nigeria, somewhere during the time I realized what part my background and expectations of white people had played into my depression.

I had accepted the reality of racism.

Part of my problems of the past was because I'd struggled to accept racism in its full sense. Yes, I knew it existed but I'd resented it. I'd hated the fact that people judged me based on my skin color, something I had no control over. I was unhappy that something that had never been an issue for me before, suddenly dictated my choices in love, friendships and a career. I'd been fighting against it, not wanting to accept that this was part and parcel of being in America.

The reality was that Racism was inevitable in America, a place where the slave trade occurred, a trade that was founded on the belief that one race was superior to another. It was not going anywhere however, I no longer had to fear it, be shocked by it, be disappointed or be depressed by it. The hole in my heart no longer had to get bigger each time I experienced it. People were going to judge me, to doubt me, to think of me as inferior, incapable of intelligence, ugly, undesirable whatever.

It was what it was, or in this case, what the country was.

But I didn't have to buy into it. I didn't have to internalize their beliefs.

I'd put these people on a pedestal, believing that their treatment of me, defined me and that they could dictate my entire experience of life. I'd internalized their rejection, believing I was unworthy and unlovable.

Now I knew who I was.

SHIFTING ALLEGIANCES

I was not worthless just because I was black. I was not undesirable just because I was black. I bled the same as them, felt the same as them and had the same right to be treated equally and with dignity. No matter what anyone thought about being black, they could never take away my humanity. No one would ever make me feel less than a human being again

I knew now that racists were like bullies. They wanted to beat you down, beat down your self esteem. They had fixed ideas of what you were and what you were capable of. They wanted you to remain in a position that was lower than them because they believed that's where you were supposed to be. Any efforts you made to get out of the box they had drawn for you or to display that you are not of that box would be met with hostility and intimidation.

But as anyone with experience with bullies knows, underlying that façade is fear and insecurity. Most bullies would back down if you stand up for yourself and I realized I could.

I COULD FIGHT BACK!

In the most recent past, I'd felt powerless against racism and had just ruminated and felt sadder and sadder about it. Now, I realized I had some power. My previous experiences had taught me how to anticipate and prepare myself for it. I could call out racist people, if they chose to behave badly towards me. I could speak up, demand equal treatment or report them. Ofcourse there was no guarantee that I'd be heard, but at least I'd feel better about myself. I didn't have to slink back or stay silent. I didn't have to be afraid or miserable anymore.

Now there were still other aspects of racism that couldn't be easily fixed such as racial profiling, police brutality and institutionalized racism but as long as I did my part to be a good, law abiding citizen who took reasonable precautions, I should be alright. Also, America had laws and if I had a good case, I stood a good chance of being heard.

The only power racism had had over me, was the one I'd given to it.

I became excited. I hadn't felt this excited since I first arrived in America. America suddenly seemed to be brimming with possibilities.

I recalled a long time ago, how I'd purposely played with people that were racist to me, specifically the Indian woman of the shop I used to frequent. I decided to do a test. As I got into the bus, I looked to see if anyone was staring at me. I took a seat by a man who seemed to be glaring at me, looked him in the eye and said "*Hello*". He held my glance for a second then turned away

I could not believe it.

I expected he'd do more than that. Slap me, push me, yell at me, something, but nope. He just turned away.

It underscored my point. Bullies could not take it when someone stood up to them. If he had dared do any of those things I'd expected, I'd have given him a hard time.

I felt empowered.

I made up my mind to do more of such things in the future.

Chapter 15

Understanding

As I faced my fears about racism, I began to feel more empowered. However, there was something that still bothered me. I wondered about the conflicting feelings I'd felt in Nigeria, of one day loving Nigeria, the next hating it. I wondered why I'd felt like a tourist in Nigeria and why my emotions felt especially heightened. I wondered if other foreigners had felt the same emotions, or whether I was the exception, the mad one.

I started researching articles about foreigners returning to their homeland and the types of emotions they experienced. This in turn, led me to study the process of immigrating and adapting to a new country. It was through this research that I found that there was a name for what ailed me, culture shock.

When a person enters a new country, he is going to experience some physical and emotional difficulties and these difficulties all contribute to what's defined as culture shock. It is essentially an emotional roller coaster.

I found that there are four main stages of culture shock, the honeymoon stage, frustration stage, depression and adjustment stage. The *honeymoon stage* is the period when a foreigner is very in love with the new country and amazed by everything it has to offer. The people seem great, their culture seems great, everything's great and the foreigner is just so happy to be there.

The frustration period is when the scales have fallen off and the individual starts seeing the new country in a different light. It is no longer exotic. He or she starts having difficulties in the new culture. He doesn't understand exactly how things are supposed to work or he doesn't agree with how things work. He might offend someone unintentionally, make a joke that falls flat or feel like he is on the outside looking in. He might begin to dislike the new culture, mock it or show animosity. Anger, hostility, anxiety and fear of being hurt are emotions that characterize this stage.

SHIFTING ALLEGIANCES

The depression stage is where the person starts feeling depressed. He sees no light at the end of the tunnel and starts to compare it to his former home. There's a deep desire to go back to his former homeland and see the people of that homeland. His previous home now seems great to his mind. He does not remember the harsh aspects.

Finally, there's the acceptance stage where the person adapts to the new culture. He becomes more accepting of the new culture and finds a way to coexist with it alongside aspects of his former culture.

I learnt that no one experiences culture shock in exactly the same way. Some might take years to go through each stage, others months. Some of the stages could bleed into each other while for others they remained, distinct. Furthermore, the degree of difficulty one suffers could be influenced by access to financial resources, emotional support and the color of one's skin. But for all of them, there were wild mood swings and a rollercoaster of emotions and these, it was emphasized was very normal.

It made sense.

I remembered how happy I was coming to the U.S. and how everything had seemed so grand. I realized that having a family in Indianapolis had helped greatly in making my transition seamless. I had a support system in place and only had to focus on my schooling and job.

When I moved, I began to experience the really difficult parts. The frustration at not being able to make friends, racism and the fact that I had no support system made everything especially difficult. I remembered the depression, *Oh how could I ever forget that depression* and the desire to go back home?

I also found that my experience in Nigeria was a particular variant of culture shock experienced by people returning to their homeland. It was called reverse culture shock and had similar emotions as regular culture shock such as happiness -at being reunited with your family again-, frustration, anger, depression and alienation.

People returning to their homeland don't realize how used they have become to certain aspects of their new culture. Also, in their mind's eye, their homeland is stuck where they last left it, when in reality it has moved on. This is why many felt like tourists in their own home. This was also why many felt depressed. Some also felt less independent than they were when they first lived there. Some called this phenomenon, the "You can't go home again" phenomenon, meaning you can never go back to the home you left. It would have changed, irrevocably.

Oh how I could relate!

To find that there was a scientific explanation for the mind fuck -to borrow an American phrase- I'd experienced was one of the greatest things to ever happen to me. I actually wept, out of relief and joy that I wasn't crazy and that everything, the sadness, depression, and pain were all normal.

I wished I'd known of this phenomenon before I came to the U.S.

I wished I could have been more prepared.

I read stories upon stories of people undergoing culture shock. I joined online communities of people sharing their culture shock experiences. People wrote about how their experiences were not what they had expected. Others talked about how they'd been frustrated with certain aspects of their adaptation such as not being understood by the natives, not fitting in, not making friends etc. Still others talked about the isolation, how their optimism had turned to depression and how they had started to reject aspects of the new culture.

I read stories of how some felt invincible or conversely too visible, how they were treated like aliens, or with hostility. I read stories of people who said their reverse culture shock was

SHIFTING ALLEGIANCES

a much more difficult transition than being in a foreign place. Some said it took years to adapt to their former home.

   I basked in these stories.
   I felt I was not alone.
   There were two things I was now clear about.
   I had been hard on myself.
   I had been hard on America.

Realizing that my emotions were a direct result of culture shock gave me some measure of peace, but it was not 100%.

There were still real issues I needed to address, like releasing my paranoia about white people. I had experienced some very hurtful things from them. *How could I look at those experiences objectively, release the pain from it and move on?* It wasn't helped by the fact that every so often, the news would bring up something about racism. It could be news that resumes with black names were routinely ignored by hiring managers. It could be studies that showed that when a black person got missing or killed, the news media wouldn't carry it but if it were a white person, everyone would know.

I could never really ignore racism.

Try as I might, I was always reminded of it.

I was constantly reminded of unfair treatment towards blacks.

But I realized that I had encountered some good kind white people. From my first set of coworkers to the man that had helped me on the ice-rink, yes the same one that I'd refused to let go of his hand. There were some good white people in the world. Lawrenceville had negatively impacted my world view and I needed to fix that. I also wondered how my paranoia may have influenced the treatment that I may have received in the past from some of them. *Surely, a girl who looked, pensive, worried and paranoid, could not have inspired warm feelings from anyone?*

When it came to my social life, it dawned on me that I'd expected to have the same life as someone who had been in this country for all of her life. That, in retrospect, was unrealistic. It was like sending an American to Nigeria, and expecting the American to make instant friendships, without being affected by the different cultural values. America was not built like Nigeria. As much as I wished it was, it just wasn't.

SHIFTING ALLEGIANCES

In Nigeria, I already had a social network. There was a shared history and a pre-approval of my personhood. I didn't have to do anything special to make friends. It just came to me. In addition, I understood all the cultural nuances, knew where to go and what to expect. I didn't have that in Lawrenceville. Combine it with the fact that people usually don't trust strangers and the racial aspect of being black, it was no wonder I had difficulties.

However, if I wanted to feel connected to America, I had to make friends. To do that, I had to go back out to joining groups, what I'd sworn I'd never do. But there was no getting around it. A person without a social network needs to start somewhere...

And so I joined another social group, one for just young professionals, but unlike the past where I had high expectations for the groups I joined, this time I had none. I just wanted to observe, see if the people were nice, talk about myself if asked and go on with my life. If it didn't work, no biggie. I had survived without friendships in the past.

I could survive again.

I really didn't expect what actually happened in my first group event. Perhaps it was the fact that I didn't seem too eager and was no longer trying too hard to make friends, but before I left, I had three phone numbers in my cell phone. Three of my new group mates asked me to call them anytime to hang out.

It had started out with me attending the event which was scheduled at a restaurant. I'd introduced myself and as soon as they heard my accent, asked where I was from. Then one of them, Dee Dee, told me she had visited a Safari in Kenya and wanted to know if I had done the same. Then I was asked if I had any family in Lawrenceville and when I said No, was told that we should all hang out.

It was actually weird how it all happened.

Amaka Lily

I went for the next event with my guard still up, still believing that the previous one was a fluke, but nope, they were still nice and I made even more friends. My calendar started filling up with things to do. I started getting invited to church events, bar events, all kinds of events.

When I started having more white friends, I began to see that some of my Lawrenceville impressions were false. For starters, the vast majority of the ones in Lawrenceville were not racist, but rather unknowledgeable about blacks. They hadn't been raised around blacks and so consequently, couldn't relate. Also, the media stereotypes didn't help matters.

So basically, some of the initial resistance I got from them was attributable to this. I found that for some if you persevered with making conversations with them, that the ice thawed. For others, once they saw that their friends accepted you, they accepted you as well. There were some who refused to hold conversations, regardless of what their friends did and still others who I got the feeling that they viewed me as a creature from outer space. But it did not hurt like it did previously.

I'd already experienced that pain before.

The best ones I found were those who were either married to, dating or grew up around a black person. These ones didn't see you as a black person first, but rather as a person. Your color did not matter to them.

Take Jesse for instance. Jesse is actually white but he grew up working class with many black people in Tennessee before he moved to Lawrenceville. Every time he sees me, he is sweet to me. He makes me feel included, jokes with me, listens when I speak and values my opinion. Essentially, he treats me like a normal girl.

Another one is Michael. He's white but sounds like a black American. I mean, his mannerisms, attitude, everything. If you heard him on the phone, you'd think he was black. He was actually the one who approached me first. I like him, but he is

SHIFTING ALLEGIANCES

sort of weird. He kind of reminds me of Ray Ray. He rails against THE MAN and doesn't want the government to intervene with his life. And he is THE MAN!!!!

These and other friendships feel so good.

It was exactly the type of reception I thought I'd get from all whites when I first moved to Lawrenceville.

It really feels good.

I overcame my aversion to bars and stopped judging them. I realized that they were places that people go to socialize and watch sports and that everyone, college students, professional people, blue collar people go there.

It is not a place solely for prostitutes and male patrons.

I realized that there were many areas where I was trying to make America "fit" what I was used to, where I wanted the country to "behave" like Nigeria would. Like when it came to morals in this country and how lax America is compared to Nigeria. It wasn't a place where "bad girls" and "shameful people" needed to hide their faces forever. They were given second chances, which wasn't such a bad thing.

As for the American justice system, as flawed and as unforgiving as it was, at least it attempted to bring people to justice.

I realized that I needed to accept America on its own terms. I needed to accept that the rules I was raised with didn't apply here, never did and never will. This was a different country. I have been living with Nigerian rules in America.

I also realized that accepting America was a constant process. Every time I thought I'd accepted America for what it was, I'd uncover another layer where I was still holding onto Nigerian ideas and principles.

I guess you can't change two decades of programming in one shot. Cultural bonds are not so easily discarded.

Amaka Lily

Epilogue

SHIFTING ALLEGIANCES

It has been six months since my trip to Nigeria.

My mother called me today, specifically to ask if I still planned to return and if so when.

It is a question that has been bugging me.

The reason I had wanted to leave America in the first place was that I was unhappy and couldn't see a light at the end of the tunnel. Now that America is no longer scary to me and I have friends, I no longer feel the impetus to rush back to Nigeria.

I am having a lot more fun than I was just a year ago. Learning about culture shock and making efforts to accept America on its own terms, helped with that. But it is not perfect. I cannot say that I no longer suffer from racism or that when I do, that I am able to successfully deal with each incident. I have made great strides. I try to take people at face value, to withhold judgment until they have shown themselves to me, but some days, I struggle. And when I hear bad news, familiar fears about my safety rise up.

Fortunately it isn't too common and I try to remind myself that every country has its warts.

My social network has grown, and it is a lot more diverse. In addition to groups, I have also been making friends from unusual places, like the mall. The other day I went out with three white, two Indian and one black friend to a bar. I have learnt to play card games.

I even shoot pool now.

As for my love life, I am doing it the American way. I have signed up for online dating sites and have gone out on a few dates. I still miss the way that Nigerian men asked you out but hey, I am in America.

When in Rome, do as the Romans do.

One of my white girlfriends told me that white guys would never ask me out the way Nigerian guys do and that it wasn't due to my race. They do it to every race. She said that white guys like to see some encouragement from women either by the latter flirting, looking them in the eye, flicking their hair or licking their lips. She said that once they see that from you, they will approach you.

I don't think I'd ever do that.

I am just not forward like that.

I am also really enjoying what the country has to offer. The other day, I went to the library and picked up 4 good novels purely for enjoyment and escapism. I appreciated the fact that I did not have to pay for these books and that I could have them for three weeks before I had to return them to the library. This was a feature that did not exist in Nigeria.

I appreciate all I have now. My apartment, the peace and quiet, the job I have, everything. I would always love Nigeria but I am here now.

I told my mother that I wouldn't be returning this year, but will definitely visit. I have decided that every year, I would make that trip back to see them. I think that staying away from my family for as long as I did contributed to my alone-ness. I feel that going back to Nigeria each year is a must to fortify myself.

I feel like this is the best decision for me. I am not making a mad dash to return home without any money. I can still continue to help my family while saving steadily. I can also plan things a bit more objectively.

Sometimes I am amazed at how different my life is. When I look back at my journals, I cannot believe the depth of despair that I was in, not too long ago.

I have made peace with my shifting allegiances. There will always be vacillation, of longing for Nigeria when America gets too hot, or for America when Nigeria gets too hot. It is how it will always be.

It is the price I paid for a better life.

About the Author

Amaka Lily is from Delta State. She was born in America and raised in Nigeria. She has lived in Warri, Onitsha & Lagos. She is fascinated by different cultures, race and cultural identity.

Writing is her passion. She has written as a hobby for the last 20 years and does not plan to stop. She also enjoys travelling, fashion and good friends.

She has a Bachelor's in Business and a Masters in Business Administration.

Amaka currently resides in New Jersey.

Printed in Germany
by Amazon Distribution
GmbH, Leipzig